THE SACRIFICE OF AVA BLACK

The Witches of Thyana

A.G. PORTER

The Sacrifice of Ava Black

The Witches of Thyana

Book 1

By A.G. Porter

The Sacrifice of Ava Black
Published by Nightshade Publishing, LLC.

Edited by Samantha Talarico
Cover Art © Open World Cover Design

Trigger Warnings: bullying, violence, depictions of death, parental loss, attempted assault

Acknowledgments

Robert Johnson of the Turtle Mountain Band of the Chippewa People. Your guidance has been paramount in telling Ava's story. Thank you for being so open about your culture. For your kindness and support I am eternally grateful.

Author Justina Luther thank you for being my accountability partner and pushing more toward my goals. More than that, thank you for being a friend.

Samantha Talarico, you have taught me so much about editing. It may stick one day.

To my loving family.

The Witch of the Woods

In the deep dark forest,
she does reside.
Where things do creep,
and things do hide.

In the deep dark forest,
she does reign.
Where things grow wicked,
in her domain.

In the deep dark forest,
should you find yourself,
surrounded by shadows,
it's too late to call for help.

For in the deep dark forest,
you are in her embrace.
A worthy sacrifice,
you will make.

A.G. Porter

Ava

It had rained in my small town of Guntersville, Alabama for two weeks straight. The local meteorologists were calling it record breaking flooding all across the state, but most of the deluge was concentrated right here. The amount of rain was stunning in of itself, but for me, it was more for the mere fact of what weather like this did to my body.

I couldn't remember the last time I'd woken up without my head feeling like someone was stabbing it with an ice pick. Having unending rain clouds hovering nearby only increased the pressure in my head. It didn't help that I'd had another episode last night; sleep paralysis. Since the migraines, they had been intense and more frequent. They were always bad and frightening, but after last night, it felt different.

I had felt the pressure start within a very intense dream. I couldn't remember exactly what happened, but pieces seemed to stay with me. There was a figure standing in a field, purple lightning all around her. She held a blade; a dagger. I could tell it was handmade, but skillfully so. Lightning flashed off its dark blade, revealing its sharpness. The image was terrifying, but it wasn't her that scared me. It was what she said.

"They are coming," her words merely a whisper, but the weight of them rang as loud as a raging river.

That's when I felt the pressure hit me and I couldn't move. I saw something out of the corner of my eye, something formed out of the darkness and emerged from the woods. Before I could react, it was on me, holding me to the ground. I could smell the dirt, feel the dampness of the soil seep into my clothes. Then it laughed. The most ear shattering sound I had ever experienced.

Sleep paralysis makes you hallucinate, my doctor had said. Some people hear things, some people see things, and sometimes it's just an intense fear upon waking. For me, it was a mixture of all of it. Whatever happened to a person's body during an episode was hard to figure out, but it was always scary.

I could still hear that laugh echoing in my ears. Rolling over, I stared up at the ceiling, willing myself to move, trying my best to drown out the sound of the ringing in my ears.

It was useless. The buzzing was insidious, coming from some dark place I couldn't reach, driving that horrendous pain deeper into my mind. If it were possible, I'd pull it out and stomp on whatever caused it, crushing it under my foot until there was nothing left.

"Ava..." My mother opened my bedroom door.

Like a vampire, I flinched as the bright light from the hall came pouring into my room. I quickly pulled my soft, purple sheets over my head and curled up into a ball. She hurriedly shut the door. She was all too familiar with my bad days.

From my cocoon of sheets and blankets, I listened to her make her way across my dark room and take a seat on the edge of my bed. She pulled the sheet from my head, revealing a mess of rich black hair and brown skin.

"Bad morning?" she asked me unnecessarily.

"It'll pass," I reassured her.

"Are you lying?" She moved a few strands of curly hair from my face so she could see my eyes.

"No, but give me five more minutes," I begged.

"You don't have five more minutes," she sighed. "Are you sure you don't want to stay home?"

"I'm fine," I lied.

"You've got a doctor's appointment after school." She kissed my forehead. "I've already talked to Dr. Abbott, and he's going to call you in a different medication."

"Alright," I sat up slowly, but the room still spun, "Sounds great."

It really didn't. The last thing I wanted was more pills.

"Please, honey," she took my hands, "if you don't want to go to school, you don't have to."

"Mom, I'm a senior," I told her. "I can't afford to get behind. Whatever is going on with me is going to sort itself out and in the meantime, I'm going to live my life as normally as I can. If I get to a point where I can't, you'll be the first to know."

"Promise?" She narrowed her sharp brown eyes at me.

"Promise." I smiled at her, but I wasn't sure how convincing I was.

Mom left me to get ready for school, which was a job when your every move felt like the entire room was spinning like a top. I managed though because the more I moved, the better I felt, especially after my shower. Too bad it didn't make me look better. Standing in front of the mirror, I could see the toll this illness had taken on my body.

My brown eyes had lost that youthful shine nearly six months ago. Right now, dark circles haunted my face, which only looked darker when accented by my black lashes. My normally sun-kissed skin was pale from lack of exposure to the outside world. I was of Mexican descent on mom's side and Mexican and Native American on Dad's so my version of pale wasn't exactly pasty, but to me, there was a difference.

The only time I was outside of the house was for school, the occasional trip to the doctor, and to go the library. It had become a sort of refuge. My head hurt too bad to read sometimes, but when I was able, I would tear through the books. Before all of this, I was busy with cheer practice and football games. My best friend Frankie and I went shopping, to parties that we really shouldn't have been at, and hung out at each other's houses.

Now, Frankie Johnston made my life a living hell. We had been friends our entire lives until this point. We were just alike in so many ways. I hated to admit it, but it was true. I'd made the losers lick my high dollar heels and laughed while they did it. Now, I was on my knees along with them.

There wasn't any one moment that made me open my eyes to the terrible shell of a person I had become. I think it was a slow burn. When my health declined, right before cheer camp began this past summer, I slowly distanced myself from Frankie and the other girls on the cheerleading squad. Eventually, Frankie called me out for bailing on them. When she wouldn't take my excuse of not feeling well anymore, she ostracized me. I could tell she had been waiting for the chance to kick me to the curb.

Soon, I was a fake who had a pill addiction and should be avoided at all costs. If someone was even seen giving me a piece of gum, they were forever banned from the cool kids' table. I was like the plague and funnily enough, I didn't care. My head killed me most of the time, so trivial things like popularity meant nothing to me.

That seemed like forever ago. Now, not having friends was lonely, I had to admit. Going from being one of the most popular girls in school to one of the most ignored had its drawbacks. On days like today, when my head felt as if World War III were taking place between my ears, it was bliss. It meant I could go to school, take notes, and come back home without worrying about mundane teenage drama.

Mom dropped me off in front of the school and reminded me, for what felt like the millionth time, that I had a doctor's appointment. Waving her off, I climbed the steps of Guntersville High School.

The brick building still had the same 1970s style from when it was first built on a grassy hill overlooking the lake. It was a patchwork of hexagonal buildings with tall glass windows. It was a decently sized school, but with over 500 students, and more every year, the city was considering an expansion or a completely new building. It all depended on money.

Some of my classmates were sitting haphazardly on the steps, under the awning, sharing stories of who got sent home from their favorite reality show, while others were cramming for a test. A group of girls a few grades below me were busying gossiping about some "skank hoe" that was going to get her "face messed up" for stealing someone's boyfriend.

I shoved my earbuds in, drowning out the chatter as much as possible. I didn't want to melt my brain this early in the morning. Nothing played through the headphones, but it relieved some of the noise. If I was listening to something, then it would probably be music my dad wouldn't approve of one bit. He loved classic rock, and I was more of an R&B person.

Lately, I was more into instrumental, mainly violin. The vocals of my regular music just grated my nerves. Dad loved playing Led Zeppelin while he was working on cars. I'd watch him from my bedroom window, wishing I felt well enough to join him.

Getting to my first class was always a hassle. My locker was located past the Jock hang out and each time I had to walk by, Rob Hastings had to say something dirty. It didn't matter how much I tried to ignore or avoid him. He was always there. It was like he had an Ava sensor because like clockwork, there he'd be.

"Ava! There you are," his thick country accent assaulted my ears, even through the earbuds. "What? No hello for your old pal? Come on! We have a lot of steamy history, you and me."

It was true, unfortunately. Rob and I had dated for a while last year, back when I was cheerleader captain and he was star of the football team. Going out together just made sense back then. Besides, he was smoking hot with beach boy blond hair and green eyes that always made me think of spring. Right now, they made me think of gangrene.

Trying my best to ignore him, I headed for my locker. My head was pounding and as I turned the knob on the lock, I was becoming more irritated; the combination wasn't coming to me. By the time Rob leaned against the locker beside me, I had messed up twice.

"Ava, I know you can hear me," he leaned over and talked into my ear, "There isn't ever any music coming out of those stupid earbuds."

I wanted to punch him. I wanted to punch him so badly that I could imagine his nose crumbling under my fist and blood running down that maroon Wildcats jersey he was wearing.

"How about you and I go out tomorrow?" he was saying as I finally got my locker to open. I wanted to shove it in his face, but he moved. "We can recreate some of our...more intimate moments, huh? What do you say?"

I was shoving books in my backpack, not answering, and when I tried to shut my locker, Rob held it open. Finally, I looked up at him. He was smiling at me, those green eyes I had once found appealing, looked menacing.

"Let go of my locker, Rob," I said, taking the earbuds out.

"She speaks," he said as his friends joined him, all laughing. "So, what do you say? Do you want to go to the Lookout?"

"In your dreams. Now let go of my locker," I repeated, my head feeling like it was going to blow at any minute, showering my classmates with brain matter.

"What? It's not like we haven't been there before, baby." He ran his eyes up and down my body. "I already know what I'm in for." He winked.

"Is that what you've been telling everybody?" I laughed, but inside I was dying. "I'm glad all of you losers like going around talking about all the girls you've nailed out at the Lookout, but I'm not one of them. I doubt you've taken anyone out there, Rob. And if you've done anything at all, it's probably been with Mr. Hand. Now get your girlfriend off of my locker or I'm going to break her."

"You, bi—" he was about to say, but was interrupted by someone who walked up behind me.

"I think she means it, man," the rough voice said. "Move it."

Rob looked over my shoulder, and I watched his face pale in an instant. He looked at his buddies, but could tell he would get no help from any of them.

"Whatever." Rob shook his head and left, followed by his football brothers.

I turned to see who had backed me up and found Gabriel Matthews standing there in all his black leather glory. No wonder Rob took off like a dog with its tail between its legs.

Gabriel's movie star black hair was down to his shoulders and his cool grey eyes looked down at me with a certain amount of interest. He really looked down at me because Gabriel had to be the tallest person in our school. He even towered over the teachers.

He scratched the stubble on his chin and I couldn't help but stare at the tattoo that peeked out from the top of his black t-shirt. It had to cover his entire chest.

People could almost swear he had failed 12th grade three times, but he was one of the smartest kids in our school. He was a shoo-in for Valedictorian, but that didn't mean he had a ton of friends. There was just something off about him that made the rest of us steer clear.

"Um, thanks," I told him, shutting my locker door, which at the moment sounded like a cannon going off.

"How long have you had them?" he asked me as I started walking toward my class.

"What?" I asked, noticing people staring at us as we walked together.

"The migraines," he said it in a way as if that should have been obvious.

"It's been almost six months," I cut my eyes at him, "How did you know I had them?"

"I could tell," he shrugged his shoulders, "I know what it's like."

"You have them, too?" I stopped at the door in front of my class.

"I'm glad you finally stood up to Rob. The guy's a jerk." He didn't answer me. "Looks like you've got a new student."

With that he walked away, leaving me reeling with all the things he said and just talking to him in general. I walked into my class, taking my seat and not really paying attention to anything my teacher was saying.

Gabriel had never spoken to me the entire time we had been going to school together. Granted, I had never spoken to him either. He was just one of those people that wasn't on my radar. Sure, I'd noticed him, Frankie had tried dating him for years, but it was clear that he wasn't interested in anyone here.

Pulling out my books and paper, I didn't notice the girl sitting next to me until she tapped me on the shoulder. I jumped so hard that I knocked the desk in front of me with my knee, which hurt like I had shattered my knee cap, and made Holley Adams, another one of my former friends, glare at me with hatred.

"What is your problem, Black?" she snapped.

"Nothing, what's yours, Adams?" I glared back, surprising myself with how snarky I'd become today. "Yeah, that's what I thought, so turn around and mind your own business."

"You've got a lot of nerve talking to me like that." She pushed back her braided hair.

"And who are you? Queen of the World?" I laughed. "I'm not in the mood for you to go on a tirade about how much better you think you are and how terrible and low I am. So shut that gaping hole in your face and turn around."

"I hope there isn't a problem back there, girls," Mrs. Swanson piped up.

"No, ma'am," the girl next to me answered. Her British accent caught everyone's attention. "They were telling me how to get to the gym. Seeing as how I am new to your lovely school, I'm afraid I am terribly lost."

"How nice, girls." This new student had clearly already charmed Mrs. Swanson. "You must be Keira Richards."

"Yes, ma'am," she beamed.

Her pearly white teeth nearly made my migraine double in pain, it was so perfect and bright. She had long, thick blonde hair and the bluest eyes I had ever seen. I'm surprised I didn't notice her when I walked into the classroom because she was drop dead gorgeous. No wonder Gabriel spotted her from the doorway. I saw that every boy in the room, and some girls, kept glancing back at her.

"Excuse me," she whispered to me. "I didn't mean to startle you earlier."

"What? Oh, it's okay," I told her.

"I was being honest about what I said to our instructor," she smiled, her cheeks blushing, "I really don't know where the gym is located."

"Oh," I fumbled with my words because having migraines makes it hard to concentrate on just about anything. "It's not that hard to find. Do you know where the snack machines are? You had to pass them when you walked to the office this morning to get your schedule."

"My host parents picked it up for me on Friday, I'm afraid." She looked even more embarrassed. "The reason I'm asking is that I have to go straight there after this class. I'm here as a transfer student. It's all based on my exceptional ability at gymnastics. So exciting."

"You sound thrilled," I pointed out.

"It's all my mother's idea," she sighed. "Anyway, do you think you can show me where to go? I've only been there once when my mother and I visited over the summer, and this school is so odd. I'm afraid I might get lost."

"Yeah, sure," I agreed.

"Don't worry about it, Keira." Holley turned around, sneering at me. "Ava here used to be on the cheer squad, but she has these episodes, so she's not anymore. So, since we're going to be cheering together, how about I show you where the gym is?"

Holley's words were like razors on my skin. Just the way she said it, it was like she didn't believe me, as if I was lying about how badly I hurt. If she only knew.

I really could not care less if she were my friend anymore, but it seemed like I was making a new one. Keira seemed like someone who was over the whole "do whatever it takes to be popular mentality," and here comes Holley to ruin it all, making it sound like I was mentally unstable. It made me angry, but what was worse, it ripped out my heart.

I hated feeling that way. I hated it when I let the bullies get to me like that. There were so many pep talks I had given myself, that having friends didn't matter. Who was I kidding? I wanted friends. It felt good to be liked.

"You know, Holley, I think I'll be just fine with Ava showing me if it's all the same to you." Keira arched her perfectly plucked eyebrows.

Holley didn't really know what to say. Her dark eyes widened with rage and just as she was about to open her mouth, Mrs. Swanson called our attention forward. Keira gave me a quick wink, and I smiled at her. Holley flipped her hair and quickly turned around.

I liked Keira instantly. Anyone who could see through Holley that fast was a friend of mine.

Mrs. Swanson let Keira and I leave a few minutes early so I could show her where to go and then get to my next class. Talk about luck. Mrs. Swanson was the sort of teacher that was a stickler for rules, so this was really out of character for her. Holley glared at us all the way out the door.

Keira talked to me on our way down the hall, the walls peppered with lockers and "Go Team" posters, and through the double doors that led to the gym lobby.

To our left and right were concession stands and restrooms. Right in the center stood a floor to ceiling glass case, full of trophies collected over the years, a testament to the school's dominance from basketball to soccer.

Keira seemed to be one of those people that rambled when they were nervous. By the time we reached the gym, I'd learned all about her upbringing in England and why she came to good 'ol Alabama to practice gymnastics.

She explained to me all about why she was starting so late in the year. Her paperwork was delayed because of a birth certificate mix up. Coach Nelson had sent her a video of the routine so she had been practicing all summer so she wouldn't fall behind. She hated missing so many football games, but she was glad to be here for competition. Ra-Ra!

We were a small state and had even smaller towns. When most people thought about Alabama, they usually thought about cotton fields and our SEC football teams, but we had a lot more to offer. Our school in particular had an amazing gymnastics and cheerleading program.

"So, are the other girls as...pleasant as Holley?" she asked as we walked past the trophy case and into the gym.

"Ha, you noticed, huh?" I snorted.

The gym smelled like floor wax and sweat. A ball trolley was in the middle of the gym, beside a volleyball net. The high ceiling held giant lights and each one of them was turned on. I shielded my eyes; the light bothered my head.

"I've been in the business for a while now." She shrugged her shoulders, looking around the gym. "There are some really nice girls and there are some really not so nice girls."

"All I can tell you is that there are a few that aren't so bad." I pointed to Coach Nelson's office. "That's where you need to be. I have to head to class."

"I'm sure I'll see you around." She smiled at me.

"Yeah, I'm sure." I smiled back.

"Black," Coach Nelson called to me as she came out of her office. She always called us by our last names. "It's good to see you in here."

"Hey, Coach." I nodded toward her.

"You have some belongings still in your locker." She clapped me on the back, sending shock waves through my head. "You can get them now or leave them in there for when you come back."

"I think I'll get them, Coach," I told her, not wanting to give her false hope.

"Richards, welcome again." She gestured for Keira to follow her.

Keira waved goodbye to me and I headed for the locker room. With the migraines, I was on permanent P.E. restriction. I wasn't complaining. On days like this, I was doing good just walking to and from each class. Still, it bothered me that at 18 I was unable to do things that I once loved. I knew if I even attempted a simple stunt that used to come so naturally to me, I'd be on the floor, throwing up.

Pushing the thoughts from my mind, I made my way toward my locker. It was still a few minutes before the next class would be here, so the locker room was bare. It was dark save for a few lights, one of which was flickering in that horror movie sort of way. The light was bothersome. So, I gave the switch a jiggle, trying to get it right itself. No luck.

Sighing, I gave up on the light, deciding I wouldn't be in here long so it was not that big of a deal. I reached my locker, put in the combination, and opened the creaky door. The maroon paint was old and chipped away on my hand. They really needed to get new lockers.

A shirt and a pair of shoes were inside the small metal compartment. The shirt was one that Rob had bought me when we went to a concert to see one of my favorite artists. Just the sight of it made me see red. I wanted nothing that reminded me of our time together.

I had been a different person then, a person who I would rather forget. I grabbed the t-shirt, crumpled it up into a ball, marched over to the nearby trashcan and threw it in. My chest was rising and falling at a rapid pace. I was furious, which was not a good idea. Anytime my emotions got the better of me, especially being angry, it sent a pressure to my head that was unbearable.

I suddenly felt sick. Rushing to the stalls, I barely made it before my breakfast came back up. My back hugging the stall wall, I slumped to the floor once it was over. After purging my stomach of its contents, the pain in my head had tripled. There was no way I could finish out the day.

I reached into my back pocket to pull out my phone, ready to call my mom for an emergency pick up, when I felt the room spin. My body slid sideways, and I hit the icy floor before I knew what was going on, sending my phone skidding across the dingy, grey tile.

My head hit with a good crack, and I felt my eyes roll in the back of my head and then my body went rigid. My eyes snapped back into place, staring out at the end of the stalls, unable to move. There was a slight haze around everything, as if I were dreaming, but there was no way I could be. If I wasn't, then why couldn't I move?

An intense pressure suddenly surrounded me. I knew there was someone else in the room with me, but I couldn't see them. The lights were still only half on, so the room was dim. Above me, they flickered. Footsteps in the distance were closing in. The closer they got, the more intense the pressure became until I thought I might be squashed beneath it like a bug.

I knew what this was. Sleep paralysis. But how? It only took place right before waking up or falling asleep. The only thing I had been doing was barfing my guts up. Had I passed out? Why? This had never happened before.

A pair of legs rounded the corner. They stopped, as if the person they belonged to wanted to take a good long look at me. Then, another pair appeared, smaller, thinner, more faint. Then another, and another. Before long, a group was standing at the edge of the stalls.

Then they rushed toward me, all of them at once. A fiery hand grabbed my throat, cutting off all the air to my lungs. I could feel them on me, straddling my body, pinning me to ground. My eyes were wide open, but I couldn't see them. Where were they? Those bone sharp fingers pinched into my skin as I struggled to breathe.

There was a smell, a stench that made my eyes water, and then I felt a pressure on my lips. It was as if they were trying to kiss me, but they yanked my mouth open with their other hand. I wanted to scream, but nothing came out, my voice lost in fear. My head was pounding; my ears ringing so loudly it hurt.

I heard it then, a laugh, the same laugh from my nightmare last night. It was deep, rough. It wasn't coming from me; it was from...that thing; the thing attacking me. Its mouth was on mine and it breathed in deeply, drinking me in. It was taking my breath. It was going to kill me. I had to fight back, but I was so weak and it was so strong.

It was useless. There was nothing I could do but lay there and wait for the end to come.

Ava

Floating. That's what it felt like. The blackness had already taken hold of me and now, I was just suspended. In what? The air? I didn't know, but I was somewhere and it was just nothingness.

There was no cold, no heat, no light. It should have been overwhelming. I should have been terrified, but I felt more at peace than I had in a long time because there was also no pain.

My head felt clear. I could form a coherent thought. For the first time in six months, my body, my mind, was free.

Are you free, Ava?

It was a voice from within the darkness, or was it in my head? I turned my head from side to side, but it was pitch black, there was no way I could see anything.

Do you want to stay here? Here in all of this blackness?

Who are you? Where are you? Where am I?

It's nice here away from the light isn't it?

I...I don't hurt. It feels...good.

Good enough to stay?

I...I don't know what you mean.

The voice was raspy, but I couldn't make out if it was male or female. It sounded far away, but it was hard to tell since it bounced off the walls of this place, whatever it was. The way its voice echoed, it made me think I was in some sort of cave.

There was something picking at the peace that had settled over my consciousness. Its claw-like fingers, digging until it hurt, digging until I realized how uncomfortable I truly was.

That's it. You see it now. You see it for what it really is, don't you?

Who are you?

Don't give in, Ava. You're stronger than...

Nothing. The voice just stopped talking. For a while I remained silent, wondering where it could have gone. I listened until I couldn't take the silence any longer.

Hello? Are you still there? How do I get out of here? Hello? Hello!

There was a rustling sound in the distance that made my entire body freeze. I don't even think I was breathing. It sounded like a bug, with thousands of tiny hairy legs, scurrying across a stone floor. I shivered, goose bumps forming all along my body.

For a while, the silence took back over. It lasted so long that I was beginning to believe I had imagined the sound all together. Then, a bit closer this time, I heard it again. I knew it wasn't just a trick my mind was playing on me; there was someone or something in here with me.

This once peaceful rest was now a thing of nightmares. I did not understand where I was or how to get out. My hands and feet could feel nothing.

Again, I heard rustling in the distance, each noise sounding closer and closer. The nearer it got, the clearer the sound became. Deep within me, I knew it was *someone*. It was that same someone who had found me lying helpless on the locker room floor. I had to get out of here, but I was at a complete loss as to how.

Over here.

The voice was back. I jerked my head around, trying to find it.

Hello? What do I do? You have to help me.

I can't.

Then why are you here?

You have to help yourself.

How?

Don't give in to the shadows. Don't find comfort in the darkness. Open your eyes.

They are open! I can't see anything!

No, Ava, open your eyes. Wake up! You have the power to fight against this. Use it! Wake up!

What?

Wake up!

Suddenly, a scream reverberated off of the cavernous walls. The blood in my veins seemed to freeze in place. Every hair on my body stood on end. Then, I heard pounding, like thunder that never ended. That was when I realized that something was running at me.

Wake up, Ava! Open your eyes!

My eyes jerked open and a brilliant light instantly blinded me. It almost looked like a mixture of blues and purples, like flashes of lightning, but then it faded to white. There were muffled voices and I think I heard someone say my name, but I wasn't sure. Slowly, faces took shape above me. There was a mess of black hair, the smell of leather, and a black tattoo.

"She's coming to," I heard someone say.

"Step aside, young man," another person said.

When I could finally see, I focused on a pair of intense grey eyes.

"Gabriel?" I questioned. "Why are you in the girls' locker room?"

Really, Ava? That's what you're going to ask? I thought to myself.

He looked back at me, an odd expression on his face, one that I couldn't really read. It was probably because I was still loopy, but I was almost certain he looked angry. I began noticing more faces around me; Keira and Coach Nelson were there. To my horror, so was Frankie.

She had the most intense sneer on her face. I wasn't a mind reader, but I was almost certain what she was thinking, "There goes Ava again, acting like she's dying. She's such a Drama Queen."

Why did this have to happen here? Why did it have to happen in front of her? This was just ammunition, and I handed it right over to her on a silver platter.

The paramedic was securing a brace around my neck.

"I don't need that," I told him.

"It's procedure, honey," he responded.

I figured it was better not to argue or resist. The last thing I wanted to do was give Frankie and her goons any more juicy gossip to carry back to the rest of the school. So, I remained silent when they put me on a stretcher, strapped me down, and lifted me onto the gurney.

There was only one way out of the locker room, and that was through the gym. The paramedics rolled me out to a group of whispering onlookers. I closed my eyes so I wouldn't have to look at them. It was that mantra you told yourself when you were little and afraid of the dark, "If I can't see them, they can't see me."

The truth was, I didn't want them to see me right now. I wanted them to see me for who I was, not what I was going through. If I could force them to sit down and listen to what I had to say, I would. Maybe then, they would be kinder. Maybe then, I wouldn't have to feel like a freak. Maybe then, they would understand. But, life is a jerk and it doesn't care what you want.

I took a glance as they lifted me into the ambulance and saw Gabriel towering over the other students, that same intense glare on his face.

I WAS AT THE HOSPITAL FOR THE ENTIRE NIGHT. I HOPED THAT IT would just be a few hours, but my family doctor, Dr. Hester, wasn't hearing of it.

"Ava, this is a very serious matter," she told me. "We need to do several tests and if I'm not happy with what I see, then you may have to stay an additional day. No arguments, young lady. We have to make sure we take good care of you."

My parents agreed. I was stuck there until the doctor cleared me. For hours we sat in the hospital room, Mom worrying, Dad answering work emails, and me pretending I was asleep. If I was awake, Mom would hover, and right now I couldn't stand it.

My mind was too busy with scenarios of Frankie trying to make my life more of a living hell. I'm sure she had something amazing up her sleeve. I guess staying in the hospital was a reprieve from her endless torture.

There was a knock, breaking my train of thought. I could hear Mom's shoes clicking on the white tile floor as she made her way to the door.

"Hi," the British accent hit my ears like a musical note. "I'm Keira, a friend of your daughter's. Well, we actually just met today. Um, these are for her."

My eyes shot open, and I watched as Keira handed my mom a bouquet of sunflowers. They were gorgeous and my favorite flower. I wondered how she could have guessed that. Maybe she had asked someone, but who?

"She's sleeping right now, but..."

"I'm awake," I announced, my voice cracking in a way that made me sound more pitiful than I was.

"Oh, well," Mom started, giving me a look that said, "You should rest."

"It's okay, Mom," I told her, sitting up. "I could use some company."

"Alright, but just for a while." She smiled, sweetly.

She moved aside and let Keira enter. Keira gave Mom a mesmerizing smile and gingerly walked over to me then embraced me in a warm hug.

"How are you?" she asked.

"I'm alright." I shrugged and tried not to flinch at the pain in my head that the movement caused. "Honey, why don't we grab something to eat?" Mom prodded Dad with her foot. "Would you girls like anything?"

"Oh, no, I'm fine, Mrs. Black," Keira told her. "My host family made a large dinner."

"Your host family? You're an exchange student?" Dad raised an eyebrow.

"Hence the accent," Keira giggled. "I'm here from London on a gymnastics scholarship for the cheer team."

"Oh..." Mom looked worried. She was well aware of how awful Frankie and her goons had been to me.

"It's alright, Mom," I jumped in. "Keira is cool."

Mom looked at her and then at Dad. He was still staring at Keira as though trying to determine if he could trust leaving her with his daughter. After a moment, he grabbed Mom by the hand.

"We'll be right back," he said, kissing my forehead, and then they left the room.

Once they had left, I relaxed immediately. I didn't even realize I was so tense. I loved my parents, but sometimes they acted like I might break. It could be overwhelming.

Keira sat in the chair my dad had just occupied and looked over at me. It was funny, but even though I'd literally just met her, I felt very comfortable around her.

"So, how are you really feeling?" She cut her bright blue eyes at me.

Keira wasn't stupid. I didn't think my parents were either, but she and I were the same age. It was easier to talk to your friends about certain things.

"Like I about died," I confessed.

"It's okay to feel bad, you know," she said in a tender voice. "We're only human, Ava. We're not built to hold it all inside."

I nodded my head in agreement, and for some reason, I just broke down crying. Keira rushed over and hugged me to her chest, letting me get tears all over her pretty black shirt.

Why was I breaking down in front of this girl? I didn't even know her. Sure, she was nice and seemed to be reaching out to me, but I've never been one to be so open. I felt this weight on my shoulders and having her come here to check on me just seemed to be that one last piece to have it all come crashing down.

"I'm sorry," I told her as I wiped my eyes dry. "I don't know where that came from."

"Don't worry," she hugged me one more time, "It's what friends are for."

I smiled, feeling better than I had in a long time. It felt good to have a friend. Still, there was a slight fear in me. Keira was my friend now, but I couldn't help wondering how long it would last. Frankie had a way of convincing people to believe just about anything. Keira seemed like a strong-willed person, but there weren't many people who could resist Frankie's charms, or her threats.

Keira stayed even after my parents came back. Before long, she had them convinced she hung the moon and stars. Even though she was new to all of us, Keira just had something about her that pulled you in, and you couldn't help but want to be near her. There was something bright about her presence that made me feel like I needed her to be here right at this moment.

Near the end of visiting hours, she stood up and announced she needed to get back before her host family thought she had run away back to London. Mom and Dad were sad to see her go, but none more than me.

Thankfully I was able to go home the next day, but Dr. Hester scheduled me for several follow up appointments. Apparently, she thought I needed every test that medical professionals had ever created. I still wasn't able to return to school until she cleared me.

Keira was kind enough to bring the homework I was missing so I wouldn't get behind. She also snuck me in my favorite Sonic treat. We made sure to discreetly dispose of the cups so my parents wouldn't have a fit about it. Dr. Hester had put me on a strict diet of no sugar, but let me tell you something—a girl cannot live without her chocolate chip cookie dough blast.

Keira kept me up to date on the happenings at school while we pretended I was eating tuna and making half attempts at History homework. As I predicted, Frankie was telling everyone I had overdosed on my migraine meds. Keira didn't want to tell me at first, but after some convincing, she revealed to me what had been spreading around campus like a wildfire.

"You really shouldn't let it get to you, Ava," Keira tried comforting me. "You know what really happened. Frankie is a vile girl and eventually, she'll get what's coming to her."

"Yeah, but in the meantime, I do have to worry about it," I sighed.

"Well, you don't have to face it alone," she told me with a pat on my hand.

"Thanks, Keira," I smiled, "You really are my only friend."

"Truly? What about Gabriel?" she wondered with a raised eyebrow, seeming really confused.

"Gabriel?" I questioned, the image of his angry face flashing in my mind's eye.

"Yes, I figured you two were friends." She shrugged her shoulders. "He's been asking me about you every day. I assumed he couldn't visit you himself, seeing as how your father might not take too kindly to such a...brooding figure coming to call on his daughter."

"Well, that's nice of him to ask," I told her. "But Gabriel Matthews and I are not friends. We've spoken like once. To be honest, he sort of creeps me out."

"Are we talking about the same Gabriel Matthews?" She looked shocked. "Because the dude's hot."

"You can be creepy and hot," I pointed out.

"True," she giggled in that musical tone of hers. "He did basically rescue you though."

"Rescue me?" I felt left out of something.

"Yes. What? Has no one told you?" Keira looked shocked. "When you started convulsing, you were screaming. Gabriel apparently heard you as he was walking by the girls' locker room door. He came rushing in and found you on the floor and held you so you wouldn't hurt yourself and then used his cell to call an ambulance."

"Oh, I didn't know." I really couldn't think of anything else to say.

That was the end of our conversation about Gabriel, but that didn't mean I stopped thinking about him. He may have come to my rescue, but I still felt like there was just something odd about him.

I told myself that I wouldn't think about it anymore, that Gabriel Matthews would just fade from my mind if I concentrated on Math. Who was I kidding? His face was there, haunting me, as I was trying to figure out what 36 times 3 was. It took me a full 10 minutes to realize I had it wrong, and that's why I had to do the problem over four times.

I was so thankful to be back in my own bed after a couple days in the hospital, but I still felt as if I had been run over with a steamroller so mind was mush. I gave up after Keira left and put on some light music until I was called down for dinner.

That night Mom made my favorite comfort food, fried pork chops and homemade tortillas. I was full and as content as I had been in a long time, even if she let the pork chops cook a bit too long and the burnt half of the tortillas. It was unlike her to let food burn, but she was tired, too.

I slept deeply, shifting in and out of a dream that didn't make much sense at first. Then, as it became clearer, I realized Gabriel was standing in that same field I had seen before, the one with the woman. He was alone though, the night sky bright and full of stars.

It looked as though he were holding something in his hands. It was shining and midnight blue. When he opened his palms, streaks of blue lightning shot outward, illuminating the surrounding field. Perhaps I should have been afraid, but I was more curious.

"Look at your hands," he said.

When I looked down, I saw my hands were aglow. The color was deep purple, with hints of vibrant pink. I was in awe. I moved my hands in front of my face, watching the light dance beneath my skin.

When I looked up again, Gabriel was standing in front of me. His grey eyes were bright, full of wonder. I had never seen him this way before now. He was beautiful. My heart lurched and the only words in my mind were, "Holy crap."

"You can do more than you think you're capable of, Ava," he said, his voice like velvet on my skin. "You must for what is coming."

"What's coming?" I asked him, still lost in his eyes.

He turned his head and when I followed his gaze, I saw the hooded figures from my nightmares. I jumped, a scream caught in my throat, and I bolted awake in bed. Sweat dripped from my brow. It felt as though the dream had only lasted for a second, but my body told me I had been struggling for a while. I felt depleted.

Groaning, I got up, washed my face, and brushed my teeth. I had a routine to stick to, and I was determined to do it. I wanted, for some twisted reason, to get back to school and live a normal life.

Why couldn't I stop thinking about Gabriel? He was never on my radar before and here I was, thinking about him, dreaming about him. Shoving thoughts of him to the back of my mind, I got dressed and made my way downstairs.

My parents both had to go to work today, so it was up to me to be a big girl and take care of myself. After making a decent breakfast, I did a bit of school work and all the laundry I had been putting off for a while. It was my least favorite chore, so I was feeling proud of myself for getting it done.

After that, I needed some fresh air. The rain had slacked off for the past few days, so I decided my exercise for the day was to take a walk around the neighborhood. I could do that and still come back in time to start dinner. I enjoyed cooking for my parents. I was actually pretty good at it.

I slipped on my favorite sweater and a pair of grey yoga pants and then pulled my hair into a bun on the top of my head. Not even attempting to look in the mirror, I opened my door and was greeted by a looming figure on my doorstep.

"Aahh! Son of a..." I jumped back, clutching my chest.

"Sorry," Gabriel looked one way and then the other.

When our eyes met, my heart did a certain dance that I had no name for and honestly, didn't want to. Naming it terrified me. Actually, the intense color of his eyes terrified me, and flashes of my dream came dancing back through my memories.

"Uh," I started, my heart still hammering like a drum and my face on fire. "What are you doing here?"

"I..." Then he stuck a container in my face. "My grandfather wanted me to bring this to you."

"Your grandfather?" This was all confusing.

"He heard you were out of the hospital and wanted me to bring this to you...and your family." He handed the container out to me again.

I took it from him and could smell herbs, like garlic and oregano. It was still warm, so his grandfather must have just made it.

"Thank you," I said.

"You're welcome." He stood there for a moment. "Are you well?"

"I'm better," I said to him. "Um, this is rather warm. I need to go set it down. Would you like to come in for a moment?"

"Sure," he said and followed me inside.

I walked back in, and Gabriel followed me to the kitchen. His grey eyes watched my every move as I set the container on the counter. He said nothing as he watched me. It seemed he was expecting me to open it, so I did.

"It's chicken parmesan," he said. "I hope you and your family like it."

"We do, thank you," I said to him. "For bringing this and being... um...well, nice to me. And, helping me the other day."

"Are you not used to someone being nice to you?" he asked seriously.

"I'm not used to you being nice to me," I pointed out. "We've gone to school together our entire lives practically, and you've said nothing to me until now."

"For one, I'm surprised you noticed me at all." His look was severe. "Also, you've never spoken to me either, so I think we're even."

I had nothing to say to that. He was right. I was too busy trying to be someone I wasn't and not caring who I hurt along the way. His words were a hard truth. I wasn't accustomed to guys calling me out on my crap.

A few months ago, I had most of the guys I knew wrapped around my pinky. I was Ava Black, a hot cheerleader, rich, and with a lot of pull around campus. I could bat my eyes and get what I wanted. Looking at Gabriel, I knew he wouldn't be that easy to manipulate. He was too strong-willed.

To me, that was intriguing for several reasons. He was fascinating in so many ways, but before I could get lost in the mystery that was Gabriel Matthews, he cleared his throat.

"I think I interrupted you," he said. "I'll let you get back to your day."

"I was going for a walk. You can join me," I offered before I realized what I had said. "I mean, if you want to."

"That would be fine." He nodded.

That would be fine? Who talks like that?

We started out the door and I made sure to leave a wide gap between Gabriel and myself. He didn't seem to notice, and if he did, he said nothing about it. We just walked down the sidewalk, not saying much of anything.

I suddenly remembered how I looked and cringed. I had learned that vanity was an undesirable trait, so I didn't focus on my looks that much anymore. Still, I felt somewhat disheveled at the moment.

Today wasn't exactly warm, but at least Alabama had odd weather and October wasn't freezing cold yet; it had just the right amount of chill that put you in the mood for Halloween. I wrapped my arms tightly around my body as a brisk breeze swirled past us.

Glancing over at Gabriel, his eyes looked up in a tree as he watched two birds dance from branch to branch; I wondered what exactly he was doing showing up at my house. Had his grandfather sent him as he claimed?

"Can I ask you something?" he said without turning his head.

His voice snapping the silence between us made me jump.

"Okay," I said to him.

"You were screaming something when I found you," he said, looking over at me. "Do you remember what it was?"

I tensed as visions of the figures came flooding back. I had tried not to think about it. Each night that sleep had overtaken me since then, I worried they would come back and haunt my dreams. I was terrified I would find myself floating in that darkness again.

He had heard me say something. I don't even remember half of what was coming out of my mouth. I didn't want to tell him what I had seen.

"No," I shook my head.

"You kept telling yourself to wake up, that they would get you if you didn't," he told me. "Like you were having a nightmare."

"I guess I was hallucinating." I felt my cheeks grow hot. "I'm really sorry."

"For what?" he asked. "You did nothing wrong. It's not your fault."

"I just hope I didn't put you in an uncomfortable situation." I fiddled with my fingers.

"Of course not, it's my job," he said and then seemed embarrassed.

"Your job?" I wondered.

"Human nature," he said, and that same intense look came over his face. "We're supposed to help one another, are we not?"

"Ava," I heard my father's voice and realized we had made our way back to my house.

Mom and Dad had just pulled up. They were getting out of the car and I saw that he had on his "Dad Face." Here his daughter stood with a very interesting-looking boy, a boy who towered over his 5'11 frame.

"Hey, Daddy." I walked over to his car and hugged him.

"What are you doing out here?" He looked from me to Gabriel. "It's cold."

"I took a walk with Gabriel," I explained. "These are my parents. Melinda and Francisco Black."

"Mr. Black. Mrs. Black." Gabriel stuck his hand out to shake my dad's hand and then my mom's. "Gabriel Matthews. I go to school with Ava. My grandfather, I believe you know him from work, Ryland Matthews, sent me over with a meal for your family. He wanted me to see how Ava was doing."

"Is that so?" Dad cocked an eyebrow. "What grade are you in?"

"I'm a senior, sir," Gabriel said.

"Gabriel is sure to be our Valedictorian," I told Dad, hoping to ease the tension.

"Maybe," Gabriel smiled. "That's if Andie Baker doesn't beat me out of it. We've been in competition since grade school."

"I know Ryland." Dad seemed to remember. "He guest lectures for Professor Hendrix."

"He does." Gabriel smiled. "My grandfather has retired, but can't seem to stay out of the lecture hall."

"He's a very gifted man." My Dad said. "And it seems you're following in his footsteps with your academic achievements. Any college prospects?"

"I've had a few offers," Gabriel stated. "My parents wanted me to follow their footsteps, go to Harvard, study medicine."

Wanted? I looked at Gabriel, realizing I knew nothing about his home life.

"That sounds amazing." Mom beamed. She clearly liked Gabriel.

"And what do you want?" Dad wondered.

"I'm fascinated with History in all forms, but mostly Anthropology and the study of people's belief systems. I have a strong interest in Native belief systems, as well, always have." Gabriel's eyes seemed to light up at the mention of the past.

"That's what I teach, Anthropology, at the University," Dad told him, a little surprised.

"Yes, I know," Gabriel admitted. "I sat in one your lectures about the Indigenous People of Mexico. I had studied some, but I didn't realize there were still so many people that spoke an Indigenous language. One in ten tribes, wasn't it?"

"Yes, that's correct." Dad looked shocked again.

Here was this tattooed, biker-looking rebel, and he was talking about researching Indigenous populations in the Americas.

"Would you like to stay for dinner?" Dad offered.

"Oh, that would be nice, wouldn't it, Ava?" Mom nudged me and I just sort of nodded so as not to be rude.

"That is a kind offer, really, but I need to get back home," Gabriel told him. "I have a few chores I need to get done for my grandfather. I'm glad that you're feeling better, Ava."

With that, he told us goodbye, climbed into his very sleek and rumbly muscle car, and seemed to vanish down the street. I stood there for a moment, looking after him. He had come into my day like a whirlwind and was gone just as fast.

The meal his grandfather made was absolutely delicious. I ate until I just couldn't take another bite. After cleaning up and then taking a shower, I gratefully fell into bed, but I couldn't fall asleep right away. I was exhausted, but my mind was whirling with thoughts of the day and most of them were about Gabriel. The conversation we had about my hallucination plagued my mind. The look on his face, his words, it all sounded so very strange. The words he'd used, "his job," made it sound like he was responsible for what? Me? For what had happened to me?

Gabriel

The rain was still coming down in sheets, so I pulled the car into the garage, next to my grandfather's black SUV. Pops drove little these days. He told me it wasn't because of the shake of his hands, he just preferred to stay home, but I knew differently. Watching the steady decline of someone you love was difficult.

You felt lost. You couldn't fix them. You couldn't make it better. It wasn't your fight. All you could do was just be there.

I found Pops at his desk in the study, his stock of white hair barely visible over the large leather-bound book. This was where he spent most of his time. Pops was a scholar, through and through. He never stopped learning and had taught me everything I knew. Without him, I wouldn't be who I was. I owed him so much.

After the loss of my parents, we were all each other had. We still were.

"You cleaned up without me," I said to him.

"You were on delivery duty," he remarked without looking up from his reading.

"Well, yeah, but you could have waited," I said.

"I am perfectly capable of cleaning a few dishes, Gabriel." Pops finally looked up at me.

"I know that," I said.

"I am having a very good day," he continued. "I want to be able to do things for myself while I can."

"I understand that," I said.

He looked at me. I had said the wrong thing. Pops knew I was only trying to help. But saying I understood what he was going through wasn't true. It was his battle. While I had my own fears of what this disease was doing to his body, it was still his body. I would never understand.

"What I meant was I just want you to know I am here if you need me," I told him. "I love you, Pops."

"And I love you." He smiled at me. "And how was Ms. Black?"

"She seemed to be in good spirits," I replied. "Her parents send their thanks for the meal."

"And were you able to speak to her?" he wondered.

"I did," I responded.

"And you still feel the same way about your initial speculations?" Pops asked.

"I do," I told him.

"I suppose I should make a few calls then," he said.

"Yeah." I suddenly felt uncomfortable for some reason.

I was sure about Ava. There were a lot of things that caused me to doubt myself. I was standoffish, somewhat shy, and other times too bold. Despite my flaws, there was one thing I knew without hesitation; Ava Black was special.

The doorbell chime relieved me from my inner thoughts.

"That's probably Trevor," I said. "We're playing some games tonight."

"Ah, yes, I remember." Pops smiled. "There is still plenty of food leftover for you two."

"Thanks, Pops." I smiled back.

Heading for the door, trying to shake thoughts of Ava from my mind, I focused on spending time with my best friend.

Trevor and I would probably would have never been friends if it weren't for Ava. She did not know the impact she had on my life.

Before Ava became someone to be feared, she had always been kind to me and others.

There was a good chance she didn't remember this, but Trevor was being bullied by Rob Hastings, and Ava had stood up for him.

I'd heard the commotion and looked up from my seat on the gym bleachers to see Ava giving Rob a piece of her mind. We were only in 4th grade, but she still looked fierce and powerful. Seeing her take on Rob was something. It compelled me to reach out to Trevor. From that moment on, we were best friends.

"You ready?" Trevor asked as I opened the door.

"You brought gummy worms?" I grabbed the bag from him. "Yes!"

"Don't be a hog," he said as we moved into the house.

"I'm not a hog." I opened the bag and started eating them.

"You are, and the last bag I brought I got like one out of it," he laughed as Kaine came up to us sniffing. "None for you, Kaine. I don't think giant wolf dogs are supposed to eat gummy worms. Don't look at me like that. I brought you something."

Trevor pulled out a large dog bone from his backpack. Kaine knew exactly what it was as soon as he saw it. Unwrapping it, Trevor handed the bone to Kaine, who quickly grabbed it and disappeared down the hall.

"You spoil him," I said.

"Yeah, well, Mom is never not going to be allergic to pet dander, so your dog is my dog." He shrugged. "And how can you not love that dog? He's amazing. I swear he knows stuff."

"You're weird," I said as we moved up the stairs to my room.

"And I'm your best friend, so what does that make you?" he asked.

"Friends with a weirdo," I laughed.

"You're hilarious." He punched my arm.

I pretended like it stung a little, but really I felt nothing. Not that Trevor was weak. He was mousey, with thin arms, but it was me. I was just born with a resistance to pain in a way that most people wouldn't understand. Trevor definitely wouldn't.

Or maybe he would. I had been tempted so many times to tell him about my past, about my parents, but I didn't want to burden him with that. He knew just enough to keep him from prying too much. It wasn't fair to him, me keeping secrets, but that's just the way my life had to be. I told no one.

For some reason this brought my thoughts back to Ava. I couldn't help but wonder if she would understand. She hardly knew me, but when the time came, if it did, would I be able to make her see that what I had done had been with the best of intentions? The thought made my stomach turn.

We made our way up the stairs and into my room. Out of all the rooms in the house, my room was the smallest, but it had everything I needed. Pops had asked me over and over if I wanted to move to one of the bigger rooms, but I told him no. This was the room my parents had picked out as my nursery. Leaving it felt like leaving a piece of them behind.

"So, how is Ava?" Trevor asked me after a few hours of playing.

I could tell that he had wanted to ask this for a while. His face said as much.

"She's doing alright," I told him.

"Did you tell her you saved her life?" he laughed.

"I didn't save her life, Trev," I said.

"You did!" he said. "It was like fate, right? You just walked by and heard a commotion and found Ava in need. You held her until 911 came. Yeah, you saved her."

"You're such a romantic," I said.

"I am not," he laughed. "It's just...I mean, it's fate, right?"

"If you say so." I shrugged.

Trevor had always been this way. He filled his head with the stories from movies and fairytales. There was always a hero there to save those in need. I didn't see myself that way. I also didn't see Ava as some weak damsel either. She was more than that. More than she realized.

His words brought back the scene of her writhing body. She was fighting with something. Something unseen. The look of terror on her face chilled me to my core. How could anyone just walk away from her and not help?

"What do you think of Keira?" Trevor asked me.

"The exchange student?" I was brought out of my thoughts.

"Yeah, we've been partnered up," he told me. "We have to do a paper together."

"I don't know anything about her," I admitted. "Why?"

"I'm just hoping she's not like Frankie," Trevor said, looking at the screen. "She seems okay, I guess. But, she hangs with that crew. I don't have the best track record with them. Not even with Ava."

"Yeah." I hated to agree with him. "You don't think Ava has changed?"

He shrugged in response. I couldn't help but wonder about this myself.

Ava

They lined the hallway, wearing long robes with hidden faces, staring at me, and I couldn't shake the feeling that they saw me as something tasty. Their eyes bore into me and I felt naked under their gaze. I picked up speed, desiring to find a way from their menacing presence, searching for the nearest exit. The further and faster I went, the longer the hallway became. More figures, more eyes, followed my every move.

I could see a faint light near what looked to be the end of the hall. My legs moved me forward, but the light came no closer. My heartbeat quickened as the hands from the figures on either side of me reached out, trying to touch my flesh. I didn't know what would happen if they made contact, but I knew I didn't want to find out.

Jumping from left to right, avoiding their hands that looked ancient and withered, I screamed in fear as I ran down the hall. I just knew that at any moment they would catch me. Then, one figure stepped out ahead of me, blocking my path. I skidded to a halt, nearly falling on my butt right in front of it.

It was dressed in the same way, a hood concealing its face, but there was something different about it, something that said it was more powerful. I gulped, contemplating a way to move around it or maybe backtracking. I'd gotten into this hall some way, so that meant there had to be an exit.

The thing pointed a long, crooked finger at me and hissed. Chills covered my body. Without even realizing it at first, I fell to my knees, shaking in fright. I could feel the thing coming closer and closer to me, all the while making these snake-like noises. I closed my eyes, praying that this wasn't real, that I was only dreaming.

Covering my face with my hands, I noticed something odd. These weren't my hands. My skin had a natural tan. The skin that covered these hands was light and fair. This wasn't me. This wasn't my body.

"Don't do this," I said, and the voice that came out wasn't mine.

I got a hiss in response.

"Please, please," I begged. "You don't have to do this."

"Oh, but we do, child," the voice hissed. "We must do this. We thank you for your sacrifice."

I screamed as something red-hot blinded me, and I jolted awake in bed. For a moment, I felt disoriented. Nothing in my room looked familiar. My surroundings were as foreign to me as some alien planet light-years away. In fact, I felt alien. I was a stranger inside my own body, looking out into the world with unfamiliar eyes.

Dreams had always been just dreams to me, but this one had felt so real. I could still feel the pain of something sharp digging its way into my flesh. The smell of old and dead things lingered in my nostrils. And, the girl, I could still feel her inside my head, or maybe it was me that had occupied her mind.

Whoever that girl was, I was her for that moment in time. I saw what she saw and felt what she felt. She was terrified, scared for her life. My heart was still racing like wild horses in my chest. It took every bit of my resolve to convince myself it was just a dream, but with all the other things that had been haunting me at night, I wasn't so sure.

I was talking like one of those people in the supernatural shows my mom watched. We were not a family of any strict religious practices. My parents said they wanted me to make up my own mind. If I had to define my beliefs, I supposed I was agonistic. Something had to be out there, but I didn't let it control my life. So, why was this dream suddenly turning me into the Winchesters? Was I having a nervous breakdown? Was it the meds?

Going back to school was nerve-racking enough. The last thing I needed was to think I was going insane or haunted. Again, being the weirdo I am, I wanted a normal school experience. Unless I wanted to spend the rest of my youth in a padded cell, I had to get a handle on things.

I met Keira at the school entrance. We waved at Mom as she drove away and then made our way inside. I wasn't sure what to expect, but one thing was for sure, I wasn't expecting people to actually be happy to see me back.

They greeted me with many hugs and genuine concerns about how I was feeling. It was a bit overwhelming, but I did my best to not ask them where they had been for the past six months. My question was answered when Frankie walked up with her posse. She was intimidatingly beautiful in her short, plaid skirt and tight white blouse.

It was no wonder people steered clear once she had marked me. They didn't want to become collateral damage.

"Look who's back," Frankie said in that high-pitched voice that seemed to rip through my brain. "How was rehab?"

"I wasn't in rehab, Frankie, and you know that." Her face was irritating me.

For six months, I had put up with her constant bullying, and I was more than tired of it. But what could I do against the Queen Bee?

"Do I, Ava?" she pretended innocence. "Do any of us?"

"I do," Keira stepped in. "And do you know what else I know? Those who live in glass houses shouldn't throw stones."

"And what is that supposed to mean, Union Jack?" she sneered, crossing her arms.

"It means I wonder what would happen if I strolled into Principal Rush's office with that purse of yours in my hands. What she would find?" Her blue eyes bore into Frankie. "I'm sure you have a prescription, right?"

"Come on, girls." Frankie suddenly looked nervous, but she pretended that Keira's words hadn't bothered her. "I'm finished wasting my time on these hoes."

"Have a good day, girls," Keira called after them, smiling.

I looked at her like my knight in shining armor. She had made Frankie run for the hills.

"How did you know about...all of that?" I asked her.

"I'm very observant, Ava," she looped her arm through mine and pulled me down the hall to our first class, "I see all."

"Oh, is that so?" I laughed.

"Yes," her eyebrow arched dramatically, "Just like I see a certain tattooed bad boy strutting our way."

Gabriel did strut, but it was effortless. When he caught sight of me, his shoulders seemed to stiffen. If I wasn't mistaken, he stood up just a bit straighter. I tried not to, but I couldn't stop myself from staring. He stopped right in front of us, Trevor close at his side.

Trevor looked at his feet like a kid who was about to get in trouble for something. His slender frame and pale skin made him look sickly. He had curly blond hair and small features. His height was fairly average, but he looked like a tiny mouse next to Gabriel. In fact, they were in extreme contrast to each other.

Gabriel was tan; Trevor was fair. Gabriel was muscular; Trevor was slim, no muscles anywhere on his body. Gabriel had intense grey eyes, Trevor's eyes, when I saw them, were dark brown. Gabriel had pitch-black hair, and Trevor's was so blond it was nearly white.

"Hi, Trevor," Keira said, which made Trevor jump. "I have some research notes for our project."

"Oh...um...hey...hi...hello," he stumbled over his words as he looked up at Keira, then quickly looked back down. "That's great."

"Smooth, Trev." Gabriel elbowed him.

Trevor smiled, looking at Gabriel like he was the big brother he had always wanted. It made me happy to know that someone like Gabriel, who would have every reason to steer clear of the likes of me or Trevor, would be kind to us. It was like seeing light after being in the dark for so long.

It sort of hurt your eyes, but in a good way, because you knew you were about to see something beautiful.

"Trevor and I are working on an English paper together," Keira explained, pulling out the notes and handing them to Trevor. "We are going to crush the competition."

"There isn't a competition," Trevor told her.

"Of course there is," she pretended to be shocked, "You and I will do such an amazing job that we'll get top marks in the class."

We all laughed.

"Well, gents, Ava and I must get to class, but you're more than welcome to accompany us down the hall." Keira batted her eyes.

Trevor looked like he was going to faint. I looked at Gabriel to gauge his reaction. He seemed unfazed. That was nearly unbelievable. Keira was insanely beautiful. Any hot-blooded male should throw themselves at her.

The four of us headed down the hall and toward my first class. People stared. We made an odd assortment, I'm sure. The gorgeous foreign exchange student, the hot bad boy, the nerdy do-gooder, and the fallen queen, all together, and not really caring what others thought.

We were like a small band of misfits, but it worked out well. Gabriel didn't say much, but when he did, it was usually to Trevor. I wondered if he was just putting up with us because he was Trevor's friend and so were we.

We didn't have lunch together, but Friday, he showed up at my table. He handed me a sandwich from Subway. I looked up in shock.

"Where did you get this?" I asked him.

"At Subway," he said, and I couldn't tell if he were trying to joke with me or not.

"Smart mouth." I shot him a dirty look, wondering what he was doing here. "What I mean is, did you leave campus to get it? We aren't supposed to do that."

"Do I look like someone who always follows the rules, Black?" Gabriel gave me a look that both frightened and excited me. He was trouble, and I liked it.

"I suppose not." I cleared my throat and opened the wrapper. "Uh, this is actually a decent looking sub."

"I guessed." He didn't look up at me.

We spent most of our lunch talking. It was the first time we had talked one-on-one since he had showed up at my house. It sort of felt like he was trying to get to know me. I realized this was the first time that I hadn't seen Keira all day. She and I had spent lunch together all week, and it made me worry that she wasn't here.

"I'm sure she's fine," Gabriel said as if reading my mind.

"What?" I looked up at him.

"Keira. That's who you're looking around for, right?" he pointed out. "I'm sure she's fine. She probably had some cheer-leady thing to do. It is Friday and we have a home game."

"Right." I shrugged.

He was right. I don't know why her absence was bothering me so much.

Maybe because Frankie was with Keira right about now, doing "cheer-leady things," and knowing that she would have to spend extra time with that monster made me worry for my best friend. I knew Keira could stand on her own, but Frankie was ruthless. If she wanted you hurt, you would get hurt.

When we were freshman, Frankie wanted the first flyer spot on the squad, but Amy Miller had that position. Amy was good, better than Frankie, and Frankie knew it. Frankie hated her, and I hated her because that's what friends do for each other. It made me feel guilty now because Amy was really sweet and had done nothing to me. Still, we gave her a hard time.

During one of the pep rallies, Amy got hurt, badly. For a while I thought it was an accident. Frankie and Holley were her spotters. They were supposed to catch her, but during one of Amy's more dangerous moves, she fell. Amy ended up breaking her leg in three places. The flyer spot was open and Frankie got it. It wasn't until a month later that Frankie confessed that she had let Amy fall on purpose.

"I mean, I figured she'd get hurt, sprain an ankle or something," she had told me one night when she had stayed over. "I never imagined she'd break her leg. But, whatever, I'm a better flyer, anyway."

It was one of the first times I realized how horrible of a person Frankie was. I was her best friend, so what did that say about me? Hadn't I done equally repulsive things to people?

"How much do you know about Keira?" Gabriel waved his hand in front of my face.

"What? I'm sorry." I looked up at him, those grey eyes staring intensely at me. "What did you say?"

"Keira, what do you know about her?" he asked.

"Oh, uh," I was confused for a moment, "I mean, about as much as I know about you. Why? Are you going to ask her out?"

I realized the thought made my blood boil.

"No," he said flatly. "I'm not interested in her."

"You seem to be," I pointed out.

"I was just curious." He blushed.

"Are you...are you interested in anyone?" I think I blushed too.

"Are you?" I could feel myself melt under his gaze.

I wanted to ask him out. I could feel the words forming on my tongue. A date with Gabriel Matthews? This was a bad idea. I mean, I guess I liked him. He was funny and kind, but I wasn't sure if my feelings for him were more than that. Besides, he didn't know me that well.

"Why?" I asked.

"Why? Why what?" He looked really confused, but he wasn't the only one.

"Why are you asking me if I'm interested in anyone?" I questioned.

"Just curious." He shifted in his seat.

I felt my face grow hot. What was I doing? Why didn't I just come out and say it? Even if I didn't know him that well, I clearly liked him. He was so charming, and he seemed like a genuinely nice guy. He was odd though, and the whole "it's my job" thing sort of freaked me out.

It was more than just him though. It was me. I was afraid. I liked him if I was being honest. However, I was scared to be vulnerable, especially with him. We had just become friends. This illness had taken over my life. I had let so many people down. I had some good days, but I also had some extremely low and dark days. I didn't want to do that to him.

"No," I got up from the table, "I'm not."

"Me neither." He looked up at me and I felt my stomach drop.

"I've got to go," I told him. "Thanks for the sandwich."

"Sure thing, Black." He tried to smile, but I could see sadness lingering at the edges.

It gutted me. I was surprised by how much that look of hurt got to me. His grey eyes looked betrayed, even though he was still smiling at me. I had to hurry away before I changed my mind and told him how I felt. Seeing him like that was nearly too much. I was certain that if I looked at him any longer, I would have done anything to bring back the light in his eyes.

Trying to push Gabriel's face from my mind, I dumped my Subway bag in the garbage and headed out the door. The fall air had turned crisp and hit me in the face like a slap. Maybe I deserved it for lying. I should have told him that I liked him.

I hardly knew him, so it was a strange thought. And I knew there was something he wasn't telling me. I don't know how I knew, but I did.

I walked across the campus, contemplating what Gabriel meant to me, heading for the art building. I wanted to take the long way around before I had to be in there with people who used to be my friends.

Let's set the record straight, I am not an artist. It was the only elective left I could take. Most of the kids in there had some talent, but then you had the handful of students, like me, who took the class because we had no other choice. Mostly, I just assisted Mr. Walker. I guess he thought the paint fumes would set me off. He wasn't wrong.

I had almost rounded the corner of the school building and stopped when I heard voices. They were low at first and the more I listened, the less I understood. Here's the thing about taking the clear-your-head route. This was the part of the school where certain things happened. People made out back here, slipped each other pills they had stolen from their parents' medicine cabinet, and any other debauchery they were brave enough to attempt at school.

I had almost convinced myself to turn around. I didn't care if it made me late, but then I recognized Keira's voice. She was whispering, but I knew it was her. There was a second voice who was a little harder to make out. Had Keira already learned about this nook in the school building? What was she doing back here? I couldn't let her get into trouble if she was up to something, so I stepped around the corner.

She had Trevor up against the wall, her hand on his chest. His eyes had this glazed over look and he was sweating. If I didn't know any better, I would say that it looked like she was hurting him, but their faces were so close together and before she noticed I was standing there, she kissed him.

"Keira!" I announced myself in shock.

She did a little squeak and jumped. Trevor swayed a little and then looked at me with a grin.

They were both caught red-handed. I couldn't help but smile.

"We were just..." Trevor said, that glossed over look still on his face.

"Yeah, I know what you were doing," I giggled like a little girl. "You should be careful. What if one of the teachers came back here instead of me?"

"The teachers never come back here," Trevor said, taking Keira's hand.

She blushed, grinning, and looked over at him. She was smitten. If I could have guessed any guy at this school to win over the beautiful foreign exchange student, it wouldn't be Trevor. He had his charms, but he was just always so shy. Around everyone. Still, the four of us had been spending a lot of time around each other. Feelings were bound to be felt.

"Well, sorry to interrupt." I knew I was blushing.

I made my way around them and started for class again. Keira said something to Trevor and then ran to catch up to me.

"Hey," she blushed, "I'm sorry I didn't tell you I liked him."

"No, it's okay," I laughed. "Trevor is super...well, he seems nice."

"Do you not approve?" She looked worried.

"What? Of course I do." I was surprised by her question. "I mean, I don't know much more about Trevor than you do. Sure, we've been classmates for a long time, but I've never talked to him until this week. He seems like a really great guy. You don't need my approval, anyway."

"Yes, I do, Ava." Keira wrapped her arm around my shoulder.

"You're my best friend. If you don't like the guy I'm dating, then I need to know."

"Well, you could do worse with the guys in this school," I laughed. "Trevor is obviously head over heels, judging by the look on his face."

I turned to look behind us and saw him still standing there with that dazed look in his eyes. He must have never been kissed the way Keira had just kissed him. His world was probably rocked, and he had to get his wits about himself before he headed off to class. I suppressed a giggle.

It was funny, but there was something stirring within me that I didn't really have a name for. It pleased me that Keira and Trevor were happy, but at the same time, I felt disappointed. I didn't even know how to make sense of it all. It was like I was jealous. Not that Keira had picked Trevor, or that I wanted Trevor, or her. I just wanted to be close to someone like that. I knew exactly who I wanted to be close to, and the thought scared me.

"Trevor is coming to watch me cheer tonight," Keira interrupted my thoughts. "Are you coming?"

"Uh, no, I don't think so." I shook my head. "The noises at football games are bit too much."

"Oh, I understand." She smiled, but it looked as though I had hurt her feelings.

I felt like a jerk. I knew that Keira truly understood where I was coming from, but I was so accustomed to seeing that look these past several months. The one that said, "I really understand, but I want you to be well so we can enjoy things together."

My parents were masters at this look. They thought they were hiding the hurt, but I could see it. They didn't want to be selfish. They knew I was in pain, but my illness had cost them so much time with their daughter.

I had already hurt Gabriel, or it had seemed as if I had. I didn't want to hurt Keira.

"You know, if I'm not feeling too bad, I'll come." I nudged her shoulder.

"Thanks, Ava." She beamed at me.

After school I went home. Throwing myself on the bed, I closed my eyes and cradled my head. It had been a long day. First, I had nearly confessed my feelings to Gabriel, and then I find out that Trevor and Keira are dating. If I were being honest, I was afraid that Keira would spend all of her time with her new boyfriend and forget about little old me.

I just needed to stop right there. Keira was my friend and she wouldn't let some boyfriend get in the way of that. Besides, I wouldn't let her forget about me. It might feel like a train was running across my brain, but I was going to that football game. I grabbed my purse and ran downstairs.

Mom was cooking something healthy in one of her many frying pans and smiled when she saw me come into the kitchen. It smelled disgusting. When my head was killing me, certain smells were like a ninja kick to my gag reflex.

"What are you making?" I scrunched my nose.

"Stir fry," she announced happily.

"Well, it smells gross," I admitted.

"But it tastes amazing," she laughed. "Are you going somewhere?"

"I was wondering if I could go to the football game tonight?" I asked, and she cut her eyes at me.

"Ava," she put down the wooden spoon she was stirring the food with, "I'm really glad that Keira is...motivating you to do more, but don't you think the football game might be too much?"

"I'll be fine, Mom." I shrugged my shoulders.

"Ava," she said again.

"Mom..." I mimicked her look.

"Don't be funny." She crossed her arms.

"Look, just let me go, and if I start feeling bad, then I'll call you and you can come get me," I suggested. "Please?"

Her shoulders slumped, and I knew I had won her over. She could never refuse when I laid on the charm, especially if my charm sounded like I was trying to be a responsible teenager.

"Alright," she gave in. "Go tell your father to take you. I'm trying to finish up this meal. Do you want any before you head out?"

"I think I'll pass." I eyed all the vegetables in the pan and made a face.

"You need to eat more veggies!" she called after me as I hunted down my dad.

Within a matter of 15 minutes, my dad had dropped me off in front of the football stadium. He gave me that same warning to call if I needed him. I waved goodbye and headed for the gate.

I was early, so I didn't have to wait in line for a ticket. After getting a Coke and a bag of popcorn, I took a seat on the bleachers. There was hardly anyone there, so I had an entire section to myself. Soon, Trevor showed up and upon seeing me, walked up the stadium steps and took a seat.

We mostly chatted about the game and about whether our team was good enough to beat our challenger. It was a conversation I didn't think I'd have with Trevor. In fact, this was probably the most I'd heard him talk, especially during a one-on-one conversation. He usually just listened.

The past week, he would sit, attentive, listening to Gabriel and Keira, mostly the latter. I would chirp in now and then, but they were the talkers. I guess Trevor and I had more in common than I thought.

"So, can I say something?" Trevor asked, a sudden switch in our conversation.

"Yeah." His tone let me know he was nervous.

"When we first started hanging out and you were being so nice, it sort of ticked me off," he confessed.

"Oh?" I felt my face grow hot.

"Yeah," he cleared his throat, "I kept going back to just last year when you were horrible to me."

"Trevor, I..." He interrupted me by putting up his hand.

"But, you're different now," he said. "I'm glad because I really like being your friend."

I gave him a big smile, and I hugged him. I'd never been one to be open with my emotions, especially not now, so this was a big step for me. Since meeting Keira, things had changed a lot. She helped me to see there were good people in the world.

"Well, I hope I'm not interrupting anything," Gabriel's voice rang in my head like music.

I turned and looked at him. His stormy grey eyes were bright, but did not indicate what he might be thinking. He had changed, but he still wore that ever-present black leather jacket. His shirt was a light grey color and fit him just right.

"Of course not," my voice sounded weird.

I didn't want him to think I liked Trevor. That made me realize I cared if he cared. Gabriel sat down beside me. I could feel the warmth emitting from his body and it sent shivers down my spine. Was I attracted to him more than I realized?

"Well, lookie here, Holley." Frankie and her squad came strutting by. "It's our little ragtag team of misfits. How adorable. I can't believe they sucked you into it, Gabe. You know you'd be better off hanging out with your own kind."

Keira was just heading onto the field and when she saw Frankie talking to us, she began marching over.

"It's Gabriel," he said gruffly.

"Oh, so forceful. I like it." Frankie batted her eyes at him and it made my blood boil. "Why don't you come sit over next to Rob and the others? I'm sure we can salvage your reputation. Then we can go to the dance together and afterwards, well, you never know what might happen."

Frankie gave him her most seductive smile. To my surprise, Gabriel looked unfazed. This was probably the first time in history that Frankie wasn't able to successfully come on to a guy.

"Just stop, Frankie," I said. "Don't you see he's not interested? You're making an idiot of yourself."

I actually felt sorry for her for a moment.

"Are you marking your territory?" she asked. "You made your way through the football team, so now you're working on the lowest rungs of the social ladder?"

"Whatever, Frankie." I rolled my eyes. My brief moment of sympathy passed.

"Oh, Trevor, I heard you and Keira were a thing," Frankie laughed. "Did you trade off doing her homework for a few rubs or something? I mean otherwise, what is she getting out of...whatever this is?"

Trevor's face went bright red, and he looked down at his feet. This caused Frankie and her pack to burst into laughter. I felt my temper flare.

"Back off, Frankie," Gabriel said to her.

"Excuse me?" She stopped laughing and narrowed her eyes at him.

"I said back off," he repeated.

"I'll do whatever the hell I want." She took a few more steps up. "There's nothing you, your pasty little lapdog, and that two-bit whore can do about it."

I could hear blood ringing in my ears. Frankie had called me a lot of things, but this was going too far. Gabriel's shoulders tensed and he looked as though he wanted to throttle her.

"You've got a lot of nerve," he began, but I put my hand on his.

"It's okay," I said. "She's not worth it."

"I'm worth more than you'll ever be, bitch," Frankie sneered.

"Oh, shut up!" Gabriel snapped. "We all know what you're worth, Frankie. And it's cheap."

Without hesitation, Frankie reared back and smacked Gabriel right in the jaw. Immediately, I stood up and got in Frankie's face so close that she stumbled back and fell. Her butt skidded down two levels of bleachers before her friends stopped her fall.

"Don't you ever touch him again! You keep your filthy hands to yourself, Frankie, or so help me God, I'll beat your face in with my bare hands!" I threatened her.

"Ava," Keira came to my side and placed her hand on my arm. "Calm down."

"You're crazy!" Frankie yelled up at me while they helped her to her feet. "You could have killed me!"

"If we could only get that lucky," I scoffed. "People like you always get what's coming to them, Frankie. Always!"

She huffed and ran down the bleachers, Holley and the others following close behind her. I didn't realize I was still shaking until Keira forced me to sit down and shoved a bottle of water in my face. It took me a minute to realize that more people had filled the stands, and members of the football team had been watching our exchange from the sidelines.

Great, I was probably going to get in trouble. My parents would never let me go to another school function for the rest of my life. It wouldn't matter if I tried explaining to them about how horrible Frankie was or that she had made my life a living hell for the past six months. They never wanted me to get in trouble.

"Are you alright?" Gabriel asked.

"You look really pale, Ava," Keira chimed in.

"Do we need to call your parents?" Trevor wondered.

I was panicking. My head hurt, I felt embarrassed, and everyone was just too close to me right now. I needed air. That sounded crazy, being outside and all, but everyone was just too close, too clingy.

"I think I'm going to be sick." I ran and barely made it behind the bleachers before I barfed all over the place.

So much for my first school outing in six months. Way to go, Ava.

I almost broke Frankie's leg or worse, and now I'm throwing up with Gabriel Matthews right behind me.

"Ava," he said. "Let me take you home."

"No," I told him. "I'm not going home early. My parents will know something is wrong."

"Then let me take you somewhere," he offered.

"No," I said again as I gagged. "I'm tired of being pushed around by her. I'm tired of feeling like crap. I'm tired of...of everything. And why are you being nice to me? You don't like me. You've made that very clear. I know you're only putting up with me because of Trevor. Well, let me give you an out. You don't have to be. We can have the same friend, but you and I don't have to be friends, okay? So, just go away."

Keira and Trevor were standing off in the distance, but I know they heard me. I felt like such a weak little girl and it really ticked me off. I grabbed a hold of one of the bleacher braces and squeezed it until my hand hurt.

"I never meant to make you feel like I..." Gabriel started.

"It doesn't matter." I closed my eyes, trying to hold back tears.

I wasn't really even sure why I felt like crying.

"Are you going to be okay?" he asked.

"I'm fine," I said, turning to face all of them. "I just need to freshen up."

With a deep breath, I walked back out and made a trip to the restroom. I washed up as best as I could, especially my mouth. Keira thankfully had some mints. Making my way back, I took my seat on the bleachers, trying to ease the pressure in my head. Gabriel and I sat with Trevor between us. I didn't speak to him for the rest of the game. I don't know why I snapped on him, but I felt horrible.

During halftime, the band took the field, and I tried my best to concentrate on their intricate moves and harmonious melodies, but it just seemed to bounce around my head, leaving more damage in its path. I almost stood up, but just as I was about to, Frankie and the other cheerleaders came back for more.

They were at the foot of the bleachers, not brave enough to come any closer, and started whispering and pointing at me. Frankie cackled the loudest and when she caught her breath, she turned and looked at me and said, "We saw you got sick earlier, Black. What? Can't hold your pills anymore?"

More people joined in, all of them aware of the rumors that Frankie had spread about me. Apparently I was a drug addict that faked an illness to get more pills. Thankfully, only half the school believed it, but it still stopped them from talking to me. Most of them were too scared of Frankie, and the others were too afraid of their parents to associate with me.

I wanted to stand up and say something, defend myself, but I was so weak and my mind wouldn't even let me formulate the words. If she only knew how bad I felt every day. If she could only understand what the pain was like, then maybe she wouldn't be so cruel.

I wished it right then. I wanted her to feel what I felt. I wished with everything in me she'd wake up tomorrow, screaming in pain because it was too much to bear. If there was a way to make her hurt, I wanted to know what it was. I always said that I wouldn't wish this kind of pain on my worst enemy, but I changed my mind.

I pointed my finger at her and for a moment, I didn't know what I was doing or what I was saying. She stopped laughing and so did her friends. It seemed forever before I said anything, but then the words came to me, "I hope you get hurt so bad one day that the pain never leaves you. I hope it hurts so bad that all you can do is scream until you're dead!"

"Ava!" Gabriel grabbed my hand and yanked it back. "What are you doing?"

"I...I don't know," I stammered.

Keira came running up the bleachers, her eyes wide with shock. Frankie's face was as pale as snow. She was terrified, as if I had just cursed her or something. Without another word, she left her friends behind and hurried toward the restrooms.

"Ava?" Keira greeted me gently.

"I want to go home," I told them and headed for the exit. "Alone. Just leave me alone."

Gabriel was having none of that. Keira and Trevor stood back this time, but he was relentless. He ran after me and caught me just as I entered the parking lot. Taking me by the arm, he spun me around to face him.

"What are you feeling?" he asked, his grey eyes searching my face.

"What?" I jerked away from him. "What are you talking about?"

"Why did you say that to Frankie?" he asked me.

"Leave me alone, Gabriel." I turned, but he grabbed me again.

"What are you feeling, Ava, you have to tell me." His grip was tight, but not painful.

"Why are you so freaking weird?" I jerked away from him again. "Are you my shrink or something? I'm feeling pissed! Does that answer your question? Now go away!"

"I can't do that." He started walking beside me as I headed down the sidewalk.

I needed to walk. My parents would be mad when I got home, but I needed it. I would explain when they stopped yelling. First, I had to get rid of Gabriel.

"You can't? Why not?" I kept walking. "It's your job? What does that even mean?"

"I just want to make sure you get home safely," he said.

"Bull," I laughed. "You're so full of it. I don't know what you're hiding from me, but you're hiding something. I can see it, you know? There's something you want to say, it's on the tip of your tongue sometimes. But instead of telling me, you just act like I'm not there."

"I don't know what you're talking about," he began, but I rounded on him.

"You mysteriously walked by the locker room just as I had a seizure," I started. "But I know that you heard nothing. There is no way you could have. You show up at my house and talk about my dreams. Then you say it's, 'your job' to help me. Either you're a stalker or it's something else. So, what is it?"

"I'm not a stalker," he said.

"Then it's something else," I pointed out.

"I'm trying to help you," he said. "You need to be careful with what you say. Words hurt. You should take back what you said to Frankie. I know you didn't mean that. That's not you."

"You don't know me, Gabriel." I walked a few inches closer. "I am not a good person. I am selfish. I am cruel. And I hate Frankie. I meant every word."

"Ava, please," he said.

"I meant...every...single...word." I moved in closer and he tensed, as if he feared me.

The look on his face seemed to have brought me back to my senses. I felt strange, as if for a moment, I wasn't quite myself. I was not a saint, but I had changed. I didn't want to hurt anyone. I remembered seeing that look in the people I was a monster to. I didn't want to be a monster to anyone else, especially not Gabriel.

"I have to go." I turned and ran home.

Ava

My parents let me have it when I showed up at home. Not only had I walked home in the dark, I had done so alone. My mother listed all the horrible things that could have happened to me, while my dad nodded his head in agreement. I thought about telling them about Frankie, but I just let them lay into me. For some reason, I felt like I deserved it.

After being sent to my room, I fell into a really deep sleep. Again, I dreamed of Gabriel in that open field. Blue lightning rolled from him in powerful waves. He told me to look at my hands, and when I did I saw a flash of deep purple and then woke up.

I rolled over in my bed and realized I had slept until noon. Groaning, I sat up. The room spun, and I immediately ran for the bathroom. On the way there, I tripped over my shoes and ran into the wall. I purged myself and then had to again.

I rested on the floor of my bathroom and thought it might be one of those days I ended up in the hospital. I didn't want to go. It was true they would usually give me something that eased the pain, but it took forever to even get it. I'd rather lie on my bathroom floor than spend it in the emergency room.

I crawled my way back to bed and pulled the covers over my head.

Mom came in and checked on me. She gave me my medication, spoke softly, and made sure I had food in my belly. I could tell she wanted to talk about what had happened last night, but didn't push it because of how I felt. She could always tell when something was wrong. Mother's Intuition, I guess.

I didn't want to think about it because then I would have to think about Gabriel. I didn't need him on my mind today.

"Ava?" Mom called for me through the door. "Gabriel is here to see you...if you're up for it."

Gabriel? No, he couldn't be here.

I felt like crap and probably looked worse. Besides, I firmly remembered telling him that we were not friends.

"I don't want to see him," I told her.

"Okay, honey," she said, but I could still sense her outside the door. "Ava, are you sure?"

"I'm sure." I grabbed my head, the pain starting to build.

She didn't say any more, and I knew she had gone back downstairs. I could just imagine what she might tell him. I was too sick, in too much pain. He'd feel bad for me, tell Mom he was sorry, and then leave. Would he come back? Did I want him to?

My phone pinged and with blurring vision, I picked it up. It was Gabriel.

I hope you don't mind, but I asked Keira for your number. Can we talk?

I didn't have the energy to text him back. The crazy thing was, I wanted to. Instead, I just powered my phone off. It was almost freeing. No one could get in touch with me until I turned the phone back on. I might or might not. The choice was up to me. There were so many crazy things going on in my life right now that I had no control over, so this one action made me feel powerful.

Mom came back in to check on me now and then, Dad too, making sure I had my medicine when I was supposed to and force-feeding me something so I wouldn't go hungry.

The pain never went away. Actually, it just worsened throughout the day. I could feel pressure building outside. Anytime that happened, I knew it was going to rain. Something about the weather increased the pain. Dad said I was like a human radar. I was better at predicting the rain than most meteorologists.

Within a couple of hours, I heard the first few rumbles of thunder. Soon the rain came, beating on the roof of the house with a mighty fist. So much for the small reprieve.

Before the migraines, I never cared about the rain. There are those who love rainy days and those who can't stand the gloom. I was indifferent, I guess. I just never paid enough attention. Now, they're some of my worst days. It brought out the beast inside my head, driving it mad and taking me along for the ride.

I'm not sure exactly when I fell asleep, but I suddenly jerked awake. It was hard to tell what had lured me from slumber, but I felt disoriented. My room was normally dark because the sunlight was another trigger for my migraines, so it was hard to tell what time of day or night it was.

Glancing at the clock, I could see the storm had slightly lost its strength at 3:00 in the morning.

Immediately, I realized that the pain had eased. I sprawled out on my bed, relief washing over me. My head was sharper, my senses not so overpowered with the pressure. I couldn't remember the last time I felt this...normal. It was as if the storm had come charging in, stealing the pain away. Closing my eyes, I nestled back in my bed, content and hoping for a few more hours of rest.

Just then, I heard glass break from somewhere in the house. I opened my eyes and looked around the dark room, listening for a moment. I wasn't sure if what I heard was imagined. The storm was coming to a close. The sounds muffled by the walls that separated us from the trickling rain and gusts of wind. Was the sound just something I thought I heard, or was it real?

Mom had the habit of getting up to check on me and then go downstairs for something to drink. I would hear her either get something from the fridge or, if she knew she'd never go back to sleep, put on a pot of coffee.

The house was dead silent save for the occasional growl of thunder. I wasn't sure, but I thought that maybe I heard movement. Straining to hear and having no success, I moved out of bed and closer to the door. There, I heard the squeak of one of the stairs. Whoever it was, they were moving carefully.

Glass breaking, slow silent movements. Did someone break into our house? I tiptoed quickly and picked up my phone. I turned it on, intent on calling the cops as fast as I could. No one was going to hurt my family on my watch.

The phone's light was nearly blinding as it came to life in my hands. I turned my back from my closed door, in case the burglar saw the light from under the small sliver of space between the door and the floor.

The phone seemed to take an exceptionally long time to turn on.

"Come on!" I whispered to it urgently.

I watched the loading notification spin and spin. Nothing was happening. I looked back at my door. There was complete silence. Did that mean I had imagined the sounds? No way, there was someone out there in the hall. I could feel them. I wasn't sure where they were, but I knew they were there.

Feeling lost, I took the phone with me and crept back to the door. I put my ear against it, thinking I could hear the intruder and pinpoint his or her location. Again, nothing.

What did I do? I had to get to my parents. I needed a weapon; something to fight off or injure someone should the occasion call for it. Making my way back to my closet, I grabbed a baseball bat I'd had in there since I played softball back in middle school.

Walking back toward the door, I dropped my phone off at my nightstand. There was no way I could get a good grip on the bat with only one hand. Besides, once I made it to my parents' room, we could use one of their phones to call the local authorities.

Slowly, I opened my bedroom door. I looked out into the dark hall, straining to focus in the gloom. It was quiet and still. Nothing seemed to move. Assuming, and praying, I was safe to cross the hall, I stepped over the threshold.

As soon as I did so, I felt that I wasn't alone. Turning around, I saw no one behind me, but I felt their eyes, just watching, waiting. I turned again, racing toward my parents' room. It was at the end of the hall, only a few feet away, but it felt like it was across the universe. I put my hand on the knob, turning it quickly, almost losing grip because my palm was slick with sweat.

Scrambling inside, I somehow shut the door with ease instead of slamming it in my haste. I breathed a sigh of relief, but knew this was no time to rest. I rushed to my parents' bed, gently shaking my dad.

He rolled over. It was more like he fell over. The moonlight was shining lightly in the window and cast over his face. I jumped back when he came into focus. A scarlet line crossed his throat. A river of red was dried down his neck and pooled into his shirt. I screamed as I took in the scene. Not only was he dead, but he also wasn't my dad. It wasn't his face. There was a stranger on his side of the bed. His lifeless eyes looked up at an unknown location. I turned to run out of the room and caught sight of myself in the dresser mirror.

My red hair circled my face in a mess of curls. Red curls? This wasn't my hair. I looked down at my hands. They were pale with thousands of reddish-brown freckles. Those large green eyes, they didn't belong to me.

Who was I? Who was this strange girl looking back at me with fearful eyes?

Fear, a type that was hard to put into words, immobilized me. It was hard to comprehend what I was experiencing. Thoughts raced through a mind I wasn't sure belonged to me.

Something moved behind me, the mirror reflecting a figure at my back. I turned around fast, raising the bat to protect myself. A hooded figure came out of the shadows, their scaled hands reaching for my throat. Swinging the bat, I connected with the side of their head with a bone shattering crack.

I bolted from the room, racing down the hall. The once familiar surroundings morphed into a home that wasn't mine. The pictures in the frames transformed into a family I didn't recognize.

As I hit the base of the stairs and ran into what looked like the living room, I stopped short. There were hooded figures in each corner of the room. They crept forward, circling me until I was in the center of a living room.

The figure from upstairs came slowly, gracefully down the steps. The robed people parted so that this thing or person could walk up to me. Words, not my words, came tumbling out of a mouth that seemed to move on its own.

"Please, don't do this."

"They all say the same thing," it spoke. Its voice like something not of this world.

The others laughed. I looked around me, afraid to even breathe.

"Please, this isn't you," I told it. "I thought we—"

"You thought wrong, precious child," it told me as a thin, bony hand moved out towards me from the shadows. "So wrong. You will make Mother so happy. Thank you for your sacrifice. For Thyana!"

"For Thyana!" the others echoed. "Thyana! Thyana! Thyana!"

I screamed as the hand touched my chest, seeming to burn right through to the bone. White-hot pain shot straight into my head as my body ignited in flames. I tried to grab where it hurt, as if that would stop my suffering, as if it would douse the fire. It only took a second to realize that there would be no relief. This was how I would die.

"Ava!" My dad shook me awake. "Ava! Wake up! You're having a bad dream."

I screamed, jolted awake, and pushed him away from me. It took me a moment to realize that she was my father and not the creepy hooded figure from my nightmare. I could still feel the burn on my skin. Instinctively, I grabbed at my chest.

Of course, I wasn't on fire. There was no hooded figure trying to murder me. It was a nightmare. A very realistic nightmare, but that was it.

"Ava!" Dad looked shocked.

"I'm sorry, Daddy," I told him, my senses clearing. "It was a crazy dream. I didn't mean to push you."

"I think you might need to see Dr. Abbott again," he stated.

"What? For a nightmare?" I got out of the bed, wobbled a bit, and then straightened myself up, trying to look like a girl who didn't need to see a shrink.

"For more than that." He stood up as well. "I know your friends have tried reaching out to you. I know something happened at that game you won't talk to me about."

"I've been in pain!" I pointed out defensively.

"I know, sweetheart," he reached for me, giving me a tight hug, "But it's more than that.

"There is something going on with you. If you won't talk to me, your mother, or your friends, then you're going to see Dr. Abbott."

He released me, kissed me on the head, and headed for the door. He turned around and asked, "Do I make myself clear, Ava?"

"Yes, sir," I said, defeated.

He left the room, and I plopped down on my bed. There was no arguing with him when he was like this. I knew it would do me no good to talk to my mom about it either. Dad's word was law.

Going to see Dr. Abbott was an undesirable option, but it was the only option I had at the moment.

He was right. I had avoided everyone. When I turned my phone back on, I had a couple of texts from Trevor. I supposed Keira had given him my number as well. Gabriel hadn't tried to text me back after I ignored him. I felt weird about that.

I had at least 20 texts from Keira. They went from concerned to irritated to downright mad. I didn't blame her. I had left angry. I had said some really nasty things to Frankie and to Gabriel. I knew Keira understood I was hurting, but I could have at least told her I was fine. I owed her an apology. I owed them all one, but I was a wimp.

Ava

Monday at school, I avoided them like the plague. Dodging Gabriel required Assassin's Creed level skills I wasn't sure I possessed. It seemed as if he were around every corner. I saw him pass by my first period class. He didn't look inside, but I just happened to look up at the same moment he went by.

My heart did ninja flips every time I caught sight of him. I couldn't tell if it was from deep shame or something else entirely.

Keira came in late. Instead of taking her usual seat beside me, she sat a few seats over. Frankie leaned over and said something, and Keira nodded her head. Frankie glanced back at me and smiled.

Great, I'd pushed her over to the dark side.

I practically ran from my last class, trying to avoid anyone and everyone I could. As I headed for the car line, my head down, I bumped into someone. I looked up, ready to apologize, but stopped short. Gabriel was looking down at me, something indescribable in his grey eyes.

I looked away, focusing on the tattoo that always peeked over the top of his shirt. There was a part of me that wanted to know what the rest of it looked like. The other part was terrified to find out.

"Have fun avoiding me all day?" he asked.

"I've got to go." I made to move around him, but he moved with me. "Gabriel, move."

"And if I don't?" He crossed his arms.

"I'll kick you in the shin," I threatened.

"Do your best," he challenged.

"I don't have time for you." I moved again and once more he met my move. "My mom is waiting on me."

"How about I pick you up for school tomorrow?" he asked.

"Are you serious?" I finally looked up at him. "I was a complete jerk to you."

"Is that an apology?" He seemed to grin.

"You're impossible!" I raised my voice, causing a few stares.

"I need to talk to you," he said seriously. "Can I do that by picking you up tomorrow?"

"I'm pretty sure we don't like each other." I shoved past him.

"I never said I didn't like you." He walked beside me, looking as if he had no difficulty keeping up with my quick pace with his long strides.

I walked as quickly as I could down the hall. People made a wide path for us. It was because of Gabriel. His tall frame was intimidating. People probably wanted to avoid getting stepped on by him.

I'm sure we looked quite humorous walking down the hall together. This big oaf of a guy, and then there was me. He was tall, dark, and handsome. I was tall and I used to be lean from years of gymnastics lessons, but now my curves were more defined. Funnily enough, I was more comfortable than I had been in a long time. When I was 20-pounds lighter, I was so concerned with looking a certain way. Now, I was just me and I liked myself a whole lot more.

"I want us to get along, Ava," Gabriel said next to me.

"Why?" I asked as I opened the door, the cool air ruffling my long hair.

"For Keira and Trevor," he said. "They like each other and we're their friends. So, we can try for them, right?"

"Okay, fine." I shrugged.

"So, tomorrow morning?" he asked. "Can I pick you up?"

"Sure." I nodded, not believing I was agreeing to this.

Just then Mom pulled up. She waved at us. Surprisingly, Gabriel walked over to the car. Mom rolled the window down and smiled widely at him.

"Gabriel, honey, how are you?" Mom asked.

"I'm well, Mrs. Black." He grinned, leaning into the car.

It was quite a task for him considering Mom's car was low to the ground. He ended up practically bent at the waist. I almost laughed.

"Hey, I just asked Ava, of course if you don't mind, if I could pick her up for school tomorrow," he said, laying on the charm. "I'll bring her home, too. I go right by your house so it wouldn't be a problem."

"Oh, how nice," she smiled, "I actually have a few errands to run in the morning so that would be great."

Mom looked at him like he was Mother Teresa. I rolled my eyes.

"Great, I'll be there right around 7:15." Gabriel stood up and slapped my shoulder like we were old pals.

Ow! What was he trying to do, dislocate my arm?

He walked away without another word, leaving me there rubbing a throbbing shoulder. I slowly got into the car and looked straight ahead. Mom started down the road before she said anything. It was almost like she was having an internal fight with herself, but the need to be a mom outweighed the desire to give her daughter any privacy.

"I'm glad you and Gabriel are on speaking terms again," she finally said. "He's such a nice boy. Rather tall and sort of ominous looking at first, but very nice."

"Uh huh," I responded. "And how did you know we weren't on speaking terms?"

"Mother's Intuition." She smiled, and I rolled my eyes. "Has he ever mentioned anything about, I don't know, getting a haircut?"

"A haircut? No. Why?"

"Oh, it's just really long. He would look so handsome with shorter hair."

"I don't know. I think it suits him."

Oh, lord, here we were talking about how nice-looking Gabriel was. I needed to change the subject. My mind didn't need to go places it shouldn't when it came to that boy. He was already dangerously close to breaking down my walls, and I didn't need to give him any help.

"It was so nice of him to offer you a ride tomorrow," she went on.

"Where are we going? The turn was back there." I turned to look at the road we'd just passed.

"Your dad got you an appointment with Dr. Abbott." Mom straightened up in her seat.

"Oh, Mom, come on," I whined. "Look, I'm friends with Gabriel again. I don't need to see that old man."

"Now you behave yourself, Ava Elizabeth," Mom scolded. "You're going to see Dr. Abbott until he says you don't need to see him anymore or what limited freedom you have will be revoked."

I slumped in my seat. I saw no use in arguing any further. I knew what she meant by talking about my limited freedom. My life comprised of school and home, but there were rare moments where I could escape. Going to the football game was a fun treat, but my true sanctuary was the local library.

It was quiet, warm, and smelled like books. It was only a few blocks from my house, so most days I walked there. Occasionally, Mom or Dad would take me. I had a favorite spot in the back. The staff had expected me every Friday after school. I guess they were surprised when I didn't show up the other day. I wondered if Gabriel was a reader. What sort of books captured his interests?

The car moved on as my thoughts raced from one topic to another. It didn't matter what I was thinking, every thought ended on one person. I sighed and leaned my head on the cool window.

The sky outside was a gloomy grey. It reflected my feelings at that moment. I hated giving into the depression, but sometimes it was easier to give up than fight. Mom seemed to sense my mood because she turned on my favorite radio station and began singing along, poking me in the side.

"Come on, you know this one." She smiled at me.

"Fine." I couldn't help but smile back.

Mom and I sang the entire way to Dr. Abbott's office. It was nearly an hour drive, so we got through a few songs. By the time we arrived, I was in a bit of a better mood.

Dr. Abbott's office was just inside the city of Huntsville in the historic district. It really was a quaint-looking area, with old brick buildings, conjoined all the way down the street. His office was at the top of a two story duplex with a red roof. The city had maintained the old colonial style well.

Looking at the structure, I couldn't help but wonder who had built it. Who had lived here, called it home, before time caught up with them and turned it into a therapist's office? There must have been a yard before the paved parking lot. I'm sure that there was once a family with children that played hide-n-seek all along the property.

Even with the modern buildings and concrete erasing what the past had created, I could still picture how it had once looked.

Walking into the office itself, I was thrust back into the present. It smelled sterile, like cleaning chemicals. Mom checked us in with the receptionist while I took a seat in one of the plush chairs.

I pulled out my phone to check any messages I might have received. Nothing. I didn't know what I expected. Keira would not talk to me right now. I sighed, putting my phone away, and concentrated on the television. It was tuned in to a local news station. They were discussing the weather, so eventually, I zoned out. It had been the same for weeks—rain. It wasn't until they called my name that I realized I had been sitting there for nearly 20 minutes.

I looked up and noticed that this wasn't Dr. Abbott's normal assistant. He was new and freaking gorgeous. Not Gabriel gorgeous, but not someone I expected to be working in a therapist's office.

"Hi, Ava," he said, and I noticed an accent. I was guessing Irish. "If you'll follow me, please."

Mom elbowed me, and I looked over at her. She raised her eyebrows and smirked at me. I rolled my eyes and got up from my seat.

He was tall, probably early twenties, with wavy brown hair and hazel eyes. His pale skin was flawless with just the right amount of pink at the heights of his cheeks.

"My name is Lorcan. How are you today?" he asked as he led me back to a small nurses' station.

"Fine," I said. "Where is Kelly?"

"She is off today," he told me. "Ava, I'm going to get your vitals and then Dr. Abbott will be in to see you."

"Okay," I told him. "How long have you worked here? I was here last month and I didn't see you." *I would have remembered.*

"For about three months," Lorcan told me as he wrapped a blood pressure cuff on my arm.

"Dr. Abbott hired me, temporarily, while I'm studying at the University."

"You're studying to be a psychiatrist?" I asked.

"I am," he told me.

"But you're not one yet?" I wondered.

"I am certified to take your vitals if that is what you're worried about." He smiled at me and I realized he was trying to joke with me, to put me at ease.

"Oh, no, I'm not, sorry," I stammered.

"It's fine, Ava," he smiled again, "Well, your vitals are good. Are you taking the medicine Dr. Abbott prescribed you?"

"Yes," I answered.

"That's good to hear," he wrote a few things down on my chart, "Any issues with those medicines? Mood swings? Unusual dreams?"

"No," I answered with a lie.

"Great." Lorcan smiled at me. It was dazzling. "Let's take you to Dr. Abbott, shall we? I like your Star Trek shirt. I'm a Trekkie, myself."

"Oh, thanks," I said and stood up to follow him. "My dad introduced me when I was little and I've been hooked ever since."

"It was my dad that introduced me to the series." He looked back and smiled. "Here we are."

We stopped at Dr. Abbott's door and he knocked. The doctor called for us to enter from the other side.

"It was nice meeting you, Ava." Lorcan smiled again and left me to enter the office on my own.

I nodded in return and then opened the door.

"Ava, it's good to see you." The doctor gestured toward a chair by the window.

Dr. Abbott's office looked like something you'd see out of an 1800s period drama. The furniture was antique. The walls were papered with gold flowers on an emerald background, and the entire room was built out of dark cherry wood. It was cozy and normally, it put me at ease.

Today, it seemed to have the opposite effect.

"So, Ava, tell me how you've been," Dr. Abbott started.

I looked up into his crisp blue eyes. They were always so kind and welcoming. Dr. Abbott was a man of at least 55, but looked 10 years younger. He had an athletic build, which I'm sure he maintained by frequent exercise. His snow-white hair was short, but shiny and healthy. It's the kind of hair that most men lost in their thirties.

"I've been...I've been fine," I decided to lie.

"Ava, do you remember the first time you came into my office? What did I say to you?" he asked me, standing up to pour himself a cup of warm tea.

"That we'll get nowhere if we don't trust each other," I told him.

"Correct you are, Miss." He poured a second cup. In one cup he placed one sugar cube and three in the other.

He handed me the cup with the three sugar cubes, remembering exactly how I liked my tea, always so thoughtful. I took a sip and stared out the window. We sat there in silence for a moment. It was grating. He knew not the push, so he was giving me time.

"I'm not trying to be evasive," I said, sipping my tea again. "I'm..."

"Fine," he finished for me.

"I mean, I am." I took a deep breath. "It's not anything I need to see you about. It's just teenage stuff."

"It may not seem like it, but I was once a teenager." He smiled at me.

"I know that." I couldn't help but smile back. "I just...I'm not sure you'd understand."

"I will try my best," he offered. "Sometimes it feels better just to vocalize our worries. Go on, give it a try."

I took one more sip of the warm brew in my hands before I told him all that had been happening at school, in my nightmares, and how I felt like I had lost my new friendships forever. By the time I was finished, it felt better having vocalized my worries. Still, I didn't know how Dr. Abbott was supposed to help me.

"Ava, I'm going to offer some advice that is rather unorthodox." He set down his tea. "Now, this might sound strange, but I would suggest what you should try is to say you're sorry."

I stared at him in disbelief. Dr. Abbott had just given me some straight up sarcasm as professional psychiatric advice.

"Wow, Dr. Abbott," I laughed. "Like I haven't thought of that."

"Have you really?" he questioned. "All I heard from you were reasons as to why you lost your temper with your friends, mainly Gabriel. You didn't offer a solution. You believe they're better off without you. Why? What if they're not? What if you're not better off without them?"

He was right. I wanted to push them away, and I was okay with that. I didn't think I was good for them.

"We must let past transgressions go, Ava," he offered. "We can't carry our sins with us throughout our lives. We must realize that salvation is possible."

"Are you giving me religious advice, Dr. Abbott?" I snorted.

"We seek redemption in a number of ways, Miss Black," he pointed out. "It is not uncommon to seek it from ourselves as well as our religious or spiritual avenues. Let go of what you have done, realize you are not that person anymore, and allow yourself happiness."

I left Dr. Abbott's office determined to call Keira when I got home. I hated when my parents were right about going to see him. It made me feel like I wasn't built to handle things on my own, but I had come to realize that it was okay if I needed help now and then. Still, I wasn't so comfortable with letting other people know I saw a shrink just yet. There were things that were just for me.

When I got into my room, I fell on my bed and sent Keira a text.

Hey, can we talk?

Sure.

Are you home?

Yeah.

Can I come over?

I can come over there.

OK.

See you in a few.

OK, see you.

I was nervous. She was ready to come over even though I had been a jerk to her. She was trying her best to reach out and I had ignored her, for days. Was she ready to forgive me or did she just want an apology? Maybe she just wanted to see me beg for her forgiveness. I wouldn't blame her.

I let Mom and Dad know she would be over. They seemed to be fine with it even though it was last minute. Mom made sure to set another plate for dinner. I'd be lucky if she'd walk through the front door, much less stay to eat supper.

Keira showed up about 10 minutes later. I watched the car pull into the driveway. I saw her get out, wave to her host family, walk up the drive, and arrive at the door. There seemed to be a bit of hesitation, but then she finally knocked. I hurriedly opened the door and stared into her intense blue eyes. We said nothing for a moment and then finally she rushed me with a giant hug.

"I'm sorry," she said.

"You're sorry?" I pulled away from her. "For what? I'm the sorry one."

"I should have given you space. I knew you were upset," she cried.

"Keira, please don't feel bad." I pulled her inside and shut the door, blocking out the cold. "I acted like a complete psycho. I'm really, really sorry."

"You're going through some stuff, Ava." She hugged me again. "I understand, really, I do. Sometimes people need space, I get it."

We walked into the living room, sitting down across from each other. She patted my hand. Her eyes wet with unshed tears.

"Yeah, well, I still acted insane," I confessed. "I'm really sorry and I totally understand if you don't want...if you don't want to be friends or hang out..."

"Now you really are insane," she laughed. "Look, I had no friends here and you're one of the first genuine people I've met here. I know we haven't known each other for very long, but...you're my best friend, Ava. Whatever it is you're going through, I want to be here for you. We'll always be friends."

"Okay, well, now you can't move back to London," I laughed. "I'll get Mom and Dad to adopt you."

We both laughed and things seemed to be right with the world. It felt good. I had Keira back. Gabriel also didn't seem to completely despise me, or at least he was trying not to. I would apologize to Trevor as well at school. Maybe I could not be an emotional basket case and have a semi-normal high school experience. It was possible if I tried not to let things build up. Thankfully, I had some really great friends that understood.

Keira stayed for dinner, and afterwards we went up to my room. I realized it was the first time she had been over. The only time we had hung out after school was when I was in the hospital.

She looked around the room, taking in how dark it was. She probably wondered if I ever got any sunlight. At least she didn't compare it to a vampire's lair like I had assumed she would. Keira plopped down on the bed and sighed.

"Your mum is an excellent cook!" She leaned back and rested her hands on her stomach.

"Unless she gets on one of her 'let's eat healthy' sprees." I laid down beside her.

She giggled and turned over to look at me.

"I'm sure," she told me. "I have something to tell you. Trevor asked me to Homecoming."

"Well, isn't that obvious?" I wondered. "Isn't he your boyfriend?"

"No, not exactly," she rolled back over, "I like him. He's not like any other boy I've liked before, but he hasn't asked me out and I haven't asked him either."

"Oh," I said, not really sure what else to say. "Don't you like him enough to be his girlfriend?"

"Well, yes, but I will not be here forever, you know?" She looked up at the ceiling. "I would hate to truly start a relationship with him and then not see him again."

"You are planning to come back and visit though, aren't you?" I felt like she was trying to tell me something.

"Of course, but you know how life can get." Keira looked at me again. "But you needn't worry about us never seeing each other again, my love! We are meant to be best friends forever!"

She hugged me tightly and I laughed. My phone buzzed next to me and I saw Gabriel's name flash up.

"Speaking of boyfriend material." She winked as I picked up my phone.

"He is not my boyfriend." I looked at his message. "Far from it."

"Oh really, then why is he picking you up in the morning?" she teased, reading the message about when he'd arrive tomorrow.

"Because we're trying to get along." I replied with an 'OK' and set the phone down.

Keira didn't bring up Gabriel again for the rest of the night. There was no more talk about boys. Instead, she told me all about her life in London, her school, her friends. It sounded amazing. We dreamed of what we would do when I could visit. My mom took her home so she wouldn't have to walk. I fell asleep, satisfied with the fact that I had patched up our friendship. It made me happy, but at the same time, I felt afraid. She'd be leaving for England at the end of this school year. Where would that leave me? She was my only friend.

I awoke the next morning to a banging at the front door. Groggily, I got up and raced down the stairs. Sleep and migraine meds were still holding on tightly to my mind, so it took me a minute to comprehend why Gabriel was standing at my door.

"Huh?" I said, looking up at him.

"Did you just wake up?" He sort of smiled down at me.

I looked at him like I had never seen him before. It still didn't register why he was there until the cold from outside crept in and jarred me awake.

"Oh my gosh! It's freaking cold out there!" I pulled him inside and shut the door.

"Nice hair," he jeered.

"Shut up," I snapped, patting down my mess of tangles.

"So, oversleep much?" He walked into the living room, looking around.

I followed him, wrapping my arms around my waist, suddenly aware I was standing in my living room with Gabriel Matthews in nothing more than one of my dad's rock t-shirts and underwear.

Tugging at the hem, pulling it down as far as I could, I slowly backed up.

"Um, give me five minutes," I told him, and he turned around to look at me.

"Sure thing, Black," he said as I continued to walk backwards.

As soon as I reached the stairs, I turned and raced up, nearly tripping over my own feet. My face had to be blood red. I hurriedly brushed my teeth, fixed my hair into a side-swept braid, and pulled on my black sweater, matching it with my dark wash skinny jeans and my black boots.

When I got back downstairs, Gabriel was sitting on the couch. He looked up from the book in his hands. He was a reader, an actual book-in-your-hands reader. That made my heart flutter. He tucked the book inside his jacket pocket and stood up before I could glimpse the title.

"Ready?" he asked, and I nodded in response.

I was suddenly extremely nervous. We walked out to his car. I hadn't really registered what he drove the last time he was here. In my driveway was a blue car that looked like it would have made any girl from the 1970s weak in the knees.

"This is your car?" I couldn't help but ask him.

"Yeah, why? Do you not like it?" He opened my door for me.

It gave a slight squeak. It wasn't the sound of time catching up with the car. You could tell it was well taken care of, as if Gabriel spent more time with the car than he did with people. No, it was a sound that said, "I was made with sound metal and by people who knew what they were doing. I was made by the hands of hard-working Americans."

"Oh, no, yeah, I like it." I slid into the passenger seat. "What is it? I mean, what kind of car?"

He smiled, shut my door, and then swiftly got in behind the wheel. He started the car before he answered. The engine came to life easily by his hands. It rumbled, stirring the butterflies in my stomach.

"It's a 1970 Chevy Chevelle SS," he said proudly. "My granddad bought it, passed it down to my dad, and then my dad passed it on to me before he died."

"Oh, that's nice. I mean, I'm sorry, but it's nice to have something...

that was his," I commented, feeling like an idiot, not understanding what the SS stood for.

"Yeah, it's nice." He nodded in agreement.

For a moment he let his eyes linger on my face as if he wanted to tell me something. Before the moment could turn awkward, he turned away.

He backed the beast of a car out of the driveway. I'm sure my neighbor, Mrs. Cora May, would have a lot to tell the ladies at church. Cora May loved to look out her window and report what she saw to anyone and everyone that would listen. Surely a questionable-looking boy in a muscle car picking up her neighbor's daughter made the cut for church pew gossip.

I smiled to myself, thinking about what must be going through her mind. Mom and Dad had left early; she would know that. Now here I was leaving with a leather-clad, tattooed boy when they weren't home. Cora May was probably dialing someone at this very moment, telling them what she saw, and speculating where we might be off to. We couldn't be heading to school in a car like this. We were surely up to something devious.

"So, you wanted to talk, right?" I asked him as we headed down the road. "That's why you insisted on picking me up."

"I do," he said, not looking at me.

"Well?" I asked him. "I'm listening and it's not like I can go anywhere. So, what is it?"

"I can't pretend like I know what you've been through these past months," he started. "But, I do know something about pushing people away. I wish you would accept the friendships that have been offered to you."

"What, like your friendship?" I laughed. "Because you've just been loads of fun."

"That's fair." To my surprise, he didn't argue. "I may not be the best example, but you haven't exactly been that nice to me either."

"Because you acted like I was gum on the bottom of your shoe." I felt my face grow hot. "So excuse me if I didn't realize you were trying to be my friend. Where I come from, we don't treat our potential friends like that."

"No, you continuously push them away, ignore them, no matter how much they reach out to you," he snapped. "I guess we're all still beneath the beautiful and powerful Ava Black, huh? We should grovel and beg for your attention like the peasants that we are?"

"Wow," I said. "Just wow."

"Ava, I didn't mean..." he started.

"No, you meant it." I turned on him. "For your information, I'm not that person anymore."

"I know that," he said. "I'm sorry, I shouldn't have said..."

"Just forget it." I crossed my arms and sat back in the seat.

Despite what Cora May might think, Gabriel took me straight to the high school's parking lot. I couldn't wait for him to put the car in park, but when he did, he turned to me.

"I'm sorry," he said, his grey eyes pleading, and suddenly he took my hand. "That was unfair of me to say. What I meant to do this morning has really blown up in my face. I'm sorry. I want to be your friend, Ava. That's what I meant to say. I know I seem...I don't know... I just want you to know that you aren't alone."

I looked at our hands and then up at him. The feel of his skin on mine was intoxicating. His palm was rough, warm, and welcoming. I didn't want him to let go, but despite that desire, I slowly slid my hand away. I didn't know what to say so I just sat there for a moment, looking at him. He nodded as if some unspoken agreement had passed between us, and he quickly got out of the car.

When we got out, a lot of people stared. I doubt Gabriel had ever driven anyone to school that wasn't Trevor, and surely not a girl. He was absolutely gorgeous and plenty of girls fantasized about him, I heard them talk, but none were brave enough to approach him, unless that someone was Frankie. I doubt she'd ever do that again. Not after this past Friday. Still, that didn't mean she and all the others wouldn't stare.

There was something dangerously appealing about Gabriel. He was the kind of guy, if you were smart, you admired from afar. If you were stupid, you'd actually risk getting close enough for him to pull you into his powerful arms, losing yourself in his mysterious grey eyes. I looked over at him as we headed up the hill to the school entrance. Was I smart or was I stupid?

As soon as we entered the building, Keira came running up to me. Her face and presence let me know right away that something was wrong.

"What? What is it?" I grabbed her arm out of fear. It was like I needed to hold on to her, to prepare myself for whatever she was about to tell me.

"Frankie," she breathed finally.

"What about her?" Gabriel asked as Trevor came up behind Keira.

"She was in an accident this morning on her way to school," Keira said, and the words felt like ice in my heart. "I saw it on my way here."

"Is she okay?" my voice shook.

"I don't know." Keira shrugged her shoulders. "I saw her being put into the ambulance."

"It looked bad," Trevor added.

I caught sight of Frankie's friends at their lockers. Holley was crying into Rob's shoulder. Amy was patting her back as tears streamed down her cheeks. The rest of the cheer squad was comforting one another as best they could. I stood there, terror strangling my heart.

"This is my fault," I said, not really sure why at first.

"Ava, what are you talking about?" Keira asked.

"I wished this on her. This is my fault," I confessed.

Ava

"Ava, don't be silly." Keira followed me out of the school.

I didn't want to be in here. I didn't want to be anywhere near here. The only thought in my mind was that I had done something bad, and I needed to run from my problems. Frankie and I were far from friends, but I didn't want anything bad to happen to her.

Didn't I, though? I had wished for this to happen. I'd wanted her to get hurt. I had said as much. I had pointed right at her and wanted something terrible to befall my arch rival.

It was ridiculous to think I was responsible for her getting into an accident, but I felt so much guilt. My mom had always said that we hold life and death at the tip of our tongues. We had to be careful with what we said. Our words could manifest in our lives in ways we couldn't imagine.

So, in a way, maybe this was my fault.

"I can't be here," I said out loud to no one in particular.

"Then let's go," Gabriel answered.

"What?" Keira looked at him and then at me.

"Let's go." He took my hand and led me back to his car.

"You're insane." Keira crossed her arms.

He opened the passenger door, and I slid in with no coaxing. Keira gaped at me as if she couldn't believe that I would just leave school like that. I couldn't believe it either, but I knew I had to leave. There was no way I would last all day at school.

"Ava?" Keira said to me as if she were giving me one more shot to get out of the car and not be a teenage rebel.

I said nothing to her. I just let Gabriel shut the door, sealing me inside his car, away from her and the feeling of dread that being there gave me. Gabriel peeled out of the parking lot, driving to who knows where.

It was quiet in the car for a long time. Rain had started to fall again and my head was pounding. It was the weather, but I also knew it was something more than that. It was the stress or the fear that I might have cursed someone, as ridiculous as that sounded.

Gabriel drove and drove. The further away from the school, the clearer my thoughts became. The pressure eased, and the notion I was responsible for Frankie's accident seemed ludicrous.

I suddenly realized Gabriel had brought us somewhere I didn't recognize. We had turned down a long dirt road with large pine trees on either side. We were on a steady incline which the old muscle car took with ease.

"Where are we?" I asked him, sitting up.

"We're headed to my house," he said.

"Your house?" I was suddenly nervous.

I wrapped my arms around my body. What in the world was I thinking, leaving school grounds with Gabriel Matthews? My parents were going to kill me!

Soon the road leveled out. We had passed the trees and were now in a clearing. In the distance stood a massive Victorian-style house. It was three stories with dark, almost black, wood siding. The roof was multi-faceted and an octagonal tower reached for the sky with its pointed tip.

Each window and seam was lined with a grey trim. If someone were looking for a setting for the next haunted house film, this would be perfect.

It was beautiful, but eerily so. The paint job might have been dark, but it was fresh and clean.

As we inched closer, I noticed that the wraparound porch was accented by beautiful fall plants. The grass was perfect and the willow trees that surrounded the property were well-maintained. A dog raised its head as Gabriel parked in the drive. I sat there for a moment after he turned the car off and opened the door.

"Are you coming?" he asked.

"Is anyone home?" I wondered.

"My grandfather is, I'm sure," he assured me.

"Will we not be in trouble then?" I worried. "We are supposed to be in school."

"We're here now, Ava." Gabriel got out of the car without another word.

He began walking up the porch steps. I was still in the car. My heart was hammering in my chest so hard I thought it might burst through. He reached down and scratched the dog's ears. Gabriel looked back at me and waved me over.

Sighing, I got out of the car and walked toward him. The dog came bounding off the steps as soon as it saw me. It was a massive thing, covered in grey hair. I swear the thing had to be up to Gabriel's chest. I stopped, but it didn't.

Before I knew it, I was on my back, the dog on top of me, sniffing around my face. I panicked. Was it going to eat me alive? I looked into its ice-blue eyes. Suddenly, I knew that this animal was harmless. It was intimidating in all regards, but I knew it wouldn't hurt me.

"Get off of her, you meathead," Gabriel chuckled and came to the rescue, pulling the dog away. "This is Kaine."

"Well, nice to meet you, Kaine." I sat up petting the dog's furry face. "You are a very big boy. What is he?"

"He's a Malamute-Wolf hybrid." Gabriel helped me to my feet.

"A wolf?"

"Hybrid. He's harmless. He thinks he's a lapdog, as you can tell. He doesn't know his own strength."

Kaine nuzzled against my leg and sat on my foot. I scratched behind his ears and he made a low groaning sound.

"I think he likes you," Gabriel laughed, and it surprised me to see a genuine smile on his face. "Come on. I want you to meet my grandfather."

I followed Gabriel up the steps and into the house. Kaine was right on my heels as we crossed the threshold.

If the outside was any indication to how the inside would look, it lied to me. The house was brightly lit. It was almost cheery. The hardwood floors looked as though they had been recently waxed. There wasn't a speck of dust on anything. A large staircase branched out to either side, leaving me to wonder where it led. It took my breath away.

Gabriel walked past the staircase and into a sunlit den. It was more like a library. The towering walls were lined with shelves of books. A deep blue carpet covered most to the floor and upon it were antique couches, chairs, and other furniture. Nearest to one of the floor to ceiling windows sat a desk. Behind that desk was a slim man wearing black-rimmed glasses.

He looked up as we entered. The man had a shoulder length mane of silver hair. His sharp grey eyes seemed to cut right through me. He stood up quickly, revealing exactly how tall he was. I was taken aback by how youthful yet mature he looked. It was such a contradiction.

Upon further observation, he didn't even seem to have wrinkles around those obvious Matthews eyes when he smiled at us. Still, there was something wise about him, something that only years of living gave you.

"Gabe," he said, his voice clear and singsong. "What are you doing back so early? And who might you be, dear?"

"Uh, Ava," I told him, nervous about getting into trouble. "Ava Black."

He gazed at me with those all-knowing eyes, and I tried not to gulp. It appeared in one quick glance he knew everything I had ever done or would do.

"So this is Ava." He smiled at me, coming around the desk. "I've heard great things about you."

"You have?" I looked from him to Gabriel.

"Oh, yes, Gabe talks about you often." He smiled, shaking my hand. "Ryland Matthews, a pleasure to meet you."

"Thank you." I smiled back even though I was a ball of nerves.

"Would you like some breakfast?" he asked, but he didn't wait for an answer, just led us out of the den.

Gabriel and I followed him as he explained to us that he had been reading all morning through his books, researching something called, "The Great Noise."

"You'll remember I mentioned my grandfather is an Anthropologist," Gabriel said.

"Oh, yes." I nodded.

Ryland continued, explaining that he needed more books.

"You know there is this great new invention, it really hasn't caught on yet, but it's called the Internet, Pops," Gabriel chimed in as he sat at the bar, and I couldn't help but smile at his childlike nickname for his grandfather.

"You youngsters and your Internet," Ryland grumbled, which sounded odd coming from someone with such a soothing voice. "There is nothing wrong with a good textbook."

I sat beside Gabriel at the bar, listening to their banter back and forth. The bar I sat at was the size of a six-person table. It was centered in the middle of what looked like a full service kitchen from the 1900s. There were modern appliances, and the floor had been refinished, but you could still see the old world charms.

Ryland, or 'Pops' as Gabriel kept calling him, busied himself at the refrigerator, pulling out eggs, milk, butter, and other items. He then grabbed a cast-iron skillet and put it on the gas stove. I watched as he took out a few pieces of bacon and threw them in the pan. He turned around, his movements fluid, and started cracking eggs into a bowl.

"So I sense there was something that lured you two away from school?" Pops cut his eyes at Gabriel as he stirred the eggs. "And I don't think it was the promise of my famous scrambled eggs."

I looked over at Gabriel. What did we say?

"Your eggs aren't famous," Gabriel tried joking.

"Gabe," Ryland's voice was stern.

"I don't know, Pops," he shrugged, "There was just..."

"It was my fault, Mr. Matthews," I chimed in and Gabriel looked at me. "I'm sorry. I was feeling...upset and asked Gabriel to...to just get away."

"I see," Ryland commented. "And, please, Ava, all of Gabriel's friends calls me Pops."

Did he? Because I sure didn't. I don't know what I was thinking getting in the car with Gabriel. I wanted to get away, but away from what? Away from my thoughts? Because they could follow you anywhere.

Still, it was my doing that we were here. I could have told Gabriel no. I could have just stayed at school. He saw me in distress, he offered a way out, and I took it. Which was extremely stupid. What did I really know about him? Nothing, that's what. We had gone to school together for a long time, but that didn't mean I knew him. I didn't know Pops either. They could both be serial killers and here I was about to sit down and eat breakfast with them. I didn't think that was the case though. Something about these Matthews men put me at ease.

Pops said nothing else and set to work cooking his, "famous eggs." Soon the kitchen was thick with the scent of bacon and other mouth-watering aromas. Ryland Matthews made cooking look like a dance. He floated around the kitchen as he gathered ingredients for home-made buttermilk biscuits.

I offered to help, but he wouldn't hear of it. He said I was a guest and guests don't cook.

"No fretting," he grinned at me, "The next time you visit, I'll let you help."

The next time? Would there be a next time? I looked at Gabriel as he chopped tomatoes. Did he want me to visit again?

"Wow, that was really good," I said, placing my fork down on my plate.

We were sitting around the dining room table. My plate was completely bare. I was convinced that Pops was a magician because there was no other explanation for how delicious that food was.

The dining room table was large enough for 12 people, but we occupied one end of it with our plates and glasses. The room was massive, with large windows that allowed in ample natural light.

I felt my phone buzz and saw that I had a text from Keira. She must have been worried about me. I was worried about me.

Hey, I just heard that Frankie is doing OK. She's in stable condition.

Thanks, Keira. Sorry I freaked on you.

It's OK. Just be safe. Don't do anything rash.

Like what?

Nothing. I'll talk to you later.

"Any news?" Gabriel asked me.

"That was Keira," I looked up from my phone, "Frankie is stable."

"Am I missing something?" Pops wondered.

He listened as Gabriel told him about Frankie and about how I thought I had cursed her. He said it in a way that wasn't poking fun, but I still felt embarrassed that he told him about my meltdown.

"You know, Ava," Pops started. "Our words are powerful, but even if you could curse someone, you don't seem the type of person who would. As horrible as it is, I firmly believe it was a coincidence."

"I'm sure you're right," I agreed.

Pops had a way about him. He was calm and reassuring. He could have told me anything at that moment, and I probably would have believed him.

"I'm so glad you were able to have breakfast with us, Ava," Pops wiped his hands on a napkin, "I do believe it is time that Gabriel takes you home so you can let your parents know where you've been."

"Yes, of course." I blushed. "Thank you."

He inclined his head, and Gabriel and I excused ourselves from the table. Pops refused to let me help clean up. Gabriel led me down the hall and Kaine suddenly came charging up to us. He had a ball in his mouth and began wagging his tail as we approached.

"Sorry, buddy, I don't have time to play." Gabriel patted the dog's head.

Kaine whined in response, as if he understood what Gabriel was saying. I didn't doubt that he did. Kaine dropped the ball, his tongue hanging out of the side of his mouth as he panted. I smiled down at him and was about to scratch his ear when he lunged at my hand. He easily grabbed my cell phone and ran down the hall.

"Kaine!" I yelled, racing after him.

"Bad dog!" Gabriel called from behind me.

I could hear his footfalls as he caught up to me. Kaine took a left, and we nearly collided into the wall as we had to turn on a dime. Pops watched as we ran past the kitchen, an amused smile on his face. The dog turned another corner, which led into the den, but he didn't stop there.

He ran from the room and out into the hallway. I watched as he hightailed it up the stairs, my phone tightly clenched between his teeth. Without hesitating, I ran up the steps two at a time, but he was far ahead of me. He took a right at the landing and then an immediate left into an open door.

Gabriel and I reached the room at the same time and burst through the door. Kaine was sitting in his dog bed, panting so heavily his body rose up and down. My phone was lying just inside the threshold. I could see that it was coated in a thick layer of dog drool, but it was otherwise unscathed.

I picked up the phone with two fingers and then glared at Kaine. He seemed to smile at me from across the room.

"Gross." I held out my phone.

"Oh, man," Gabriel chuckled. "I'm sorry, Ava. Let me go wipe it off."

He took the phone and retreated out the door and down the hall to what I assumed was the bathroom. Kaine got up from his bed and walked over to me. He sort of bowed his head and then looked up at me as if to say he was sorry.

"It's alright." I kneeled down and scratched behind his ears. "I know you were just wanting to play."

Kaine moved closer to me and licked my face. I laughed and wiped my cheek with the sleeve of my shirt. As I did so I noticed the room I was in had a very intricate mural on the wall. The room itself seemed to be a study. A medium-sized oak desk sat on one side and behind it was a large bookshelf. On the other side were shelves lined with jars and oddly shaped containers filled with plants and other items.

The wall opposite the door was what I was interested in the most. Besides the marble fireplace that adorned the center, the entire wall was painted with a majestic, though very disturbing scene. It depicted people, Vikings, both men and women, in a battle with forces dressed in dark cloaks. Fighting with the Vikings, not against them, were Indigenous People. I couldn't tell what tribe they were, but all of them were in a heated battle. One figure stood front and center, pointing a withered hand at a warrior.

My heart did a flip, and my palms began to sweat. Those figures reminded me so much of the phantoms that haunted my nightmares. I instinctively took a step back, but then another image in the mural caught my eyes. There was a young girl behind the cloaked beings. Her raven black hair seemed to dance in a whirlwind, hiding her face. She wore what looked like traditional garments of her tribe and was chained to what I assumed was an altar at the base of a tall fortress. Many of the robed figures surrounded her, and one had a knife in their hands. The knife immediately caught my attention, the bone white blade and black handle. I had seen that before.

I moved closer, and with each step, the stranger I felt. Finally, when I was just inches from the mural, I reached out and let my fingers trace one of the hooded figures.

The wall was textured. I could feel every fiber, groove, and indention against my skin. I looked over at the Viking warrior the woman was pointing at with her grotesque finger. He was tall, broad, a gleaming sword in his hand. His face was obscured, half hidden in shadows, but I still could see that he was a handsome young man.

I could also see the look of determination carved into his features and bravery in his stance. He was ready for the beast that stood before him and the woman I was assuming he was risking everything to save. There was something about him that captivated my thoughts and imagination.

I looked at the contours of his face, the line of his jaw, the veins of his smooth neck. There was a tattoo that peeked out of the top of his leather suit, one that had been battered from the fight.

Who was he? Who was the raven-haired girl? She looked as if she might be part of the Native tribe, but I wasn't sure. I needed to know.

Looking up, I saw there was a figure, a woman, in the sky. She was domineering and a light shone around her. I could only assume she was far more powerful than anyone else in this scene. She made me think of a goddess. She seemed to protrude from the ground. Her features were vague, as if the artist wasn't sure how to paint her. However, what stood out the most was the crown of animal bones that adorned her head. She was fierce, looking out over the battle, her hands reaching forward, as if waiting to take everyone and everything with her back to that dark hole in the earth she came out of.

The scene changed as I moved on. The young woman was now free of her bonds. The man and his companions were scattered at her feet. Some were on their knees, seeming to be fighting their way back to their feet, readying themselves for more.

Another scene and she was battling the figure with the crown of bones. Colors of red and white swirled around them. The Viking warrior was upright, battling more robed figures as the young woman kept this goddess at bay.

Finally, in the last scene, the Native woman had pushed the monster back into the earth. I could tell it had taken many lives to do so. In fact, the young Viking warrior was now in her arms, his chest a gaping wound.

The goddess seemed to scream up from her cage, pulling at the earth, rage in her eyes, but she was safely sealed away. There was a barrier of white light that prevented anyone from stepping over.

I could feel my heart breaking at the sight. There was so much bloodshed. Why? Who was this goddess? Who was this raven-haired woman with this much power? What had happened?

"Ava?" Gabriel said from behind me, causing me to jump.

"What?" I spun around.

"Sorry, I didn't mean to scare you," he said to me and then looked up at the painting.

"What is this?" I asked him, turning back around.

He walked up beside me and handed me my phone. Gabriel looked at the mural for a good while before he commented.

"This has been in my family for ages," he started. "Centuries ago, my ancestors were part of a ruling Viking family."

"Really?" I was curious about how this related to the painting.

"Yeah, it's true," he continued. "My ancestor, Herleif was an Earl."

"Impressive," I laughed.

He smiled at me and then continued, "There have always been warriors in our family. This mural was a battle that Herleif fought in the 10th century, when the Vikings came to North America, along with the Beothuk Tribe. Legend says that the two opposing peoples had to band together in order to fight a common enemy."

"Those things?" I pointed at the hooded figures.

"Yes," he said. "The Witches of Thyana. Their goddess of earth and life."

The name sent shivers down my spine. I had heard that name before, hadn't I?

"The Vikings, when they first came to what is now Newfoundland, began trades with the Beothuk people," he continued. "Things were fine, but then went downhill quickly. Young girls from both the Viking clan and the Native tribe went missing. Of course, they blamed each other. It wasn't until one of the Beothuk girls, a Medicine Woman in training, came forward with a vision. She said a dark force, one that had latched itself to Herleif's clan, was taking their young women."

"Why were they taking them?" I asked, looking at the young girl.

"Well, if you believe in things like this, the Witches of Thyana stole souls to feed their goddess," he explained. "Apparently, she had a taste for young maidens."

"Young maidens?" I don't know why the story was upsetting me, but it was.

"Yes, any maiden with exceptional talents," he explained. "According to the lore, Thyana liked the taste of human souls, especially those with unique abilities."

"That's why they wanted her." I pointed to the mural.

"Yes, according to the stories, Tepkunset was a very powerful wielder of magic. The Imprecors wanted her for their 'Mother' so they took her."

"Imprecors?" I wondered.

"It's just a term for a curse, but that's what the lore calls them," he said. "They were definitely a curse."

"Yeah," I stared at the mural once more, "And it looks like she sealed Thyana away?"

"She did. She defeated them, but we aren't sure how. The legends also say that Herleif vowed to never let an Imprecor hurt another maiden or anyone else for that matter," Gabriel told me. "They say he formed a secret society, the Mavors, to battle the forces of evil. They made a blood-bond with the Beothuk Tribe, that if ever they needed one of the Mavors to fight with them again, they would be there. It's said that his family were the chosen guardians of the next Medicine Woman of the Beothuk Tribe."

"Your family then, right?" I looked at him.

"Yes," he nodded. "It was our people who had brought the darkness to this land in the first place. We owed a debt."

"And, was there another Medicine Woman?" I asked.

"The Beothuk Tribe actually died out from what we can tell," he said. "If they have descendants, they are scattered thanks to European invasion."

"That's awful," I said, thinking about my own ancestors and what they must have faced at the hands of White invaders. "How would the Mavors ever find the next Medicine Woman if they needed to?"

"The blood-bond is sealed in magic," he explained. "They would find her, even if it took them their entire life, they would find her."

"He loved her, didn't he?" I pointed at the warrior in Tepkunset's arms.

"Yes," Gabriel nodded his head, staring at the mural, "Erik fell in love with Tepkunset. He loved her so much that he gave his life for her."

"I'm taking this too seriously, aren't I?" I laughed.

"I do too, sometimes," he told me.

"Did she love him?" I asked.

"I think so." He shrugged. "Every legend says they were bonded the moment they saw each other, but their differences kept them apart. They were never, ever truly together and then Erik was killed in battle."

"That's so tragic." I felt sad.

"It is," he said. "But isn't that something? To have a love that is so strong it is still talked about hundreds of years later? I want something like that."

I turned to look at him and felt my face flush with heat at the thought. Who wouldn't want a love story that epic? Even if he didn't believe in Medicine Women, witches, and ancient evil beings, he seemed to at least believe in love.

His eyes searched my face, as if he wanted me to say I agreed. When he looked at me like that, I wanted to trust him. I wanted to reach out and touch the tattoo that was always just there, above the line of his t-shirt, and I almost did. I wanted to just be there with him.

Gabriel took a step forward and brushed a stray strand of hair from my face. It shocked me. I was not expecting such an intimate reaction from him. My hand itched to reach out to him. My face reddened and I suddenly felt hot, but instead of letting his spell completely mesmerize me, I stepped back. He seemed to snap out of whatever magic that had held him captive and then said, "Are you ready to go?"

I nodded, not trusting myself to speak. Gabriel led me back down the stairs and out of the house. I didn't see Pops on our way out, or Kaine, so I assumed he was still in the kitchen cleaning up our mess.

The rain had started back up again, so we made a mad dash for the car. I nearly slipped in the mud, but managed to stay upright. Gabriel was laughing at me as we climbed into the car. I playfully punched his shoulder, which hurt me more than it hurt him, I'm sure. His arms were like brick walls. I held my hand as the pain ebbed away and was thankful that I hadn't hit him any harder.

It was around 11:00 by the time Gabriel pulled into my driveway. My parents weren't home yet, so I was glad I would not have to talk to them about being home early or about Frankie.

Frankie. How was she? I'm sure she was fine or Keira would have told me otherwise. Looking back, I realized how stupid it was for me to think I'd had anything to do with her accident. I was just Ava Black. I had no power over anyone else's life.

"Gabriel," I said before I got out of the car. "Thank you."

"For what?" He looked genuinely confused.

"For...being there," I told him.

"Are we friends?" he suddenly asked me, leaning over, making me gulp.

"Um, I guess we are," I said, afraid to move, wondering what would happen if I did.

"That's going to be...interesting," he said and then sat back up. "I'll see you later, Black."

I just sort of nodded and got out of the car. He had reverted back to weird Gabriel, and I wasn't sure what to think of it. It was going to be interesting? I guess he wasn't wrong.

Gabriel

My heart was still hammering in my chest as I watched her run through the rain up her porch steps. I could still smell her. The scent of lilac lingered in the air. Maybe it was her shampoo. A warm feeling spread across my chest. Before I jumped out of the car and ran after her, I put it in reverse and headed home.

Squeezing the steering wheel to calm my nerves, I tried to get the look on her face out of my mind. Her dark eyes stared back at me through thick lashes. The closeness of her face, the smoothness of her skin, was right there in my memories, tormenting me with impure thoughts.

And I said we could be friends. What was I thinking? I wasn't. That was the only explanation. Oh, that was wrong. I was thinking, and it was all about Ava Black.

She was so enthralled with the mural on the wall. The way she had looked at it, like she could stare at it for hours. That's how I felt when I looked at her.

The thought hit me like a gut punch. I could feel the tiny flame explode into a raging fire in my chest as it crept up my neck and settled in my cheeks. Ava Black had a hold of me, and I didn't know what to do about it.

My phone rang, and I dug it out of my pocket to answer it.

"Hey, Trev," I said. "What's up?"

"Huh, we're supposed to be running today," he said.

"Oh, yeah, crap, I forgot," I said. "Are you still at the school?"

"Yeah," he replied. "We can meet at the gym in town if you don't want to meet here since you kind of bailed in the middle of the day to whisk Ava off somewhere."

"Yeah, did anyone notice?" I wondered.

"Not anyone that matters," he told me. "Keira was worried sick. I thought she was going to send out the hounds. Anyway, I'll meet you at the gym by the doughnut shop because that's not tempting at all."

Laughing, I hung up the phone and turned the car around. I had been running with Trevor for the past few months. He had applied to a few departments within the military to work in cyber security and had received interest. The actual CIA had come to his house, interviewed him and his parents, done background checks, and even talked to me and Pops.

He was smart; it was impressive. But, now he had it in his mind that he was going to be sent overseas somewhere and needed to get in shape. I pointed out that he could do cyber security from here on American soil and would probably not be involved in some James Bond type situation.

"I've read about this type of stuff, Gabe," he had told me. "They could send me anywhere. And, there is a physical. I don't want to fail if I get recruited."

So, I agreed to train with him. He had actually worked up a bit of muscle, but Trevor was naturally thin. He had a long way to go. I wasn't sure what the physical test entailed, but maybe we could get him ready for it. He was determined, so I would not stand in his way.

He was a computer genius, so if our government really wanted him, I don't think they would care much about the fact that he couldn't run a mile.

I pulled into the gym parking lot and grabbed my gym bag out of the trunk of my car. We usually trained at the school gym, but this was a pleasant change. It was one of the chain gyms that had been recently built, so all of the equipment was nice and everything was functional.

The one at school was always busy and most of the time it was crawling with the jocks, like Rob Hastings and his pack of bumbling idiots. Just thinking about that jerk made my blood boil.

Trevor was already there and ready, so I hurriedly dressed and met him at the treadmills.

"How is Ava?" he asked.

"She's okay," I told him.

"Does she still think she cursed Frankie?" he asked.

"I don't think she ever thought that." We started warming up. "She just felt guilty."

"Yeah, but Frankie will be fine." Trevor shrugged. "Karma ignores people like her."

"Trevor." I looked at him.

"I'm not saying I wanted her to die," he laughed. "That's not what I meant at all. I'm just saying that Frankie is one of those people who will have the perfect life. Her family is loaded, she'll get into a good school, marry a rich guy, and probably never have a worry in her life. She'll never have to pay for being a crap person."

"Yeah, well, it sounded like you wanted her to pay with her life for a minute there." I eyed him. "That doesn't sound like you."

"I just said that's not what I meant," he said, not looking at me.

We didn't say anything else about it and continued our workout. Trevor was unusually quiet. I supposed he was mad that I had assumed he had wished death on one of our classmates.

Not that I was defending Frankie. She was a horrible person. Especially to Trevor. There had been times she wasn't that nice to me either, but mostly she basically harassed me. It was gross and really sad to be honest. There was a part of me that felt bad for her.

Still, that didn't mean I thought death was a suitable punishment.

Trevor had faced a lot more at the hands of Frankie and people like Rob. I wasn't going to pretend like I understood what it was like to be him or what he dealt with regularly. People just left me alone. I understood why. My presence turned many people off. I was a big guy and according to Pops, I could look a little menacing.

Trevor didn't have that advantage. It wasn't right for me to judge how he felt.

Suddenly Trevor dropped the weight he was about to lift and slumped to his knees. I caught him and looked at his pale face. His dark eyes looked nearly black, and his skin felt clammy.

"Hey," I said. "Trev? What's wrong?"

"Whoa," he said, and his eyes focused on mine. "Whoa, sorry. That was weird."

"Are you alright, man?" I asked.

"Yeah, I think so." He shook his head. "I just got dizzy for a minute. I'm fine. I didn't eat a lot today. Maybe I need one of those doughnuts."

"Funny." I narrowed my eyes at him.

"I'm fine, really," he said, shaking me off. "But, I'm also okay with calling it a day."

"Okay." I wiped the sweat from my forehead. "Are you alright to drive home?"

"Yeah," he told me with a laugh. "I'm fine. I promise. I'm telling you. I just need to eat something."

We grabbed a doughnut, and I made him eat it before letting him leave. He thought I was being ridiculous, but I told him to get over it.

"Bye, Papa Matthews." He waved as he got into his small Ford Coupe.

I laughed as he drove away. My smile faded as soon as he was out of sight. I had never seen Trevor like that. He was out of sorts. And then the dizzy spell. I didn't like it.

On the way home, I grabbed a pizza. Pops probably had cooked a delicious meal, but I needed something really greasy and unhealthy. That's what you did after you hit the gym, right?

I made it inside the front door as the first rumble of thunder sounded overhead. Kaine came whining at my feet.

The hair on my arms stood on end. This was a different kind of whining. My heart sank. Fear flooded my body.

"Pops?" I called, making my way through the house. "Pops!"

I hurried into his office and didn't see him. My fear intensified, moving from room to room, still not finding him. I ran upstairs and barged into his bedroom.

"Pops?" I called and then heard the shower running. "Pops?"

He didn't answer when I knocked on the door, so I pushed my way inside. I found him huddled in the shower's corner, trying to pick himself up.

"Pops," it came out as a frightened whisper.

I grabbed a towel and opened the glass door of the shower. Making my way in, the water soaking me instantly, I wrapped the towel around him and pulled him to his feet. I turned off the water and helped him out of the shower, carefully moving over the slick tile.

I sat him down on the toilet and looked at him. He had a small abrasion on his forehead, but looked otherwise unharmed. His body was shaking.

"Pops, are you alright?" I asked him.

"It's passing." His voice was low. "I'm sorry."

"Please don't apologize." I could feel the tears stinging my eyes.

I grabbed another towel and wrapped it around his body. He seemed to be thankful for the extra layer of warmth and pulled the towel tighter around him.

"Maybe I should take you to the hospital?" I offered.

"No." He shook his head. "It's just an episode."

"Pops, your head." I pointed at it.

"I'm not even bleeding," he told me. "They can't help me, Gabriel. I'll call Dr. Jones in the morning, I promise. Right now, I just want to get into some warm clothes and rest."

"Alright," I relented. "Let me get you something."

I went into his room and grabbed him a pair of his usual pajamas. After helping him dry off and getting him into his clothes, I led him to the bed. He eased in under the sheets with a grateful sigh. I gave him his nightly medication, and it wasn't long before he was asleep.

Kaine and I sat next to him for a few hours as the storm moved in, keeping vigil. When my eyes grew heavy, I made my way to my room and took a much needed shower.

Falling into my bed, it wasn't long before sleep encased my mind. As I faded into the inky blackness, I saw flashes of dark blue light.

Ava

I walked into the house, head pounding, but it was nothing compared to the hammering of my heart. He had been so close, and I would be lying if I said I wasn't wondering what it would feel like to kiss him. I'd had boyfriends, but none of them had made me feel the way Gabriel just did, and he hadn't even touched me. Sighing, I pushed myself off the door and into the dark living room.

Mom always left a light on in here, so it surprised me to find it so dark. I could have sworn it was brightly lit when I left with Gabriel this morning. As I went to flip on the light, nothing happened. Irritated, I tried it again. Once more, nothing happened.

Outside there was hardly any natural light to filter in through the windows. The clouds had sufficiently buried the sun in its murky puffs. Still, I could make out most of the details in the living room.

I was about to feel my way toward the end table, to search for a flashlight, when I heard a voice and a felt a hand on my shoulder. Screaming, I turned around and punched at whatever I could find.

"It's me! It's me!" I heard Keira's voice through all my wailing.

"Keira? What are you doing?" I yelled at her.

She flashed her light from her cell phone in my face. Her expression was just as terrified as mine. She lowered her light and looked at me sheepishly.

"What are you doing in my house?" I questioned her. "How long have you been here?"

"I just got here," she told me. "I've been trying to call you and you didn't answer. I got nervous. I thought...well, I thought maybe something had happened to you."

"I was at Gabriel's," I said, crossing my arms. "What could have happened to me?"

"I don't know." She shrugged her shoulders, looking around. "I mean, you don't even know him that well and you took off with him. I was just afraid, when I couldn't get in touch with you, that he might have...I don't know. I just wanted you to be okay."

"So your response was to break into my house, and what? Rescue me?" I couldn't help but laugh. "What if I was being murdered when you came in? You're 95 pounds soaking wet, you would have been killed, too."

"Well, I had to try, didn't I?" She looked at the floor and then looked at me.

I burst out laughing. I laughed so hard I started crying. After a moment, Keira joined in with me. We fell onto the couch, laughing until our stomachs hurt.

"Thanks," I said to her, wiping at my eyes. "Few people would face down a potential killer to make sure I was safe."

"Don't mention it." She smiled. "I'm sorry I broke into your house."

"How did you break into my house?" I looked at her curiously.

"It was rather easy," she said, just as the lights flickered back on and then back out as a roll of thunder sounded outside. "Geez, this weather is insane. And I thought it rained a lot in London!"

Keira and I spent the rest of the day catching up on schoolwork by candlelight. If I was going to skip school, the least I could do was not get even more behind. Right when I could no longer focus on Pre-Cal, Mom came through the door. She was carrying bags of groceries. Keira and I ran to help her. She didn't question what Keira was doing here. I think she was just glad that I was actually hanging out with someone.

As soon as Dad came home, the storm was in full force. It was making me a bit nervous. I wasn't one that normally let storms freak them out, but this one had really strong winds. Dad brought out the battery operated weather radio and turned it on. We sat around the kitchen table, playing board games and eating snacks.

Mom called Keira's host parents and asked if it were alright if she stayed here until the storm passed. They were perfectly fine with it. I was too. I liked having Keira there. She made me happy despite the pain. It was a pleasant distraction. Maybe she wasn't as much of a distraction as Gabriel, but still.

Around 11:00pm, the storm dissipated. With it being so late, Keira's host parents thought it would be best for her to stay the night with us, and Mom agreed. She would have normally never agreed to that on a school night, but she didn't want anyone to risk driving. Keira wasn't planning on staying the night, so I let her borrow some pajamas and something to wear to school the next day.

She was slimer than I was, but luckily, I had some of my old clothes she could wear. I told her she could have them because it just wasn't my style anymore. And, honestly, I would probably never fit back into them again. I was fine with that. I had embraced my new curves.

We finally got into the bed around midnight. We had a guest room, but Keira stayed in my room. My bed was large enough for both of us. Mom warned us not to stay up talking, but we couldn't help it.

"You never told me what you and Gabriel did while you were away," she pointed out just as I was about to fall asleep.

"We really didn't do much," I told her. "He just took me to his house."

"Really? What does it look like?" she wondered.

"It's massive," I confessed. "It's like something out of a Bram Stoker novel, but it's still really pretty. I met his grandfather. He was really nice. I met his dog, too, who almost ate my phone. I swear that dog was a human stuck in canine form. He was so intelligent. We had breakfast and talked. He told me a lot about his family's history. It was interesting and..."

"And what?" Keira prodded.

I was about to tell her about the mural on the wall, about how the figures were the same ones I had seen in my dream, but I decided against it, mostly because it sounded insane. There was no way I dreamed about an ancient being from ghost stories and myths.

"I thought he was going to kiss me," I finally said, and she gasped. "He didn't. Maybe I was just reading into it. He leaned over and right when I thought he was going to, he just asked if we could be friends."

"Did you want to kiss him?" she asked.

"I don't know," I shrugged my shoulders, but my stomach flipped at the thought and I shifted around in the bed.

"What is it?" Keira propped up on her elbow and looked at me.

"Gabriel is...he's gorgeous and was oddly sweet today," I began. "But there's something about him. I can't put my finger on. It's like this part of me wants to dive in headfirst because I know it would be amazing, but then there's the other part of me that...senses something sort of off about him. Like he's not telling me something really important. I know it sounds crazy, but it's like I can tell that he is that sweet and charming person, but he's hiding something."

"We should always listen to our gut instincts," she offered.

"Yeah, maybe." When I didn't say anything else, Keira laid back down.

After a moment, she was fast asleep. I knew it would take me a bit longer before sleep would catch up to me. My mind was being pulled in a million different directions. There was Gabriel and the thought of what might be between us, and then there were the figures, Imprecors, and the legend of his ancestors that seemed to be calling to me.

The story had been bouncing around my mind all night. I knew it was just that, a story, but something about the robed beings stirred a keen interest inside me. While Keira slept, I pulled out my phone and researched the Imprecors and the Witches of Thyana. I didn't find anything in particular about them, but I did find things about the Beothuk Tribe, their encounters with the Vikings, and their near extinction from European settlers. Everything that Gabriel told me was true, at least the believable parts.

What I could find out about Thyana was interesting, but not really helpful. She was the Viking goddess of nature. She had devoted followers, but it didn't say anything about them killing young maidens for her. Her name was so familiar to me. Maybe I had heard it in school or one of my Dad's many history lessons.

Frustrated about not finding out more about the Imprecors, I put my phone down and finally drifted off to sleep.

I was worthless the next day. Luckily, so were most of the teachers. They yawned and downed coffee. What made things worse was that Gabriel wasn't there. When I sent him a text to check on him, he said he wasn't feeling well.

We didn't have much work in any of our classes, all except for Mr. Ryan's Pre-Cal class. I swear the man made it his life's goal to torment students. That was, unless you were a cheerleader or football player, but especially a cheerleader. He always gave me the creeps, the way his eyes lingered on us when we wore our uniforms. I guess I didn't mind it before, when I ruled the school, because I could get away with anything in his class. Now, I realized how disgusting that was.

As soon as we put our butts in our seats, he was handing out a pop quiz. I was not at all prepared for this. I glanced over at Keira and she rolled her eyes. Trevor was already getting started, his pencil moving over the paper with purpose. Keira and I met eyes again. We were both jealous at how easily schoolwork came to Trevor.

"Miss Black!" Mr. Ryan's nasally voice jolted me to attention. "Eyes on your own paper!"

"They are," I said.

"Oh, really?" he snarled at me, crossing his skinny arms over a wide gut. "Then why are you looking around?"

"I was just—" I started, but he cut me off.

"Detention, after school today," he snapped.

"What? I didn't do anything!" I huffed.

"Do you want to make it two days?" he challenged.

"No and it shouldn't be one because I wasn't cheating," I seethed. "But I guess that doesn't matter to you since I'm not a half-dressed cheerleader!"

The room went completely silent. Jaws were on the floor, and I heard someone snicker toward the back.

"Get out," his face was tomato red. "Hand in your paper, which you will receive a zero on. Go straight to the office."

I stood up, grabbed my paper, and slammed it on his desk. Without so much as a backwards glance, I yanked open the door and slammed it behind me. I was mad, fuming even, but I didn't mean to do it. As soon as the door hit the frame, the glass in the small squares that decorated his door shattered, hitting the floor with an ear-splitting clash.

I stopped for only a second, hearing someone curse and Mr. Ryan yelling. I just kept walking after that and headed for the office.

They called both of my parents to the school. By the time they arrived, I had calmed down and now felt really nervous. I had never been in trouble at school. Even when I should have been caught a million times, I always got away with it. Now, I was in some serious crap. Not only had I been accused of cheating, I insulted and made some serious accusations about a teacher, and I broke his door.

Mom and Dad spent a long time in the principal, Mrs. Rush's, office. Too long because I spent quite a while squirming in my seat. The receptionist, Mrs. Terry, kept glancing in my direction. I'm sure this was her train of thought, "She used to be one of the good kids. What happened to her?"

I was never one of the good kids. I was just superb at hiding who I was. It was shameful to think about and I may have deserved to get in trouble back then, but this time, I was innocent.

I had already given my spiel to Mrs. Rush. She didn't look impressed or sensitive to my plight. I felt she had always been a fair principal. She didn't throw favoritism to anyone. However, I had damaged school property.

The door opened and Mrs. Rush called me inside. Gulping, I walked in and took a seat in between my parents. I didn't dare look them in the eyes.

"Ava," Mrs. Rush began as she took her seat on the other side of the desk. "We have never had an issue with your behavior before. I find it shocking that you are sitting in that chair at the moment. Be that as it may, we have a zero tolerance policy when it comes to things of this nature."

I didn't say anything. I didn't trust myself to speak. Tears were already burning at the corners of my eyes.

"However, seeing as this is your first offense," she started, and I looked up, "you are only required to finish out this week with after-school detention with Mr. Ryan. Your punishment will be entirely up to him. This is much better than suspending you, which would have gone on your permanent record."

"I understand, Mrs. Rush," I told her. "I'm really sorry I lost my temper. I didn't mean to break the glass. And, I wasn't cheating! I'm not a cheater."

"I know." Her voice was gentle. "Your detention will start tomorrow after school. For now, I think you should go home."

"Yes, ma'am." I lowered my eyes again. "Thank you, Mrs. Rush."

Mrs. Rush walked us to the door. Thankfully, the exit to the school was only five feet from the office door, so we could leave without drawing unwanted stares from my classmates.

Mom and Dad were silent all the way to the car and all the way home. This was worse than having them yell at me. I had no idea what was going on in their heads. Were they so disappointed in me they couldn't even look in my direction? I felt worse than worse at the thought.

When we opened the door to the house, that's when Dad lost his cool. He yelled at me for about 45 minutes straight. I was mad. I was angry that he didn't see my side of things. I yelled back, defending my actions. It was a bad idea. He really lost it and grounded me for a month.

I stormed off to my room and slammed the door. Throwing myself onto my bed, I had a good angry cry. More than anything I was shocked Dad had lost his temper on me. He was always the calm one.

"Ava?" Dad came knocking on the door a little while later.

I thought about ignoring him and pretending that I was asleep, but I didn't want to go to bed mad at him. Even if I was angry with him, I wanted to see his face. I wanted him to look at me like he always did, like I was his little girl and not a disappointment.

"Yeah," I called, my nose stuffy from all the crying.

"Ava, honey," he came in and sat on my bed, "I want you to know that I love you."

"I know, Daddy," I sat up, leaning my back against my headboard, "I love you, too."

"This just isn't like you, Mijita." He took my hand in his.

"I told you, Dad," I started. "It wasn't my fault. I didn't cheat on my quiz. Mr. Ryan is just a big, fat jerk."

"I never thought you cheated," he assured me. "What upset me is the way you went about defending yourself. Your mother and I have always taught you to stand up for yourself, Ava, but the way you handled it today was not acceptable."

"I'm sorry." I felt tears well up in my eyes. "I really am. I was just so...mad. I'm sorry."

"I may have overreacted with the whole grounding thing." He smiled sheepishly. "I'm not going to ground you all month, but you are grounded for the rest of the week. No phone, no Keira. But, do something like this again and it will be a different story."

"I promise, I won't," I said.

Dad hugged me and I cried into his shoulder. It was late and mom was already in the bed, but Dad convinced me to go downstairs to eat a bowl of our favorite cereal. Afterwards, I took a shower and crawled into bed. I was emotionally drained. I slept hard that night. If I dreamed, then I didn't recall a single thing about it.

I saw Gabriel as soon as I walked into the school the next morning, and memories of how close he had been to me made my face flush. I was almost about to smile when I caught sight of Mr. Ryan. He sneered at me, crossing his arms. Just seeing him made my blood boil. I stomped past him and stood next to Gabriel and Trevor.

"Are you feeling better?" I asked him with concern.

"Yeah," he said, sort of gruffly, giving me this look I didn't really understand. "I gotta go."

He left me and Trevor standing there, staring after him. His abruptness stunned me. He had seemed to warm up to me the other day, and now I was revolting again. Trevor looked at me and shrugged his shoulders.

I wanted to run after him and ask what his problem was, but resisted the urge. If he wanted to act like a big baby, fine with me. Huffing, I made my way to my locker after a quick goodbye to Trevor.

I had been eager to see Gabriel, and now I felt like an idiot. I thought there had been some kind of peace brokered between us, that we were friends. If I were being honest with myself, I had hoped there might have been something more.

"I think Mr. Ryan is murdering you with his eyes," Keira said as she came walking up, as I put books in my backpack, nodding in Mr. Ryan's direction.

"I don't care," I huffed, even though I did. "I feel like murdering him for real."

"I didn't hear that." Keira plugged her ears. "That way when the police come to question me, I can honestly say I never heard you say anything murderous about Mr. Ryan."

The day was full of gossip. People talked about Frankie and how she was doing. It was all very tragic, even though the official report was that she was going to make a full recovery. They also talked about my outburst in Mr. Ryan's class. By the end of the day, I'd learned that I had a brain tumor that was causing rage episodes and Frankie was on life support.

During a free period, I hid in my normal spot in the library. The school library wasn't as cozy as the one in town, but Mrs. Dean did everything she could to make the white washed concrete walls to feel welcoming. We had become closer over the course of the semester and she had come to expect me to occupy the reading nook she had created in the YA Fiction section.

I waved to her as I walked in. She smiled in return and I hurried to my spot. I stopped short when I found Trevor there. He didn't notice me at first, but then looked up when I began walking closer.

"Hey," he smiled.

"What are you doing here?" I asked as I sat in the seat opposite him. "I'm normally here alone this time of day."

"This is my study period," he said. "I'm normally in the computer lab, but they're replacing some servers so everything is shut down. So, here I am. I can go if you need some alone time."

"What? No," I shook my head. "I'm not trying to run you off."

We sat there for a moment. It was awkward. We usually had Keira or Gabriel as a buffer. Trevor and I didn't have the best history. I wasn't the nicest person to him, but I wasn't exactly the meanest either. Still, there were times when I could have stepped in when Frankie and Rob were bullying him and I didn't. To me, what I did was worse. Guilt hit me hard.

"Gabriel isn't himself today," he said to me.

"No, he's not," I said. "Do you know why? Was it something I did?"

"No, I don't know why," he said. "But I'm sure it's not you. He likes you."

"Right," I said.

I wasn't sure how to take that. Trevor surely meant that Gabriel liked me as a friend, but the thought of Gabriel confiding in him about me made my cheeks flush.

"Miss Black," I turned and saw Mr. Ryan standing behind us.

He was holding a small bag in his hands. It looked like a travel bag that one would carry toiletry items in. Why he was carrying it in the library, I have no idea.

"I don't believe it is appropriate for you to be back here with Mr. Bishop alone," he said, sneering down at us.

I wanted to say so many things, but I was already in so much trouble. If I did anything else to get in even more trouble I was bound to be suspended. Instead of starting a fight, I sighed and began gathering my things.

"And why not?" Trevor said suddenly. "This is a place for all students. Ava and I are friends, Mr. Ryan. What's inappropriate is for you to look at two teenagers and think something is going to happen between them in the library reading corner."

My mouth fell open as I stared at Trevor. Mr. Ryan's face went ghostly white and then scarlet. He huffed, but said nothing as he turned around and stormed away. I was nearly sure he left a trail of smoke in his haste.

"That was amazing," I laughed. "Thank you."

"He's a creep," Trevor said. "And you're welcome. That's what friends do. We stand up for each other."

"Trevor..." I started.

"We've talked about this before," he told me. "I'm glad we're friends. I don't care about what happened before. I know that wasn't the real you. This version, this Ava, this is the real you and I like her."

"Can I still tell you I'm sorry?" I asked. "Because I am."

"I know that," he said. "Which is why you didn't even have to say it."

Trevor and I sat in comfortable silence for the rest of the class.

I lingered in the hallway as the last bell of the day rang like a gong. Keira assured me I would be just fine, but I claimed there was no way I could last through detention with Mr. Ryan.

He already had a ton of work for me to do. I cleaned, filed, and then cleaned some more. The entire time he sat at his desk, peering up at me over his thick-rimmed glasses. I was so creeped out. Having his eyes on me made my skin crawl. There was this suspicion that he enjoyed watching me dust the shelves in his unnerving little dungeon of a classroom.

When the clock showed 4:00pm, I practically ran for the door.

"Same time tomorrow, Miss Black," he called after me.

I didn't respond. I just grabbed my belongings and hurried down the hall. I made my way outside into the light of the evening sun. It was dim, golden, and felt like heaven on my skin. I was so thankful to see it after all the rain.

Mom said she was going to meet me in the parking lot. I checked my phone and had a text from her that she was running late.

Great.

I made my way to the parking lot. I would just wait on the grassy part between the gym and the parking spaces. There was a short brick barrier between the two that I could perch on until she got there.

To my absolute horror, Rob and his football buddies were getting ready to leave after practice as well. Someone hit him on the shoulder and pointed at me. Rob turned, grinned, and made his way in my direction. I sat down and pretended I hadn't seen him.

As he and his friends approached, they brought to mind a pack of wolves that had just gotten a whiff of fresh blood.

"Well, hey there," Rob called. "How was detention with Ryan, huh, Ava? Rough. Did you make sure to show a little cleavage? I heard he likes that."

"You're a pig, Rob." I narrowed my eyes at him.

"What? You didn't mind showing it before. What's different now?" He laughed and so did his friends.

"Ava..." I stiffened as I heard Gabriel behind me.

What was he doing here? I turned to look at him. He was wearing a black tank top and a pair of running shorts. Was he exercising in the gym? Was he in some sport? I was so confused.

"Oh, is this why you're suddenly so modest?" Rob laughed. "Is Gabe making an honest woman out of you?"

"This conversation is boring." Gabriel's jaw muscle clenched, then he said, "Let's go."

Gabriel marched down the steps and grabbed my hand, pushing past the group, easily moving Rob from his path. Rob's nostrils flared with irritation, a sign he wasn't done. I was speechless as Gabriel manhandled me down the parking lot.

I was actually pissed. He spent all day ignoring me. Even when we sat outside for our break, he said nothing to me. Now he wanted to play knight in shining armor?

"Now, wait, I'm just playing," Rob laughed. "I think it's great that the two freaks have found love, or whatever this is. But, I get it Gabe, I really do. Ava, she's hot as hell. If you can get past all the craziness, she'll blow your mind in the sack."

I turned around, ready to give him a piece of my mind, but Gabriel rounded on him before a word could come out of my mouth. He put his index finger on Rob's chest.

"Bored." He seemed to barely move a muscle, but when he shoved Rob backwards, he went flying.

Rob's body seemed to skid forever, but finally stopped nearly halfway to his overpriced truck. His friends looked at him in shock and then back at Gabriel. No one knew what to say. Rob seemed to be fine, just out of breath and thoroughly embarrassed.

"Let's go, Ava," Gabriel said after a moment.

I followed him to his car in silence. We got in, and I watched as Rob's buddies help him off the ground.

"Your mom supposed to pick you up?" he asked.

"Um, yeah," I told him.

"Text her and tell her you got a ride," he practically commanded. "You can't stay here."

"Okay," I said, even though I wanted to argue with him.

He was being weird and bossy, but he was so mad I didn't want to say anything at the moment. I didn't bring up what had just happened the entire ride. I kept glancing at him though, wondering how he could have possibly done that with such little effort.

Gabriel pulled his loud car into my driveway, and I put my hand on the door handle.

"Ava," he said. "I'm sorry I got so angry."

"Is that all you're sorry for?" My anger came bubbling up to the surface.

"What?" He seemed confused.

"I thought we were friends?" I asked him.

"We are," he told me.

"Then why have you ignored me all day?" It felt like such a childish question. "You have, don't even deny it. You have avoided me like I have leprosy, and then you come sweeping in like a dark and broody version of Captain America? What is your deal?"

"I...I don't have an explanation," he confessed.

"You are so frustrating." An irritated laugh escaped my throat. "Until you figure out what the hell is going on with us, I don't want to be your friend. I don't want you picking me up. I don't want you trying to rescue me from any situation. I can take care of myself. I don't need your help. Just...just stay away from me."

He said nothing. He only nodded, which infuriated me. I was mad at Rob, I was angry at Gabriel, but I was furious with myself. I meant what I said, but at the same time, I didn't want him to stay away from me. Or, at least, I didn't want him to agree to it. I wanted him to fight with me.

I stormed out of his car and ran for the house. Just as I reached the steps, rain began to fall.

My dreams that night were full of dark shadows and screaming girls. It was a blur of images and colors. The painting in Gabriel's house must have really gotten to me. The dark-haired woman was there. Tepkunset was me and I was her. I could see through her eyes as the dark figures came for her in the night.

She and I struggled against them as their leathery hands grabbed for her arms and legs. They bound her, rope biting into her skin. She cried out in pain as blood ran down her arms. I cried with her.

"Hush, child," that same chilled voice I had heard before said to her. "It all shall be over soon."

"Demon," she spat at the monster.

I felt myself speak to this thing out of Tepkunset's mouth, but it wasn't my voice that came out. It wasn't even in a language I could speak, but even so, I understood. If I wanted to say something, I couldn't. I was just a spectator, as I had been in the dreams previously.

"We are no demons. We are the Witches of Thyana," the figure hissed. "You will be a worthy sacrifice for our Mother. There is great power in you."

"You are mad." Tepkunset struggled against her restraints. "I do not have the power you seek."

"Do not lie," it laughed. "You have power. It is in your words. Your words bring forth the future. Have you never noticed? Anything you say, anything you wish aloud, it all comes to pass."

I could feel as Tepkunset's mind began to race. She was thinking back to all the times her words had seemed to predict the future. She thought it coincidence or fate. Never in her wildest dreams would she think that it was her bringing these things, sometimes horrible things, into reality.

Her grandmother was the Medicine Woman in her tribe. She had taught Tepkunset from a very young age. Her grandmother would tell her that she was very strong with the spirits. Had this been what she'd meant?

And then when the White men came to their land, her ability to foresee things had become stronger. Her grandmother believed they had brought a darkness with them. Young women, from both peoples, were being taken. It had nearly caused a war between them. It wasn't until Tepkunset offered a vision of dark figures that they realized it was something else hunting their daughters.

"They will come for me!" she cried into her arms. "My people and the White men! You have taken too many daughters from us. They will come."

There was a sudden rumble in the distance. Tepkunset knew it was the sounds of horses and feet of men.

"Father!" she called. "Erik!"

Erik. She called for him in her time of need. The boy with the dark hair and eyes like a stormy sky. He had made sure to speak to her every chance he'd had when their people banded together. She enjoyed his company, the lingering of his stares, the brush of his skin on hers when she had passed him a cup of water, their tender and brief kiss when they found each other under the moonlight.

The figures took a piece of cloth and gagged her. I knew why. If she really had this power, then she could use it against them. They couldn't risk her speaking their failure into existence.

"If you want to save them, you will give yourself willing to our Mother," the figure commanded her, but Tepkunset shook her head. "Very well," the figure laughed. "It shall be a pleasure killing them in front of you. Especially the boy whose name you call."

"Sister, they arrive," another figure called to the one over Tepkunset.

Sister? These things were female? If it weren't for that revelation, then I would have been resigned to calling them "it" for as long as I had the displeasure of dreaming of them.

"Good," she smiled, "Let us end this."

Tepkunset began fighting harder against her restraints. One of the sisters pushed her back down on the stone slab they had placed her on. Her head was forced down so roughly that it felt as if they were going to crack her skull like an egg. She tried crying out, but all that passed through her gag was a stifled moan.

"Velia," a sister said to another. "Let us bring her to Mother."

"No," Velia hissed. "We must make them watch. They deserve this, Letta, you know this. I want to see what she does when we kill the boy. I wonder if she will cry when I pull his spine from his skin. Then we will kill her entire family."

"The sacrifice is more important than your personal vendetta, sister," the thing growled.

"What's the point of this long life if we do not enjoy in its small pleasures?" Velia seemed to laugh. It was hard to tell by her garbled voice.

They grabbed the stone piece that Tepkunset laid upon, but not with their hands. There was a force they controlled, one that was unseen. The stone slab silently moved across the floor as it followed behind them and out of the door.

The sky outside was a brilliant shade of sickly green and grey. This sky was brought on by dark magic, tainted by the unnatural forces the sisters brought with them.

In the distance I could hear the clanking of metal upon wooden shields, the screams of the injured, and rumbles from what I couldn't fathom. There was a war taking place while these beings carried out their ritual for sacrifice.

"Demons!" a voice cried out, ripping through the sounds of war. "Release her!"

"Your beloved is here." Velia acted as though she were pleased to see him. Maybe in a way she was. Maybe this was exactly what she'd hoped for. "Have you come to watch us gut the little goddess?"

"I've come to end you!" he cried out.

The stone slab that Tepkunset was tied to raised vertically behind the sisters, giving both of us a view of the battlefield and Erik. Many of his clansmen surrounded him, all wearing leather armor, faces painted for battle, and brandishing gleaming swords, axes, crossbows, and a weary look in their eyes.

When Erik's eyes met mine, or rather, Tepkunset's, I felt a jolt in my chest. Love like this, it was rare and pure. It was a love that is only found once in a lifetime. Tepkunset would give anything to be with Erik and I knew he had to feel the same. Why else would he face literal evil for her?

Just seeing her face fueled Erik to move forward. His handsome features twisted into a wild, panicked version of itself. I couldn't help but notice how similar he looked to Gabriel, or rather, how much Gabriel looked like him, his ancestor. He charged, and that same unseen force stopped him in his tracks. He was stuck in the middle of the field, his sword arm raised, one-foot forward.

Tepkunset pulled against her restraints again, tearing at the already broken skin. I wanted to cry out, but she was too busy trying to free herself.

"Did you think your mortal blade could stop me?" Velia laughed. "Puny, pathetic humans!"

She raised her hand and then brought it down. A half-dozen men flew backwards, hitting into the row behind them. Velia clenched her hand and the woman beside Erik grabbed her throat, eyes filled with terror, and fell to her knees.

"Stop! Stop it!" Erik pleaded with her.

The woman made one last choking sound and fell forward, landing on her face in the dirt. Erik glared up at Velia, his eyes burning with pure rage.

"Hand me the blade," Velia said to her sister.

One of them handed her a knife. The handle was bone white, and the blade was black as night. It wasn't hard to see how sharp yet primitive it looked. The blade must have been handmade from some sort of dark stone, and I didn't want to think about who that bone belonged to.

Velia made her way to Tepkunset, standing over her. She raised the blade high above her head, readying herself for the strike. Looking through Tepkunset's eyes, all I could see was that black blade and knew that her life was about to end.

"You made this weapon to destroy us," Velia sneered. "And now, we use it to offer you to our Mother, goddess Thyana. How poetic."

"No!" Erik screamed.

"We offer the sacrifice for your glory," Velia screamed, the blade held high. "With it we shall await your blessing for your faithful servants."

They looked at Tepkunset's tear-stained face. "Thank you for your sacrifice."

"Stop!" Erik yelled again.

The knife came jutting forward, about to hit her chest when Tepkunset's body seemed to explode with a bright yellow power. I could hear her thoughts. She was saying it over and over: "You will not hurt me. You will fail. You cannot touch me."

Velia stumbled backwards, nearly falling. She looked at Tepkunset with wide, expressive eyes. They were muddy and red. Her face a map of lines and desiccated flesh.

You will untie me, Tepkunset thought.

She was embracing her power. All that teasing had been Velia's undoing. She had given Tepkunset the answer to save herself and the people of her tribe.

Velia stepped forward and undid Tepkunset's bindings.

"What are you doing?" Letta jumped to her feet.

Tepkunset looked at the other figure and used her power to force her to her knees.

"You don't want to do this," Velia was saying through her efforts. "I can see what you're capable of now, Tepkunset. Mother must have chosen you to join us. We could do many wonderful and terrible things together. Be a sister. Be a Witch of Thyana."

Tepkunset's hand was freed. She removed the gag from her mouth and at that moment spat in Velia's face.

"I am no fool, Velia," she said to her. "Your promises are hollow. You would kill me the first chance you got. All of this, the darkness you brought upon our land and people, it has ended. Let him go."

At that moment, the earth shook with a powerful force. All of them, every being, stumbled and fell to the ground. I saw her then, the goddess from the painting, emerge from the ground. She was fierce, beautiful, and terrifying. I shielded my eyes and realized it was Tepkunset who couldn't look upon her. Again, I was only an observer.

"You will bow to me, little goddess," a voice boomed.

I bolted straight up in bed. My body was shaking, and I rubbed my wrists, looking at them, expecting them to be bloodied, but they were not. My skin was unmarked the way it should be, no wounds of any kind. There was a creak in the floorboards and I nearly jumped out of my skin. My eyes shot forward, and I turned on my side table light. I expected to see the sisters in front of me, reaching out with their scaly hands, but I was completely alone in my room. Shivering, I pulled the sheets closer to my chest.

"It was just a dream," I tried to tell myself.

Ava

The dreams continued for days. It was always the same thing. I watched Tepkunset taken by the Imprecors, realizing her abilities, and it always ended with Thyana emerging from the ground.

Each night I would get more from the dream. I would watch Thyana try to convince Tepkunset to join her. When that wouldn't work, they would fight. It was like watching a battle of might and will. Their powers manifested in bolts of lightning and unseen forces that could lift trees straight from the ground.

With little to no sleep, I was on edge for the rest of the week. My friends could tell, but I just said it was because of Mr. Ryan. Each day of my detention, he had something worse for me to do. He even made me clean the science labs and all the equipment. He didn't even teach science.

Once, he made me go to the teachers' lounge and warm up his food like I was his maid. I thought about spitting in it. I was bone dead tired and sore from all the cleaning by the time Friday rolled around.

Gabriel had granted my wishes and steered clear of me. I told myself it was for the best. We clearly didn't get along and all of our interactions usually ended with us arguing. That couldn't be healthy.

Still, when I caught sight of him in the hall, my stomach did this weird little dance.

"I hope you've learned your lesson, Miss Black," Mr. Ryan said, as I was finishing up my sentence.

I looked up at the clock. Just 2 more minutes and I'd be free.

"Yes, sir," I said, even though I didn't respect that man one bit.

"But, by all means, mess up again," he laughed. "It's been great having a lovely personal servant, cleaning up after me. You'll make a good wife one day."

I wanted to say so many things, but I knew it wasn't worth it. I would do anything to avoid being his "servant" again, even if that meant listening to his sexist remarks.

At that moment, Keira appeared at the door. She was like a knight, come to rescue me from the evil ogre. I hurriedly tossed the cleaning products into the basket and set it on the counter.

"Keep your nose clean, Miss Black," he said as I walked out the door.

"Go die in a hole, Mr. Ryan," I said under my breath.

"You alright?" Keira wondered.

"I am now," I shrugged as we raced out of the school door, "Glad to be out of that weirdo's evil lair."

"He is awful," she agreed. "What did he say to you?"

"Just being a creep," I told her. "I hope he trips over a Lego on his way to pee in the middle of the night, or you know, just never comes back to school again because he got lost in the woods."

"You are so funny," she laughed. "Are you ready?"

"Can I go home before we head out?" I asked her. "I need a shower."

Keira had talked me into going out. It was the only Friday that was an off day for the football season. She wanted to go explore the town. She had been so busy with cheerleader activities, she hadn't had the opportunity yet, and she wanted to do so with me. I wasn't going to deny her that, and I was excited to have a friend to do things with.

Not long after I grabbed a quick shower, I swung by Keira's place and picked her up. It had been a while since I had driven. I almost wasn't able to talk my parents into letting me drive. After much convincing, I was finally able to take my poor neglected Kia Sorrento out on the town.

After an hour of fighting Friday night traffic, we made it to Huntsville, and I was glad to be here for something other than a therapy appointment. It was a bustling city full of rocket scientists, doctors, and some really great shopping malls. We were downtown, the part with expensive restaurants and bars that served $20 cocktails, but there was one place that was a haven for all—Henry's Game Room.

Henry's Game Room wasn't a recent addition to the city, it was first a pool hall and then about 15 years ago it was converted into a sort of Chuck E. Cheese for teenagers and adults. It had been ages since I had been there. I was excited.

We got in line at the counter; the noise from conversations and gaming machines were a bit overwhelming, but I was just taking it in slowly.

"Are you okay?" Keira asked, concerned.

"What? Yeah," I smiled at her, "Let's do this."

We paid for our tokens and hit the games. Soon, Keira ran into some friends she had made at school. They said their hellos to me, but mostly talked to her. Of course, I knew who they were, but none of us had really said much to each other in a long time. It felt weird being the person on the outside with kids I had grown up with.

"Gabriel!" I heard Keira call. I froze at the game I was playing. "Is Trevor with you?"

"Yeah, he's by the Mario Kart machine," he told her, his voice higher than usual as he tried talking over the noise.

"Ava, I'm going to say hi to Trevor, okay?" she asked.

I nodded and tried concentrating on my game. I could feel Gabriel still standing there, right behind me. Just then a waitress came up. I saw her out of the corner of my eye as she enveloped Gabriel in a massive hug. My stomach felt tight all of a sudden.

"Gabe! How you doin', suga?" the hostess greeted him cheerfully as she let him go.

She was probably around 23, cute, short, with curves in all the right places. Her curly red hair seemed to glow with a life of its own.

"Hey, Cherry," he said in that deep timber of his.

Cherry? Really? A redheaded girl with apple cheeks and flaming red lips was named Cherry?

She seemed so sweet. So why was I wanting to get away from her and Gabriel?

"Can I get a table and this many tokens?" He handed her forty dollars.

"You sure can, darlin'." She grinned from ear to ear. "And who might this be?"

I realized I had turned completely around to listen to their conversation. Well, wasn't I rude?!

"Ava," I said after a moment, trying to sound nice, but I'm not sure if it worked.

Was I jealous? Oh my gosh, I was!

"Well, it's good to meet you, honey." She smiled. "I'll be right back with those tokens."

The place was loud. It was full of an array of gaming machines that ranged from Super Mario Kart to pinball. The atmosphere was thick. People were laughing and having a good time. Had it always been this loud? I looked up at Gabriel and noticed he was staring at me.

"Too much?" he asked, and I realized I was rubbing the side of my head.

"No," I said and put my hand down. "Gabe."

"I've known Cherry for a long time," he explained.

"Clearly..." I had to stop. I sounded like an insecure girlfriend.

He stared down at me as if he wanted to say something. I looked back, wondering why I wasn't able to break eye contact with him.

"Here are your tokens." Cherry came up, breaking the spell. "I've got you guys a table if you want to follow me."

"Do you...uh...do you and Keira want to sit with us?" he asked.

"Um, sure," I said and stood up to follow him to the table.

I had no explanation for why I accepted his invitation. It was an out-of-body experience. He asked, and it was as if someone else said yes.

We sat at the booth together. It was tucked in a corner, but we could still clearly hear the noise. I looked around, at the menu, at the napkins, at the Star Wars poster above our table, anywhere but at him.

We hadn't spoken since I'd told him to stay away from me. We were not doing a good job of that right now.

"Are you hungry?" he asked.

"Um, I haven't eaten yet," I told him.

"Do you guys want to order a pizza to share?" he asked.

"Yeah, sure," I said, picking up the menu, using it to shield myself from him.

"See anything you like?" he asked, peering over my menu.

"Oh, yeah," I cleared my throat, "I like pretty much everything on my pizza, so you just order what you like."

Cherry came back and Gabriel ordered the pizza. Keira and Trevor rescued me then. They filled in the awkward silence with their easy chatter. When the pizza came, it had a little of everything on there. I had a feeling that Gabriel did that just for me. It was probably the best pizza I'd had in a long, long time. After we were full, Keira dragged us out to the game floor. To be completely honest, I was never a gamer and had no idea what some of these were. This was just a place I used to come and hang out. Keira was eager so I wanted to give them a try for once.

We commandeered the Mortal Kombat machine. After a few rounds, I was kicking everyone's butt, even Gabriel's. He looked at me incredulously when I won for the fifth time.

"I'm just pushing buttons." I shrugged.

"That makes it even more frustrating!" he laughed.

He was smiling, something that was a rare occurrence. I couldn't help but smile in return. I think we played every game in the place at least 10 times, and he had to go back for more tokens.

"Ava?" I heard a deep voice beside me as we were making our way back to the table.

I looked up to see Lorcan Walsh standing in front me. He was accompanied by a few friends, a girl and two other guys. They looked at him and then at us.

"Oh, hey, Lorcan," I said to him.

I suddenly felt nervous. None of my friends knew I saw a therapist. Not that I was ashamed, it was just hard to explain. When you tell people you're in therapy, they automatically think you're crazy. If they knew, if Frankie ever found out, she would use this against me.

"Hi, I'm Lorcan," he shook hands with my friends, "I know Ava from a summer internship at the university."

"Yeah, we did one for the psychology department," I went along with the lie.

"Really? I don't remember you, Ava," the young woman said to me.

"I don't either," one of the boys smiled, "I'm sure if I saw you, I'd remember."

"She's in high school, Reese," Lorcan warned. "And it was a brief internship with Dr. Abbott."

"Right," I said, and I felt Gabriel move up closer behind me.

When I looked at him, I could swear he was giving Reese a death stare. Was he being protective? I didn't like it. He had no right.

"Do you guys want to join us?" Lorcan asked. "We're about to fail miserably at pool."

"Sure!" I agreed immediately and walked toward the pool tables, leaving everyone, even Lorcan, behind.

I was pissed. Gabriel didn't have a claim on me. I sure didn't need his protection. If he wanted anything from me, he should have said so instead of acting like a jackass.

I had no idea how to play pool, but I grabbed a stick from the wall and went over to the pool table. Lorcan smiled at me as he took another stick and began gathering billiard balls into the triangle.

"Want to team up?" Gabriel asked me. His eyes looked almost pleading.

"How about girls versus boys?" Keira suggested. I could tell she was picking up vibes.

"That sounds intriguing," the girl with Lorcan said coolly. "I'm Kat, by the way. You've met Reese, my incredibly rude twin, and the other one there is Bron. He doesn't talk much, mostly because he's deaf."

Bron signed something to her and even though I didn't know ASL, I could tell it was profane. Kat laughed and blew him a kiss.

Bron was insanely intimidating. He looked like a classic movie henchman. He was a big guy with light brown hair and deep green eyes with a scar across his thick jaw. He stood a few inches taller than

Gabriel, which made him look like a giant. And he hardly moved. He just stood there like a statue. I wasn't even sure if he was breathing. I almost wanted to touch him to see if he was real.

The way he stared at me, not like I was attractive, but like I was something strange, made me feel like a sideshow attraction.

Reese gave me what I assumed was his most flirty smile. He looked a lot like his sister, perfectly smooth skin, rich black hair, and eyes dark as the night's sky. They were tall, slender, and looked like they had stepped off the runway at a fashion show the way they were both dressed.

Kat floated around me, capturing my attention. She was like a ballerina the way she glided past Gabriel, giving him a sly smile, and took down another pool stick. Her dark brown eyes seemed to drink him in.

"Ready?" she asked.

Gabriel said nothing as he took his place with the guys. His jaw was set tight as we began to play. By the time we were done, the girls had won three out of five games. If it weren't for Kat, we more than likely would have lost. She was amazing, Keira was just okay, and I scraped by on sheer luck.

I kept hitting the ball too hard. It was mostly due to being upset. Lorcan tried helping me and each time, I noticed Gabriel's face turn a little red. Or, maybe I was just imagining that part. Maybe I wanted him to notice.

Soon, we had to say our goodbyes. It was getting close to my curfew and if I was late, my parents would ground me again. Considering I had just been released, I didn't want to push my luck.

As Keira was exchanging social media contacts with everyone, I hung back to talk to Lorcan.

"Thank you," I said to him. "For not telling everyone how we actually know each other."

"That's not my story to tell." He smiled. "And, you're welcome. It was nice seeing you outside the office. Maybe we can do it again."

"Um, yeah..." I felt heat rise up my throat. I wasn't sure if he was flirting with me, but thankfully Keira called my name. "Bye."

I waved at everyone and we made our way to the ticket counter to exchange our hard earnings for some cheap toy. I ended up picking the pink dragon because it was fierce and cute at the same time and I wanted to believe that could be me.

Keira and Trevor led the way to the parking deck. I watched as they held hands and giggled up the street, not seeming to have a care in the world. It made me smile. I was happy for them.

"So, it was fun hanging out with you guys tonight," Gabriel said from beside me.

"Was it?" I turned on him, my anger rising to the top. Perhaps I was being unfair, but I really didn't care.

"If it wasn't, I wouldn't have said so; I don't lie." That seemed like an accusation.

"What is that supposed to mean?" I put my hands on my hips, the stance of a woman ready to brawl.

"Lorcan," he pointed behind us, "He was lying and so were you. That's not how you know him."

"Well, it's really none of your business, is it?" I shot back.

"No, I guess not." He stared down at me, his grey eyes storming.

I turned to leave, but his voice stopped me.

"It was my grandfather," he said. "The day I was out of school; it was because of him. You asked me how I was feeling and I didn't know what to say so I just bolted. I'm not proud of that, but the way you looked at me, full of concern, if I would have stayed there, I might have poured my heart out."

"Is everything okay?" I asked him, walking closer. "Is Pops alright?"

"He's doing better," he took a deep breath, "He looks healthy, right? He hasn't been for a long time. He has Parkinson's. It was a bad day."

"Why didn't you tell me?" I questioned. "We are supposed to be friends, right?"

"I want to be," he confessed.

"But, you can't be? Why?" I asked him. "Am I that bad? Maybe I am. I was never the nicest person before all of...before now."

"You were always nice to me," Gabriel said, taking a step closer. "That's part of the problem."

"What do you mean?" He was so confusing.

"My first day of school was in Mrs. Baker's third grade class, and she put me in a seat behind you. You had your hair in French braid pigtails and you were wearing a purple shirt with a unicorn on the front. When Mrs. Baker told everyone to make me feel welcome, you turned around and said, 'Hi, I'm Ava. First days are scary, but don't be afraid. You are brave.' I never forgot you."

"My mom still has that shirt," I took another step closer to him, "It was my favorite. She said she had to bribe me to take it off so she could wash it. You remembered that? Really? I never thought you even noticed me."

"I've always noticed you, Ava," another step closer, "Which is why being your friend is..."

"Not a good idea?" I offered.

"Terrifying," he said.

We were on a nearly deserted street right beside the opening to the city park. Keira and Trevor had left us behind. It was dark save for one street lamp. Still, I could see the fire in his eyes. They seemed to draw me like a magnet because I felt my feet moving forward.

"I'm not scared," I said, my voice thick with emotion.

"Liar." He smiled and took a step closer to me.

Oh wow, was this it? Was he going to kiss me? I was ready. I was more than ready. My heart was beating so hard I could feel it in my eyes.

Gabriel placed his hand on the side of my face, running his thumb over my cheek. He tilted his head, leaning closer. Just as I was about to close my eyes and give in to the moment, a movement caught my eye. For a split second I saw something standing just beyond the entrance to the park. It was in the shadows, but I knew what it was.

Screaming, I grabbed Gabriel's arm and stumbled backwards. I nearly fell in the street, but he caught my shirt and pulled me back. Clinging to him, I peered around his shoulder to the spot I where I had seen it.

"Ava? What's wrong?" He spun around, looking in the direction I was staring.

Tears burned my eyes, and I had to blink them away to get an unobstructed view.

"I saw...it was...I saw it," I stammered.

"Saw what? What's the matter?" He grabbed my face in his hands. "What is it?"

"I'm going crazy," I wrapped my arms around my body, "I'm losing it."

"Ava, talk to me." He shook me gently.

"You'll think I'm crazy, too." I lowered my head.

"I won't," he tried to convince me.

I tried pulling away from him, but he held me firmly.

"Don't do this," he begged. "Don't open up to me and then shut me out."

"That mural," I started. "It...it got to me. I've been dreaming of those things, the figures. Well, that's not right. I dreamed of them before I saw the mural. And, then, when you showed me that painting, it just...bothered me. I see her in my dreams, Thyana, I see her fighting with Tepkunset. And, then...I've seen them...kill...these girls...I... You must think I'm crazy."

Gabriel didn't say anything for a moment. I knew it. He thought I was insane. Instead of running away from me, he pulled me into a tight hug. It was the most sincere gesture. He wasn't doing it for him. He was hugging me so I'd feel safe and cared for. Did he believe me?

"Let's get you to your car," he finally spoke.

I let him lead me, my body still trembling the entire way. We finally caught up to Keira and Trevor. They knew something was wrong, but I just told them I wasn't feeling well. It was such a normal occurrence, they didn't question it.

Gabriel squeezed my hand as I got into my car.

"Can we talk tomorrow?" he asked.

I nodded, not wanting him to let go, but knowing he had to. As we drove back home, I began to calm down and then I felt silly. Embarrassed. I had acted completely insane. Keira talked about how much of a good time she'd had all the way to her house. I just smiled and nodded at all the right places so she wouldn't think I was slowly having a mental breakdown.

"Are you sure you're alright to drive home?" she asked as she got out.

"Yeah, I'm fine," I told her. "I had so much fun tonight. Thank you for inviting me."

"Of course!" she laughed. "Let's do it again soon, yeah?"

"Yeah." I nodded in agreement.

When I finally got home, my parents were both wide awake on the couch. I knew something was wrong as soon as I saw them.

"What is it?" I asked them.

"It's Mr. Ryan, honey," Mom told me. "He was...he's dead, Ava. They found his body sometime tonight."

"What? How? What happened?" My voice rose an octave.

"I don't know, not really," she sighed, "Cora May called me. She's only heard some details. She said something about maybe he had fallen."

"Fallen? Like down the stairs?" I wondered. "At his house? The school?"

"I have no clue," she answered. "I'm sure we'll know more soon. I just wanted you to know."

"This is horrible," I remarked. "I mean, it was no secret that I didn't care for Mr. Ryan, but I never wanted him to...die."

"Of course you didn't," she said, soothingly, rubbing my back as I sat on the couch with them. "Do you need anything? Do you want to talk?"

"No," I said. "I don't really know what to say."

"Did you, did you have a good time with Keira?" Dad asked.

"Yeah." I felt numb. "We saw some other friends there, Gabriel and Trevor, we...uh, we had a good time. It was nice."

Until I saw a monster from my nightmares and you told me one of my teachers died.

"Maybe you should get some rest," Mom suggested.

"Yeah," I responded.

"Good night, Ava," D ad told me. "Try not to stress over this. We love you, honey."

"Okay." I walked up to my room in a daze. "Love you, too."

I laid back on my pillow, knowing that sleep would have a hard time claiming me that night.

Gabriel

❧

"Are you alright?" Trevor asked me as I drove him home. "You look pissed."

I said nothing to him for a minute. He was right. I was angry. It was hard to tell what had upset me more.

"Was it that guy?" Trevor wondered. "Lorcan or whatever?"

The mention of his name sent white hot rage coursing through my body. It wasn't jealously. That was a lie. It was complete jealously. I saw the way he looked at Ava, and I didn't like it. In fact, it made me so mad I would have no problem turning the car around, walking back into the arcade, and punching him square in the face.

Clearly, Ava wasn't interested in him. That shouldn't be my only reason for resisting the urge to drop kick him from the top of the parking deck. I was thinking like a madman. I needed to calm down.

And it wasn't just that. Ava had been upset. She had seen something in that park. She was terrified. Seeing her like that scared me. And it pissed me off. I felt this need to do something about it. I wanted to make it better. I wanted to fix it.

Pops said that was one of the best, and probably the most difficult, things about me. I couldn't leave things alone. Relentless, he called me.

I wouldn't stop until I found a solution. Sometimes it drove me mad, because what did you do when something couldn't be fixed?

"No, it wasn't him," I lied.

"Was it Ava?" he pressed.

"No," I said.

"Gabriel, we've been friends for a really long time," Trevor said to me. "I can tell when you're upset. I can also tell when you like someone. I don't know how because you've never liked anyone. Still, somehow, I know you like her. So, what's going on there?"

"I don't know," I sighed. "It's...complicated."

"It doesn't seem complicated to me," he pointed out. "Ava likes you; most of the time, you like her. You're both moody, broody, and unfairly good-looking. What is the problem?"

"Hilarious, Trev," I snorted.

"One of my many talents." He smiled. "Look, whatever is going on, figure it out because you look stressed."

That was an understatement. There was so much going on in my head I couldn't think straight half the time. I was in a constant state of fear that something was going to happen to Pops. He seemed to be doing better since his fall, but I watched him as if he were a piece of paper about to blow away in the wind.

"I'm fine," I told him again. "What about you? Anymore fainting spells?"

"What? No. You make me sound like a southern belle," he laughed. "I told you it was only because I hadn't eaten that day."

"Right," I nodded.

Trevor was another worry. He could tell me he was fine, but I didn't believe him. Something was going on. He had his moments where he was himself, but other times, he just wasn't. While I hadn't witnessed anymore moments of fatigue, he was agitated and short-tempered.

I supposed I could write it off as stress. We were all under a lot of that. This was our senior year. He had prospects he was counting on, trying to impress his parents, and he had a new girlfriend. I suppose that was what Keira was to him.

I didn't want to be one of those friends that changed as soon as his best friend got a girlfriend. Keira was nice, a bit too bubbly for my taste, but we got along well. And the most important thing was that Trevor really seemed to like her.

He had pointed out that I had never liked anyone, but kettle meet pot, really. He had never shown an interest in anyone. Then Keira comes in and he's completely swept off his feet. It was a bit jarring. It made me wonder what it was about this girl that had captured my friend's attention.

I pulled the car into Trevor's driveway. His mom and dad were sitting out on their porch even at the late hour. They weren't necessarily waiting on him. This was just something they always did.

Trevor's parents had him later in life. His mom had told me that Trevor was their miracle baby. This was after years of IVF treatments, lots of tears, complications, and prayers, she had said. Finally, at thirty-six, she found out they were going to have Trevor.

She told me they were the old parents, but they were okay with that. I honestly thought it was the sweetest thing, and they were absolutely the nicest people on the planet. I'm a softy.

I waved at them as Trevor bounded up the steps and took a seat beside his mom. As soon as I was out of sight, the same feeling of unease and anger crept its way back into my chest.

Hurrying home, I raced inside and headed upstairs to stare at the mural. Pops was at a lecture tonight, so it was just me and Kaine. The large dog settled at my feet as I continued to look at the battle depicted on the wall, as if it would suddenly make sense of everything.

Ava said she had seen them, the Imprecors, she had dreamed of them, even before seeing the mural. That should sound crazy to me, and to most people it would. I believed her. How could I not? She was so frightened. That look on her face would haunt me for a long time.

I had to talk to her. There was so much I wanted to say. Some of it I didn't know if she would understand. I didn't understand it myself. What I hoped she would remember was that feeling that had passed between us earlier tonight.

Slumping down in the chair, my eyes still on the mural, my mind raced back to the memory of my hand on her face. We had been mere moments from finally expressing how we felt, or at least I had. Surely she felt the same.

I heard a noise down the hall, something that sounded like the creaking of the stairs. Kaine stood up. A low growl rumbled through his body, and the hair on his back stood on end. My heart beat quickened.

Slowly I stood up and eased open the middle desk drawer. Pulling out the revolver that was kept there, I held it to my side and walked toward the open door, careful not to make a sound.

Kaine came up beside me, and I put my palm out to him. He waited as I had trained him to do. Peering into the dimly lit hallway, I saw nothing, so I moved forward. I signaled Kaine, and he followed me.

We moved through the hall and down the stairs. The sensation of being watched came over me as I entered the living room. The exposed flesh on the back of my neck prickled with goosebumps. It was as if a phantom hand had brushed my skin. There was noise, like the sound of whispers in my ear. I whirled around, pointing the gun in the sound's direction, but nothing was there.

The sound seemed to travel into the foyer. I followed it, Kaine right behind me. I could hear the scuttling of feet or what sounded like heavy cloth being dragged on the floor. I rounded the corner, gun raised.

"Gabriel!" Pops stopped short.

"Pops." I instantly dropped the gun.

"What's wrong?" He pulled out his own weapon. A small, but powerful handgun he always kept at his side.

"There was something in here," I told him. "I think. I don't know. I heard something. Kaine seemed to sense it, too."

"Did you do a search?" he asked.

"I was about halfway through," I told him.

"Let's keep looking," he said.

After we looked through the house and found nothing, we met in the study. My eyes were back on the mural, and Pops was busy mixing a few things together for a tea. He said it would calm my nerves. I think he just wanted me to go to sleep. It was probably full of melatonin.

"I know I heard something," I said.

"I believe you," he said as he continued to mix ingredients. "That's why we keep protection around the house."

"Something else happened tonight," I said, looking over at him.

"Oh?" he asked as he brought over the tea.

"Ava," I said, taking the cup. "She saw something."

"What did she see?" he asked.

I pointed at the mural. He looked at it and then back at me.

"Gabriel," he said.

"She said she has been dreaming about them," I continued. "Before seeing the mural. Pops, if you could have seen her face. She saw something. I have to talk to her."

"If you're sure," he said.

"I am," I said confidently.

"And you're not letting your emotions..." he started.

"I have never let my feelings about Ava interfere with my responsibilities." I felt defensive. "I am sure."

"Alright," he sighed. "I'll make a few calls."

Ava

The next few days were a complete whirlwind of emotions. The school was in a state of dreary sadness. Students cried, teachers tried their best to comfort them, and all that was on the lips of everyone in town was the death of Mr. Ryan. The weather reflected what everyone felt. Dark clouds covered the school and rain poured with no end in sight.

And me? Well, I felt guilty. I'd never liked Mr. Ryan, but I felt awful for being such a jerk to him before his passing. I knew it was silly. Nothing I said or did could have changed what happened to him, but it still clung to me like a wet piece of paper.

Of course, I only knew things that were taking place at the school because of the texts from my friends. With the onset of the weather, I was in severe pain. I was never really able to talk to Gabriel like he had wanted because I was either asleep or hurting. When I actually had a moment of relief, I would read the messages from the group chat between Gabriel, Keira, Trevor, and me. It was full of what was going on and what homework I needed to make up. To be honest, it was a bit overwhelming, but I was thankful they cared.

On the third day of being stuck in bed, either that or running to the bathroom to dry heave for the millionth time, I received a private text from Gabriel.

How are the dreams?

My heart hit hard in my chest. I told him the truth.

No better.

One of the only things that gave me any sense of peace was remembering his hands on my face and his lips so close to mine. I wasn't sure what any of that meant. He had said the thought of being together was scary. I didn't think that was the best way to start a relationship, if he even wanted to start one. Maybe he was just physically attracted to me. That has happened before. Still, what he'd said about pouring his heart out to me made me want to believe there might be something more. What was I letting this guy do to me?

I'm sorry. I wish there was something I could do to ease your pain.

You don't think I'm crazy?

Of course not.

I guess...

Ava, I believe you.

How? I saw something that wasn't there...

It was real to you. That means something. We'll figure it out. I'm here for you.

Thanks, that means a lot.

You mean a lot to me.

Did you mean to send that?

Yes.

I thought this was a bad idea and you were terrified?

It is.

Well, that's not confusing....

I need to tell you something. When you feel better.

You can't do that! Tell me now!

It's better in person. Feel better. I'll talk to you soon.

I slumped back in my bed, willing my head to stop trying to kill me. I wanted to know what he had to say. I wanted to be able to walk out the door and just be normal. I wanted so many things and at the top of the list, I wanted to make out hard with Gabriel Matthews.

As the week wore on, I was actually feeling a bit better. The weather was still lingering, but I could feel the pressure ease. Even Mom made the comment that I looked like I had a little color in my cheeks. I was more than glad too because she said if I went another day in this much pain, she was going to take me to the hospital. I wanted to avoid that because I knew my doctors would keep me until they ran a slew of tests.

On Saturday morning, I awoke to a beautiful day. The clouds were nice enough to let the sun give us a wave now and then. I didn't feel like my old self, whatever that felt like, but I was functional.

"Can I go out?" I asked Mom as we were making breakfast.

"Are you sure you're up for that?" Mom eyed me over the bowl she was using to whisk the eggs. "You're just now feeling better. I'd hate for you to have a relapse because you pushed yourself."

"I'll be alright," I tried reassuring her, then I tried for a bit of sympathy. "I want to take advantage of the days I actually feel like doing something."

"Well, I suppose so then," Mom said after a moment. "Where are you going?"

"To Gabriel's," I said smoothly, or at least I tried.

"Gabriel's?" She looked up from her bowl. "I didn't realize you were that close."

"It's new," I told her.

"He's expecting you? And his grandfather?" she asked.

"Yeah, we talked about it this morning."

"Okay, I guess it's alright," she nodded, "I'll drive you over after breakfast."

"Can I drive?" I wondered.

"That might be pushing it," Mom said.

"Please?" I asked. "If I start to feel even just a tiny bit sick, I'll come straight home."

"I suppose," she finally relented. "But straight home, young lady."

About an hour later, I pulled into Gabriel's driveway. My mouth felt dry. I was nervous. I was unsure how our interaction was going to play out considering this was unfamiliar territory we were in.

Steadying my nerves, I climbed the steps of the porch. With my heart hammering in my chest, I knocked on the door. It took only a minute for him to open it, Kaine at his heels. A wide smile spread across my face, one which he returned. I didn't even get to say anything before he pulled me into a tight hug.

"I'm so glad you're feeling better," he whispered in my ear, sending tingles down my spine. Kaine came up to my legs, waiting for a pet. I didn't deny him a scratch behind the ears.

"Is that Ava?" I heard Keira from the den. "It is!" She came running forward, pulling me from Gabriel's arms and hugging me. "Oh, darling, you look so tired. Are you feeling better?"

"I'm alive," I remarked and then looked at them both. "Uh, so, what's up?"

"Gabriel and I are lab partners in Biology," she explained, pulling me into the den, Kaine at my heels, whining. "We're working on this project that's due Tuesday. She just assigned it to us! Can you believe it?"

"Mrs. Meeks can be a pain," I agreed.

"I just dropped in on Gabriel," she laughed. "He wasn't expecting me at all, but I want to get this over with. I hate waiting."

There were papers and books strewn all over the table in the den. Keira settled down on the couch, pulling me down beside her.

"Oh, we should call Trevor!" Keira exclaimed. "I'll order pizza. It'll be like an impromptu party. Your grandfather wouldn't mind, would he?"

"Where is Pops?" I asked him.

"Errands," he explained. "Sure, call Trev."

Errands? Had Gabriel invited me over here knowing full well that his grandfather would be out all day? Maybe he'd be gone for only a few minutes, but maybe not. I looked up at him as he sat down across from us, picking up some of the papers, avoiding my gaze.

Trevor showed up about 30 minutes later, pizza in hand.

"I get a tip, right?" Trevor asked. "I delivered the pizza."

"Ha!" Gabriel remarked, grabbing the box and taking out a slice.

"Here's your tip," Keira walked up to him, kissing his cheek.

"That's it?" He grabbed her and kissed her lips.

She laughed, pulling away and grabbing a slice for herself. Watching their public display of affection only made me wish they would disappear.

It wasn't long before Keira and Gabriel completely lost focus on the project. We had been there all day, just talking, mostly about Mr. Ryan.

"It's just horrible how it happened." Keira shook her head.

"What do you mean?" I asked. "I thought he fell, like down the stairs or something?"

"Oh, he fell," Keira answered.

"Maybe we should talk about something else," Gabriel offered.

"Wait, what happened?" I pressed.

"He went on his usual walk, according to what I heard from the teachers, down one of the trails by the lake," Keira explained. "The trail he was on was close to the mountain edge. You know those trails go all over the mountainside, or Mrs. Meeks said so. Anyway, he didn't make it back to his car before it started storming. He lost his way and fell over the side of the mountain. A Park Ranger found him after his wife called and said he wasn't home yet. They found him in a hole, a crevice in the side of the mountain, his body broken to pieces."

"Keira," Gabriel warned.

"I'm just repeating what I heard." She threw up her hands.

I sat there, taking it all in. It was a terrible way to go.

"I have to go," Trevor blurted. "My mom's texting me."

"Want to give a girl a ride home?" Keira batted her eyes at him. "My host parents dropped me off."

"Your chariot awaits, my dear." He gestured toward the door.

"Bye, my love!" Keira hugged me tightly and then whispered in my ear, "Don't do anything I wouldn't do. Or, you know, live a little."

"You're awful." I gently shoved her toward Trevor.

They waved goodbye as they headed out the door, Keira hanging on Trevor's arm. Gabriel stood there watching after them for a moment. When he turned to me, the look in his eyes made my heart skip about two beats.

In three quick strides, he'd marched over. I stood up quickly, unsure of what was about to happen, afraid my breath smelled like garlic from the pizza. Instead of sweeping me into an epic kiss, he took my hands in his.

"I have to tell you something." He looked at me seriously.

With my hand in his, he led me upstairs. We walked into the room with the mural painted on the wall. The sight of it made my stomach flip. Gabriel walked forward and pulled an enormous book from the shelf, placing it on the desk that sat in the middle of the room.

"I think it's time you see this." His voice was thick, laced with excitement and nerves.

"What is it?" I wondered, staring at the dark leather cover.

It had faded gold-colored lettering on the front. Even if the words were more visible, I don't think I would have been able to read it. I was sure the words weren't English or any other language I had ever seen.

"It's my family's history," he answered. "You've heard some of it."

"About the Mavors?" I wondered.

"Yes," he answered and opened the book. "You remember I told you that one day a new Medicine Woman would be born, Tepkunset's heir?"

"I do." I crossed my arms over my chest.

"And that if she was ever born, she would have a guardian, a guardian from my bloodline, that would find her?" he asked as he flipped open the book. "This book was put together by my ancestors and the Beothuk Tribe, mainly Tepkunset. They said there would be signs of who she would be, of what she could do."

"Okay..." I began feeling really uncomfortable with the story.

"It's been nearly 500 years since Tepkunset's death and that long since another woman from the tribe has been located, mainly because the Beothuk people have been nearly annihilated," he went on, eyeing me with determination. "My grandfather, Pops, and I are the only Matthews left. It's up to me to find...to find her. This is my job, Ava. This is what I was meant to do. I am supposed to find her. She will have her same abilities to speak things into existence, and the Imprecors will be drawn to her power."

"Gabriel, you're freaking me out," I backed up, "It's like...do you believe in all of this?"

"You do, too," he responded. "You've seen them."

"What?" I took another step back. "I...I was hallucinating...that's all. I feel like I still am."

"You weren't," he moved closer to me, closing the book, "You saw them. You've been dreaming of them. This is real. The Imprecors are real. The Mavors are real. I...I am one of them. I am a guardian. You're her, Ava."

"Even if that were true, how would you know that?" I asked him. "I'm not powerful. I can't do what she did. So, how do you know?"

"You are Tepkunset's descendent. I am Erik's descendent. We were meant to find each other. I think...it's like...well," he stumbled along, trying to find the right words, "For years I tried to deny it. I didn't want to think that fate would choose this for me. That's why I never talked to you, not until I looked at you one day and just knew. I knew."

"You knew what?" I asked.

He closed the distance between us and grabbed my shoulders. His hands were firm, but he wasn't trying to hurt me. He stared at me for a moment and then leaned in and kissed me, deeply. I went to push him away, but his lips felt so right on mine. For a moment, I gave in. I wrapped my arms around his shoulders, bringing him closer to me.

"No," I shoved him back after a moment, "Just...stop. I...I need to go."

I raced down the stairs and toward the door. Kaine was on my heels, but Gabriel was the one who caught my arm.

"Ava, wait." He spun me around.

"No!" I jerked away from him. "You're insane. Do you hear yourself? You're talking about the supernatural. You're talking about us...destined to meet...to what? Fall in love? Be together forever? Fight witches? Fight a goddess? I'm only 18! You're only 18! We hardly know each other. All of this is just...way too much."

"Ava, please," he called out again. "I know you sense something about the dreams, about this story, about...about me."

"No, just leave me alone." I walked out the door and ran into Pops as he came up the steps.

"Ava, are you alright?" he asked when he saw my face.

"I need to go," I pushed past him, fighting back tears, "I need to go home."

I raced to my car without looking back. I had to get out of there. I had to get the feel of his lips off of my skin. Gabriel Matthews was inside my mind, my soul, and had been for a while, and now I found out he was completely nuts. Just my luck.

When I awoke that Monday morning, I debated faking a migraine and staying home. With my luck, Mom would want to take me to the hospital. My only choice was to go to school and face down Gabriel. Sighing, I climbed out of the bed and got dressed. Mom dropped me off at the front of the school shortly after that.

Trying my best to avoid him, I raced to my locker, grabbed my stuff, and dashed into my first period class. Breathing a sigh of relief, I settled into my seat. Looking to my right, I noticed that Keira wasn't there. I sent her a text to find out if she was coming.

Can't. Sick. I think I have strep or something. Host parents are with me at the doctor.

That sucks.

Big time. You have to tell me all about you and Gabe after I get out of here. I want all the gory details about what went down after we left.

I put my phone away without answering her. Class was about to start, but the truth was, I didn't want to rehash any of it. Was I supposed to tell her everything? She would think we were both insane.

After class, I saw Gabriel walking down the hall. My heart dropped into my stomach. He was making his way toward me, but I ducked into the girls' restroom.

I thought about staying there for the rest of the day, but hanging out in the restroom was not my idea of fun. I let the late bell ring, not caring my teacher was going to chew me out for interrupting class. Taking a deep breath, I was about to walk out of the door when Rob pushed his way in.

"What the hell?" I stepped back.

"I saw you come in here," he smiled down at me.

"So you decided to follow me into the girl's restroom?" I asked.

"Seems to be the only way I can get you to myself," he sneered.

"What do you want, Rob?" I asked, crossing my arms over my chest.

"I just want you back, baby," he moved closer to me. "You know me and you just make sense."

"Not interested," I tried moving passed him, but he blocked me. "Move it, Rob."

"What do you see in that freak anyway?" he asked. "Matthews is some kind of roid-raging lunatic. He's no good for you. Let me show what a real man is."

Rob moved in close, touching my cheek. I jerked away from him, slapping his hand. His eyes filled with anger and quicker than I could react, he grabbed the back of my head and pushed me up against the wall.

"Get off of me!" I yelled.

"That's not what you said a few months ago," he said close to my ear.

Anger and fear coursed through my body. Panic was rising up in my chest as his hands moved to my waist.

"I said to get off of me!" I screamed.

Suddenly Rob went rigged. His eyes seemed to glaze over and his arms dropped to his sides. He looked almost docile. My mind was tail spinning. I snapped my fingers in front of his face.

"Rob?" I called to him.

He didn't respond.

"Rob?" I said again. "Can you hear me? Say something!"

"Something," he said.

A wave of panic crashed over me. I didn't understand what was happening. Not that I had time to process it because Rob seemed to be coming to his senses. That same lustful need seeped back into his eyes. Before he had a chance to react, I brought up my leg and kicked him directly in between his legs.

He fell to the ground, clutching his privates. I grabbed his head and rammed my knee into his face. I heard a loud crunch so I knew I had broken his nose. Blood spurted everywhere as he hit the floor.

"What the hell did you do to me?" he looked up at me, his face a bloody mess. "You're a freak. Just like Matthews."

"Don't you ever touch me again," I said as I walked away.

I left the bathroom and headed straight for class. I probably should have told someone, but Rob was the golden boy. Besides, something other than his physical assault on me had just happened. I doubt Rob was brave enough to tell anyone what took place either. How would he explain my sudden control over him? My brain didn't even want to process it as Gabriel's words haunted my mind.

Even if that weren't the case, his dad had a lot of pull in town seeing as he was a police officer. In small towns, no one believed the victim. Not the right people anyway. It would all be a lot of fuss and Rob would get away with it.

I might be shaking. My soul might be shattered into a million tiny pieces. I might even be on the verge of tears, but I wouldn't let him or anyone else see them. I had my vengeance and Rob would know it every time he saw his crooked nose in the mirror.

The next day Mr. Ryan's funeral took place. The school was nearly bare, substitutes replaced most of the staff, and they released the school early so anyone who wanted to could attend the funeral. I couldn't bring myself to go. The last thing I had said to him was forced politeness, and the last thought I had was wishing his death.

Guilt hit me like a bat to the face. And then a thought settled in my mind.

Go die in a hole, Mr. Ryan.

That's what I had thought. Those horrible words had passed through my mind. I knew I didn't really want him to die, but in that moment I was so angry. I wanted to cause him pain.

I had initially thought that Frankie's accident was my fault. I believed my words had power over her life. Then what happened with Rob the day before was fresh on my mind. Did I now believe that I had caused Mr. Ryan's death? That would mean I put weight into what Gabriel had told me, that I had power. And, if I did, what kind of power was this?

I shuddered, pushing the thoughts from my mind as I climbed into my mom's waiting car. I looked up at the school and saw Gabriel standing at the top of the stairs. His grey eyes seemed to know what was passing through my mind.

For the next couple of days, it was the same routine. He'd show up and I would dodge him. Keira was still sick at home, so I really didn't have to explain anything to her yet. Trevor wasn't stupid. He noticed I wasn't around much. He asked me if I was okay one day and I just simply nodded and ran for the car.

Trevor texted me one morning saying he had come down with the same thing Keira had. It wasn't surprising. They spent all their free time together, and Trevor had been looking a little pale. I felt awful that he was unwell, but now I had no one to talk to at school.

That following week, Frankie came back to school. It was an enormous shock. I had no clue she was coming back. She walked in, dressed to the nines, with a cast on her arm. Other than that, she looked great.

She looked the same, but something was different. Of course she still strutted the halls, but she was more reserved. I thought maybe she was just trying to get sympathy, but I couldn't be sure. It wasn't like I was going to ask her.

Seeing her reunited with her friends made me want Keira to come back, but the last I'd heard she was still having a hard time of it. Apparently, she'd contracted strep and walking pneumonia at the same time.

As the week wore on, I was getting better at just keeping my head down and going to class. Rob avoided me like I was the monster from his nightmares and told everyone he had an accident at home and that's how he broke his nose. Fine by me, I never wanted to see his disgusting face again.

When I would get home, I'd turn my phone off and get my homework done. After dinner, I would watch something on Netflix until I fell asleep. Even though it seemed like I had this figured out, each day that went by I felt a little more hollow.

The next day, I was paired up with Anniston, a small mousey girl, during History and we had to compete with other groups in Coach Tucker's trivia showdown. By the time the game was coming to a close, the only other team left was Frankie and Holley. They stared us down like a pair of lionesses, ready to devour their prey.

"We've got this," Anniston whispered to me.

She was right. It was neck and neck for a while there, but in the end, we came out the victors.

"Great job, girls," Coach Tucker said. "You both get 10 extra points on tomorrow's exam."

"Good game, Ava," Holley came walking up to us after class, "Must be on some wonderful drugs today."

"Shut up," Anniston said. "You don't have to be so mean all the time, Holley. Y'all used to be friends."

"Go throw up, Anniston," Holley snapped and the other girls laughed, but I noticed Frankie wasn't one of them.

Anniston was a tiny girl. She had been so since we were kids. She had knobby knees and was probably only 80 pounds. There was no way she had an eating disorder. Holley just enjoyed making fun of people in the cruelest way possible.

"Bye, Holley." I turned back around to my locker.

"So, I heard you and Gabriel are a thing," she continued. "Or you were...now you're ignoring him. What happened? Did he give it up and now you're done with him like you were with Rob? I guess you haven't changed that much. You're still a slut."

I spun around and slapped her across the face. She had no right to talk about Gabriel. She had no idea what I was going through and how much...how much I missed him.

She was so shocked that all she could do was stare at me, holding her jaw. Holley made a move toward me, but Frankie stepped forward. Despite all the crap that Frankie and her crew had done to me, I had never been violent. Oh, I had wanted to, but I kept my hands to myself.

"Leave me alone, all of you," I said to them through gritted teeth, feeling a strange sense of anger pass through me. "Leave Anniston alone; as a matter of fact, leave everyone alone. I get that it makes you feel better to hurt people, but I, for one, have had enough of you and your goon squad. Take this as your final warning."

They suddenly stood up straight, their sneers wiped from their faces. I noticed all of them had the same glassy-eyed look. Without another word, they left us standing there.

"That was epic!" Anniston exclaimed. "You are so cool, Ava!"

I didn't feel cool. I felt off, to be honest. There was a lot going on inside of me right now, and I just needed to get out of there. Quickly pulling on my hoodie, I raced out the door and literally ran out of the school.

There was no way I could go back, but I didn't have a way home. Instead of heading to class, I ran behind the gym, tears obscuring my vision. A sprinkle of rain started coming down. As I rounded the corner, I felt a hand on my shoulder. Jumping, I spun around and came face to face with Frankie.

"What do you want?" I nearly screamed.

"How did you do it?" she asked me as rain beat down on her perfectly styled hair.

"What are talking about?" I stepped back.

"The pain," her voice shook, "It never leaves. You wished this on me. You said you hoped I knew what it was like."

She was crying. She took a step forward and pointed to her back.

"It won't go away," she wailed. "It hurts, every day. I try to pretend like it doesn't. I can't sleep. No matter how much medicine they give me, I hurt."

"Frankie, I didn't do anything," I told her, even though there was a fear swelling up inside me.

"You did, Ava," she told me as she cried. "You did this. You have to undo it, please."

She stepped forward and grabbed my hands. It was like all of her fear and suffering washed over me. I wanted to pull away, but she held onto me so tightly.

"Undo it," she pleaded again.

"I...I don't know how," I told her, terrified of what I was saying.

"I was afraid you would say that," she said, laughing in a way that made me a little scared. "We were never friends, were we? Not really. I did so many cruel things and I'm a bad girl, but I'm not as cruel as you, Ava. I would never do this to someone."

She turned and left me staring after her, thunder clapping loudly overhead.

Ava

Frankie's words hung in the air as I continued to watch her walk away. She honestly thought I had caused this accident or the pain, maybe both. All of Gabriel's claims came rushing back to me. I shook my head, trying to clear it.

I began walking down the road to the park, the rain still coming down steadily. I pulled my hood over my head and shoved my hands in my pockets. Mom was going to kill me, but I had to hope she would understand. Maybe I would get lucky and none of my teachers would notice. I was hardly there as it was, so maybe they wouldn't miss me.

When I entered the park, I made my way to the playhouse. Climbing inside one of the tunnels, I was safe from the rain. I began shaking as I realized how cold I was. Rubbing my hands together, I tried for warmth but gained nothing except tired fingers.

What the heck was I thinking coming out here by myself and in a thunderstorm? Just as the thought crossed my mind, another crack of thunder sounded overhead. I shuddered, some from the cold but mostly from the implications of things that were getting harder to deny.

I pulled out my phone and opened a message to Gabriel. What was I going to say? "Hey, I thought about it and I think you're right. We are soul mates, destined to rid the world of demons from hell and preferably before they suck my soul out or whatever."

Yes, totally sane text message to send to someone.

I slumped, sighing, and put my phone back into my pocket. Irritated, I got my phone out one more time and opened a message to him again.

Can we talk?

Of course. When?

Now. I'm at the park...left the school...long story.

I'll be there. Give me five.

Now, I was nervous. He was on the way and didn't even question the fact that I wasn't in school. Briefly, I wondered how he was going to sneak out. It was Gabriel though, I'm sure he'd find a way. I don't think any of the teachers would stand in his way if he just got up and walked out.

Suddenly, I heard something hit the playhouse. I jumped and peeked outside. The wind was picking up, so maybe it was just a limb from a tree. My heart pounded. That's what I wanted to believe. I felt scared, like actually afraid. It had nothing to do with the storm that was moving in either.

I eased back into the tunnel, on my hands and knees. My breath came in heavy, deep gasps. There was something out there; I felt it.

"Hello?" I called out to no one and then rolled my eyes. "Yes, Ava, be that stupid girl in a horror movie, greeting the monster."

I moved a bit closer to the entrance, but just as I was about to take another step, a shadow moved across the opening. Yelping, I jumped back. It was more than a shadow. It was a cloaked figure. They were here.

I backtracked as fast as I could. Tumbling out into a square room, I could sort of stand up. My head didn't exactly touch the roof, but it was close. Backing up, I planted my back against the wall. I looked around the playhouse. There were three escape routes: the one I came in from, one that led to the slide, and the one that led to the monkey bars.

I knew I wasn't going the way I'd come. I didn't want to cross the monkey bars, or fall, either. The slide seemed my only genuine option, but that meant going through another room. I just wanted to get out of here.

Taking a deep breath, I crouched down and looked at the tunnel again. I screamed as I saw a figure crawling quickly toward me. I hurriedly ran for the tunnel that would take me to the slide. I moved so fast I hit my head on the entrance. Feeling dizzy and still scared out of my wits, I moved into the tunnel, crawling as fast as I could.

I made my way to the second room, staggered to my feet, and saw the entrance to the slide straight ahead of me. The room was spinning, and it felt like the slide was so far away. I moved forward, but my feet felt like weights. I stumbled and finally made it to the steps.

As I reached the top, I felt wet, clammy hands grab my ankle. Screaming, I kicked out, trying to free myself from their grasp. Nails, sharp as knives, dug into my flesh. Screaming again, I used my left foot to kick out as hard as I could, three times. I heard a gurgled whimper and they released my foot.

I went hurtling down the slide, face first. It curved to the left and then right. I came tumbling out into a puddle of water. Two hands grabbed my shoulders and pulled me upright. Yelling in fear and anger, I started punching and kicking.

"Whoa, Ava, it's me!" Gabriel grabbed my wrists. "What happened? Are you alright?"

"They're here! They're in there." I limped, stepping forward. My ankle was covered in blood and my head hurt so badly I couldn't see straight. "They're in there!"

Gabriel picked me up and carried me away, running. My head was swimming and before I knew it, I threw up, all over both of us. He didn't seem to notice, but I was squirming to get out of his grasp. Thankfully, I had eaten nothing that morning, so it was mostly stomach acid. Still, if we weren't being chased by witches, I would have been mortified.

Suddenly, Gabriel stopped. I thought he had finally noticed the smell until he spoke.

"Trevor," he spoke and the sound of fear in his voice made me look.

Keira and Trevor were standing in our path. My mind was whirling with pain and questions. They were supposed to be at home, sick. As I looked at Keira, she did look unwell. There was a touch of yellow to her skin and dark circles haunted her eyes. Just then, figures moved forward, out of the shadows of the trees. Fear took over my body and I clung to Gabriel.

"I should have known," Gabriel said, and I could feel him holding me tighter.

"Yes, you should have, Guardian," she said the last word in a taunting way.

"Keira?" I called to her. "What are you doing?"

I watched the hooded figures slither up beside her. She reached out and pulled Trevor closer to her. I thought she was trying to protect him, but to my shock, a hint of green light seemed to illuminate her skin where her hand touched his arm. At her touch, Trevor flinched and his eyes went vacant.

"If you hurt him..." Gabriel started.

"You'll what?" Keira asked him. "As you can see, you're a little outnumbered here."

"Keira," I said as my mind was clearing. "Please don't hurt him."

"What do you want?" Gabriel asked.

"That's easy," she smiled, "Give us Ava and we'll give you my boy toy."

"You know I can't do that," he told her, pain in his voice.

"Then I'll kill him," she said, as if she were talking about the weather. "You know I will."

The green light under her skin brightened and Trevor whined. I could feel Gabriel's arms tighten around me.

"Put me down," I said.

He looked at me for a moment and then set me on my feet. I was wobbly and my vision was still blurry, but I stood. Keira relaxed her power over Trevor and the tension in his face eased.

"If I go with you, you'll release Trevor?" I asked.

"Ava," Gabriel started, but I put up my hand.

"Of course." She smiled.

"And you won't hurt him or Gabriel." It wasn't a question.

"I suppose I don't have to," she said. "Even though we would like to."

"These games are tiring," one of the things hissed beside her. "What would stop us from killing both of them and taking her by force?"

"It is not what she wants," Keira told it.

The thing seemed to bristle with unspent energy. There was no way I was going with them. I was stalling and hoping that by doing so, Gabriel would think of something. I looked at him and I could see a dark blue light behind his eyes. Had I imagined that? It reminded me of the power that illuminated him in my dreams.

"Why are you doing this, Keira?" I asked her suddenly. "Answer that and I'll come with you. Why align yourself with them?"

She eyed me suspiciously. I could see the green power that lived inside her course through her body and settle in her eyes. It scared me. I didn't recognize her. Here was someone I thought I knew, someone I had shared my hopes, dreams, and secrets with, thinking she was my friend, like a sister, and she was really just a thief.

"I like being on the winning side." She smiled again.

"We are...were friends," I tried reminding her, and I noticed that I sounded like one of the girls from my dreams.

"Oh, darling, that's so sweet," she laughed, making fun of me. "We can be. Just walk over here. I'll let poor Trevor go, and we can be on our way."

"Why? So you can sacrifice me like they did all those other girls?" I asked her. "I saw them in my dreams, all the way back to Tepkunset. Those girls were her descendants, weren't they?"

"Ava, there is so much you don't know." Keira's nostrils flared. I could see her patience was wearing thin. So was mine.

"You came to my house, Keira, you stayed the night, ate dinner with my family, told me things about yours," I tried reaching her. "You are my friend. You don't have to do this. It's not too late."

I stepped forward and extended my hand. Gabriel stirred beside me. The Imprecors moved uneasily, tensing, looking as though they were ready to pounce. I saw something flash across Keira's eyes, but it was fleeting.

"Why can't you see there is nothing for you here?" Keira asked me. "What holds you to this place? Gabriel? You two are like oil and water. Your friends? You have none. Your family? A hovering mother and a controlling father? Have you ever wondered why your life is in shambles, your body is betraying you, and the people around you just don't really like you? It's because of the power inside you, Ava. They can sense it and it scares them. There's a darkness inside of you. How else could you have cursed Frankie and killed that perverted teacher? Your body is screaming at you to open up! Be free! Let go of the things that are holding you back. I can show you how to do that. Mother can."

"Doesn't she just want my power?" I asked her. "Doesn't she just want to...eat it?"

"That's how you'll serve her." Keira smiled at me and I felt sick. "You can join her, be one, and live forever, you and mother."

"I have a mother," I retorted, feeling that familiar surge rush through my body, her words terrifying me. "And a father who loves me."

"I can fix that problem," she sneered. "If that's what's holding you here."

"You will not touch them!" I yelled at her, feeling power run up and down my body.

"There it is!" She clapped her hands. "Let it out! Come for me or I'll go for them."

As soon as those words left her lips, I could feel something ignite inside me. A rush of energy started from my toes and coursed up my entire body. It felt like I was on fire, but the pain was fleeting. Without really knowing what I was doing, all I could think of was wanting them to just move. To move away, far away from us.

Energy, like lightning and the color of a purple night sky, seemed to explode from me. Keira, Trevor, and all the Imprecors were knocked off their feet and flew at least 20 feet backwards. Keira slammed against a tree with Trevor falling on top of her.

"Trevor!" I went to run after him, but Gabriel grabbed my arm.

"There's too many, and you just expensed a lot of energy," he told me.

"What are you..." I felt myself grow weak suddenly. "He needs us."

"We have to go." He looked pained.

"My parents," I said to him.

He pulled me in the opposite direction of the group, and we ran for his car. It didn't take him long before he had it started and we were speeding down the road. I noticed we were not going to my house.

"Gabriel, my parents," I repeated to him.

"We have to get out of here, Ava," he responded.

"Not without my parents." I grabbed him, crying. "You take me there now! Or so help me I will jump out of this car!"

"Okay, okay." He pulled out from under my grasp, trying to get back control of the car.

He turned the vehicle around so fast I thought we might flip, but thankfully he was a pretty decent driver. It seemed to take ages to get there. I knew Mom was working from home today and Dad had a doctor's appointment, so he was supposed to be home, too. We would just grab them and go. I would explain on the way. They would just have to listen to me or I'd get Gabriel to knock them both out if we had to.

Gabriel pulled in my driveway, and I was out of the car before he had it in park. He called after me, but I ran as fast as I could and burst into the house.

"Mom! Dad!" I called, running toward the living room. "Where are you?"

The living room was empty, so I ran into Mom's office, but she wasn't there either.

"Ava?" I heard my Dad call and my heart sank. Something was wrong.

About that time, Gabriel came up behind me. He tried stopping me, but I ran to the sound of my dad's voice. It was coming from the kitchen. Fear threatened to overtake my limbs, but I kept moving on pure adrenaline alone. I didn't want to see whatever was in there, but I had to go to him.

Running through the open archway, I slipped on something and fell hard on the tile floor. I came face to face with my mother who laid in a pool of blood. I screamed, but no sound came out. After a moment, I reached out and touched her. She was still breathing; I thanked the heavens.

"Mommy?" I cried, shaking her. "Wake up! Please!"

I felt Gabriel enter the room. I looked up at him. "Help her."

"Ava," I heard my Dad. "Get away from her."

I wasn't sure if he was talking to me or Gabriel, but I made my way to the other side of the kitchen island. There was so much blood, I wasn't sure where his began and hers ended. When I rounded the counter, I saw him sitting up, leaning against it, holding his side.

There was a sword, an actual sword at his feet. It was confusing, but my main concern was him. I rushed to him, unsure of what to do but thankful he was still alive. I grabbed my phone out of my pocket and went to dial 911. Dad reached up and took the phone from my hands.

"What are you doing?" I didn't mean the words to sound so angry. "You both need help."

"You have to listen to me," he said; his dark eyes looked so strange to me suddenly. "I don't have a lot of time, sweet girl, and I need to you listen to me."

"Daddy?" I felt so scared.

"I know who you are, Ava, what you can do," he told me. "I have known for a while now. Your...mother and I both have. You're going to hate me and that's fine, you should, but I need you to listen. You are good, you hear me? It doesn't matter what they tell you, you are good. You're the reason I believe there is hope in all of this."

"Ava," Gabriel came up behind me, "Step back."

My dad looked up at him. There was something there, it wasn't necessarily hate, but it wasn't kindness either. He didn't like Gabriel at all.

"You know she doesn't need you, Guardian," my dad said to him. "But you better do your job."

"I will," Gabriel said.

"I am so sorry." Dad looked back at me.

"Daddy, we need to get you some help, please," I pleaded.

"It's too late for that, sweetheart," he told me.

"Sweetheart..." I heard my mother's voice.

She was standing up on the other side of the island. Her features looked so foreign to me. A face I had seen a thousand times now looked like it belonged to a stranger. Mom held a strange-looking dagger in her hands. The handle was bone white, and the blade was black as night. I recognized it as the one I had seen in my dreams. It was the blade that Tepkunset had made

"Mom?" I called to her.

"Oh, Ava," she smiled, moving a bit closer to us, "Are you that dumb?"

"You're not my mom," I said.

"I haven't been your mom for about a year," she said thoughtfully. "I am so glad you finally figured out who we are, so we can all stop pretending. This human skin is so heavy. Soon, I can shed it."

My mind was whirling. I wanted to give in to this crushing fear and hopelessness, but I knew if I did, Gabriel was as good as dead and I would be served up to Thyana. I had to get a hold on my emotions, even if my entire world was shattering right before my eyes.

"Mother sent a few of us out to potential heirs, converts," she said. "I was lucky enough to get you. And, look, with all of my nurturing, you turned out to be who we were looking for. Now, come to Mommy so we can go home."

"Did you do this?" I pointed to Dad.

"We were having child rearing disagreements." Mom rolled her eyes. "That human skin he's wearing has made him weak. We have no place for that. He had to go. Well, she, we do not convert men. Disgusting, vile things."

I suddenly picked up the sword and pointed it at her. "That's close enough."

"Ava, you wouldn't hurt your mom, now, would you?" she asked.

"You're not my mom," I reminded her.

"Fair enough." She smiled.

"Give me that dagger," I told her, focusing my energy on her.

"Why would I do that?" she asked.

"It's what made this wound on him, right?" I asked her. "I've seen it in my dreams. I have a feeling it would do some major damage on your kind."

"You always were a smart one," she told me. "But that doesn't mean I'm giving it to you."

"Give me the dagger," I told her again, focusing even harder.

"I told you..." Suddenly her eyes became unfocused and her body tensed.

"Take him to the car," I told Gabriel.

"Ava," he started.

"Take him to the car, Gabriel, please," I begged him.

He nodded and picked up my father. Dad winced and cried out, blood running out of the wound like a faucet, but Gabriel did as I asked.

"Bring the blade to me," I told my mother.

She moved a little, but she was fighting hard. I could feel it. The energy coming from me was like an unseen arm, reaching out and holding her in place. When she pulled, I moved with it.

"Drop the blade on the floor." I figured I would try something else.

Mom's face contorted, but she opened her hand and the dagger clattered to the floor. Keeping the sword pointed at my mother, I slowly walked forward, trying not to break the control I had over her. I could feel myself tiring, so I picked up my pace. Grabbing the dagger, I stood up and looked at her.

My heart shattered. She was my mother. She had raised me, cared for me, held me when I was sick, talked to me about crappy friends and even crappier boys.

"If any part of my mother is still in there, you'll stay here," I told her. "You'll let us go."

I could see her body tremble. I didn't know what that meant, so I just left her there. Rushing out of the house, I joined Dad in the backseat and Gabriel took off. He looked at me in the rearview mirror, a million questions in his eyes.

"We're taking him to my house," he told me. "No doctor will know how to treat him. Maybe Pops will be able to help."

I nodded holding Dad's head in my lap. He slipped in and out of consciousness, his words making little sense. Gabriel had given him a shirt to put over the wound. I held it in place. My first aid knowledge was limited, but I knew the less blood he lost, the better. Or, at least I hoped that was the case for whatever he was.

For a while, memories played over in my mind. I tried to recall a time when I thought my parents might not be my parents, but nothing stuck out. Sure, we had our disagreements like all families did, but they never seemed out of the ordinary to me. How powerful could I be if I didn't even know my own parents were part of the Imprecors?

Then I wondered why Thyana had sent them to raise me? Mom had said that she sent them out to potential converts. Did that mean all the girls in my dreams, Tempkunset's descendants, had parents that were imposters as well? Why? They had been killed, sacrificed to her. Did some of them join her? Were the Imprecors, those shriveled beings, girls that had been converted? Would that eventually happen to Keira?

"You have to pull over," my dad blurted.

"We're getting you help," I told him, or I guessed it was 'her.'

"You have to, now." Dad tried sitting up, but managed to clap Gabriel on the back. "You know what happens when we die."

Gabriel nodded and pulled over. We were on a lonely road lined with pastures and sparse trees. As soon as Gabriel stopped, he got out and helped Dad out of the car. Dad pointed to a pine tree and Gabriel sat her against it. Dad's breathing was rapid and shallow. The wound seemed to have turned putrid all in a matter of minutes.

She breathed in deeply, seeming to enjoy the night air as it filled her lungs. I knew what she was doing and it gutted me. She was saying goodbye, to living, to me. I knelt beside her, taking her hand.

"I love you," she told me. "I know you might not believe me. How could this evil being love, right? I do. You taught me that, Ava. Mother sent me to you, to turn you, to convert you, and I was determined to fulfill her wish should you prove to have potential, but you broke my heart and then mended it. Do you want to know when? I had only been this human for a few months, and you came to me while I was replacing a busted pipe in the kitchen, such a mundane human task. You told me about a boy at school who was saying things about you to his friends. We talked about it and afterwards, you said, 'You're one of the good ones, Daddy.' That's all you said, and I knew; I wanted to be your real your Dad, your real parent. I'm not exactly male, but I'm not exactly human, either. I spent the next few months undermining everything your mother and Thyana tried. Any influence they had on you, your arrogance, your pride, your anger, I would do my best to break it because I knew you were one of the good ones, too."

I didn't know what to say to her. Tears flooded my eyes and fell down my cheeks. I buried my head in her chest and sobbed against her for what seemed to be the longest time, but I knew it was only seconds. She lifted my head and kissed my cheek.

"You have to stand back," she told me.

"I don't want to," I sobbed.

"Ava..." Gabriel gently lifted me to my feet, and we backed away.

"There is so much more I want to tell you," she smiled at me, "Just know that I will always fight for you."

With those words, her body burst into flame. I was so startled, I jumped back. Gabriel held me steady. In the distance, we heard a horrible sound, something that sounded like the scream of a thousand voices. My skin crawled with energy.

"We have to go," Gabriel said, and we rushed to the car.

Just as we took off down the road, something hit the roof. We swerved along the road, but Gabriel straightened the wheel before he lost control.

"Son of—" he said.

"For people who don't want me dead, they sure do like trying to kill me." I held onto the door with one hand and the dash with the other, trying to brace myself.

Gabriel grunted and floored it. We were flying down the small road at breakneck speed. I wasn't much for praying, but I found myself asking whatever deity listening to please let Gabriel keep this thing on four wheels.

"Almost there," Gabriel said, but I think he was talking mostly to himself.

There was another horrible screech and we both flinched. I covered my ears as the sound intensified. Gabriel shrunk into himself, but he kept driving. He turned sharply and I knew we were just moments from his house. Right when the house came into view, something big and dark came out of the woods and hit the car at full speed.

I had just enough time to shout Gabriel's name as the car went sailing through the air. My body lurched as the car rolled onto its side, flipping once and then twice. It landed on the roof and skidded nearly all the way up Gabriel's driveway.

It finally came to a stop, and I felt something warm trickling down the back of my head. I laid on the ceiling of the car, not sure if I were breathing or not. I turned to see Gabriel still in the driver's seat, hanging upside down, a large gash on his forehead. I remembered thinking, "Well, at least one of us remembered to buckle up," before the darkness took me over.

Ava

I could hear noise and voices, unsure of where it was coming from. It took me a moment to remember where I was and what had happened. Groaning, I pushed myself up from the busted windshield, feeling glass digging into my hands. Gabriel was still unconscious, his arms dangling limply from his body.

I made my way over and just as I reached him, something banged against the passenger side door. With my heart in my throat, I whirled around. One of the Imprecors was trying to pull the door off its hinges. I searched for the blade and saw it just inches from the window. I grabbed it just as the thing pulled apart the door like popping open a soda can.

It reached inside, but I sliced it with the dagger, making contact with its forearm. Smoke exploded from its skin and a sizzling sound, like bacon cooking, sounded throughout the car. I watched as a large burn formed on its already disgusting flesh, as if I had dropped acid on it.

"This doesn't have to be so difficult, girl," it said, and I recognized its voice as the one from the park. "Just come with us."

"Not happening," I told it.

It growled and hissed and moved forward, but as it did so, something seemed to stop it from progressing. While it was afraid of the blade in my hand, it was the force preventing its movements. A barrier had been formed and the Imprecor could not cross it.

"What have you done, girl?" it asked.

"That's not me," I confessed.

Soon, many more of the Imprecors joined its companion. None of them, thankfully, could go any further than the edge of the passenger side door. I saw Keira make her way to the front.

"What magic is this, Ava?" she asked. "Have you been holding out on me?"

"It's not me," I told her.

"This is getting old. Come here." She tried reaching in as well, but I swung the blade, catching her across the cheek.

Keira howled in pain, lunging at me in anger, but got thrown back by the protection that surrounded me.

"You're not welcome here," Pops stated as he walked down the driveway.

To my utter shock, Lorcan and several others accompanied him. Two men rushed forward and opened Gabriel's door. They quickly and easily pulled him from the car. Blood was dripping from his head and down his face. The sight was unnerving, but I took comfort because he was still breathing.

Lorcan reached down and helped me out of the car. I wanted to ask him what he was doing there along with a million other questions, but we had other matters to deal with. Turning, I watched Keira stalk the unseen perimeter. She reached out and I could hear a sizzling sound. Jerking her hand back, she hissed and glared up at us, the damage from the blade had already left an angry wound.

My mother, or who I had believed was my mother, emerged from the crowd. She looked at Keira's hand and then she did something strange. She smelled the air, like an animal. She walked a few paces left and then right, sniffing.

"Impressive," she said. "This wasn't here before."

"It's new," Pops told her.

"Strong?" she asked with a smile.

"Very," he replied.

"No fun," she pouted.

I didn't recognize her at all. It didn't stop me from wanting to run to her, to grab her shoulders and shake her, ask her why. Instead, I just stared at her, knowing that my life, the one I'd had before, was over.

"We'll come back," Mom said to us, looking right at me.

"Don't forget, Ava," Keira said. "We still have dear Trevor."

"Hey, Keira, you have something on your face," I pointed to my cheek with my middle finger. "Just there."

She sneered at me, and while her reaction was satisfying, my heart still sank all the same. I had to do something. I had to save him. There was nothing I could do at the moment and she knew it. She made it a parting jab. With that, they seemed to melt into the night.

I wanted to sink into the ground, to just give into the crushing weight of darkness and sorrow, but I knew that was out of the question.

"Gabriel?" I turned to Pops.

"He's in excellent hands." He took my arm and led me to the house.

I watched Lorcan and the others as they followed us. I recognized them as the friends who had accompanied him at the game room that night. The beautiful girl who moved like a dancer, Kat, looked different, fierce and focused.

When we finally made our way inside, I followed them through the house and into a room I had passed before but had never been inside. It was a freaking medical unit. It was small, but it seemed to have all the bells and whistles. The two guys who had pulled Gabriel out of the wreckage, Reese and Bron, were tending to him as he lay on one of the two hospital beds. I started to go to him, but Lorcan stopped me.

"Let them work," he said. "They know what they're doing. Trust me."

"I don't even know you," I told him, pulling away from his touch.

"Ava," Pops came to me. "Will you trust me then?"

I looked at him and then at Gabriel. Bron was cleaning his wounds and Reese was listening to his heart and lungs. They really seemed to know what to do. Finally, I nodded my head. When I did, I could feel blood running down the back of my neck. I reached back and came away with bloody fingers.

"Let's get you looked at," Pops told me. "Kat can help."

Kat seemed to materialize at my side. "Come with me, Ava, let me help."

She led me to the other bed and gently leaned me forward to get a better look at the wound.

"That looks nasty," she said. "I'll have to stitch it and cut a little bit of your hair."

I didn't say anything. She must have taken that as permission to get started. Kat worked silently, moving around me so quietly, I hardly noticed she was there. She took out a few things and had me lean over again. I watched a few strands of my hair fall away. Any other time, vanity would have taken over and I probably would have panicked watching my long black locks hit the floor. Right now, I didn't feel much at all.

That was until she poured some type of cleaning solution into the wound. I winced, grabbing both my knees and squeezing.

"I'm sorry," she said. "I can give you some medicine for the pain."

"Will it make me sleepy?" I asked her.

"No, it's only for the wound," she explained. "I'll have to administer it with a needle, but it won't make you drowsy."

"That's fine," I told her.

After a few pinpricks of pain, she began stitching the wound. I could feel it somewhat, but it wasn't unbearable. It was nothing compared to what was going on inside. When Kat was done, I stood up and swayed on my feet. I caught myself on the bed and saw my reflection in the metal medicine cabinet.

A funhouse effect had warped my features, but I could still see the haunted look in my eyes. I was sure even without the distortion, I wouldn't quite look like myself. I didn't feel like myself either. Apparently, not being who we say we are was going around today.

"Are you alright?" Kat asked.

"I'm fine," I said.

I wasn't. She knew that, and so did I. It's just what people said when they didn't want to talk about things that were bothering them. I tore my eyes away from the girl in the metal cabinet and looked over at Gabriel.

He seemed to be resting, his face cleaned and his wound stitched. Reese and Bron had worked quickly and efficiently. It made me wonder how many times they had done something like that.

Lorcan was standing in the corner, just watching. All of them knew something about what was going on, but none of them told me. A man walked into the room and my heart nearly jumped out of my chest. Dr. Abbott stood there, no shame in his eyes for his betrayal.

Without really thinking about what I was doing, I stalked over to him and punched him right in the mouth. Bron stepped forward and I turned to him, ready for whatever the big man wanted to do, but Dr. Abbott put up his hand.

"Easy," he told Bron. "I deserved that."

"And more," I said as I turned back to him.

"I don't expect you to understand, Ava." His once caring blue eyes looked sinister to me now. "But I had a job to do."

"That makes me feel so much better." I held back tears.

"I need you to understand something," he said. "I'm not here to coddle your feelings."

"Callum," Pops warned, but Dr. Abbott went on.

"As you saw a few moments ago, we're up against something much bigger than all of us," he told me. "I suggest you pull yourself together."

I walked closer to him, glaring, feeling the power I'd had before building inside me, and said, "Fuck you."

The energy in my body pulsed, and everyone in the room staggered backwards. I reined it in as much as I could once I realized what I was doing, but Dr. Abbott still went sailing into a shelf and onto the floor. He landed with a satisfying thud.

"Ava," I heard Gabriel call.

I turned to look at him, still unconscious on the bed, and the anger faded from my body. I wanted to be mad at him. He had betrayed me just as much, if not more, than anyone else. Still, seeing him lie there, the wound on his head, knocked the fight right out of me.

A part of me wanted to go to him. The anger inside wouldn't let me. I turned and made my way to the only place that felt familiar—the study. Once inside, Kaine came bounding out of his bed and sniffed at my heels. I scratched behind his ears and stood in front of the mural.

Time seemed to slow down and speed up. I wasn't sure how long I stood there, but eventually I began pulling every book off the shelf I could read. Some were lost causes because they were in languages I would never know how to speak.

By the time the sun rose outside, I knew more about the Matthews history than I knew about my own. They were Vikings, or Norsemen, as they preferred to be called. I found a family tree. Gabriel could trace his line all the way back to Scandinavia, in parts of Norway. It surprised me when I saw Bron's name on there. He was a very distant cousin, but they were related.

I could feel a headache forming between my eyes. Closing the book, I rested my head in my hands. Hearing a knock at the door, I looked up. Lorcan stood in the doorway, two cups in his hands. Anger flashed through me and he seemed to notice.

"I come in peace," he held the cups up, "Besides, I'm sure you could use something to drink."

When I said nothing, he ventured further into the room and placed a warm cup of tea in front of me. I hesitated for a moment, but it was too tempting and I was extremely thirsty. Picking up the warm brew, I only took a moment to give it a quick cooling blow before I took a big gulp.

"What do you want?" I asked him.

"I don't want anything," he said, taking a sip himself. "I came to see if you were alright."

"Oh, peachy." I stared at him.

"And your wound?" he asked me. "Are you in pain? Kat can give you something if you'd like."

"I'm fine," I told him.

"Right," he said, staring at me. "Learn anything interesting?"

"Interesting? Yes. Helpful? No," I said.

"I'm sure you have so many questions," he began.

"You think?" My words were laced with anger.

"We would like to offer you some answers, Ava," he said. "If you'll speak to us. We are on the same team and want the same things."

"And what is that?" I asked him.

"To end the Imprecors," he told me. "To stop Thyana."

"I want to save my friend," I said.

"Of course," he nodded, walking to my side of the desk, "We will help you do that."

Lorcan kneeled down in front of me; his hazel eyes looked more green today and there were faint dark circles under them, giving his fair skin a bruised look. He hadn't slept either.

"I know this is asking a lot of you at the moment," he suddenly touched my hand, "but we are just asking for a miniscule amount of trust. We can help each other."

Looking at him, the tenderness in his voice, the softness in his eyes, I wanted to trust him. He really seemed like he was being sincere, but at the moment, I didn't even trust myself.

"Ava," I heard Gabriel's voice as he entered the room.

Lorcan looked up but didn't immediately let go of my hand. I moved away from him and stood up.

"Are you alright?" I asked him.

"I've been better, but I'm fine," he told me, still looking at Lorcan. He had something in his hands. "Um, Pops set up a room for you, and Kat has given you some clothes to change into. If you'd like to shower, I can show you where it is."

"Okay," I told him and moved toward him.

"Remember what I said, Ava," Lorcan told me. "We just want to help."

Without another word, I followed Gabriel down the hall. We passed many closed doors until we reached one near the end of the hall. As soon as he opened the door, I turned to him.

"We have to find Trevor," I said to him.

He seemed taken aback, but he nodded. "I know. We will."

"When?" I felt fear and guilt well up inside me.

"As soon as it's safe," he answered.

"When will that be, Gabriel?" I wanted to shake him.

Trevor was his friend first. Why wasn't he just as terrified as I was? Why wasn't he already out there looking for him?

"You have expended a lot of your energy," he said. "You're still learning to use your power. If you were to face them right now, there is a good chance they could overpower you. Do you want that?"

"Of course not," I told him.

"You need rest," he said.

"Look who's talking," I said, taking in his disheveled appearance.

His face was bruised, his eyes haunted, and his black shirt still had matted blood on it. I was sure as soon as he'd come to, he had rushed to find me.

"Eat something, rest, take a shower," he seemed to plead with me, handing me the bag of toiletry items and clothes. "When you've done that, I promise we will find him."

There was a crack in his voice. I knew he didn't mean to show it, but he was afraid. I should be angry with him. I was angry with him, but that didn't mean I wanted to see him in pain. Reaching out, I touched his hand.

"Don't," he pulled away, "Don't comfort me."

He left me there, moving faster than I thought most people were capable of doing. I felt as if he had slapped me in the face. Pushing the hurt down, I entered the room. It was nice, but nothing extravagant. A nice comfortable bed, nightstand, dresser, and a desk. I opened the door I assumed was the bathroom and was thrilled to see I had my own toilet, too.

I turned the shower on and made the water as hot as I could stand. Peeling off my stiff and bloody clothes, I climbed in and let the water and steam envelope me. Dark water ran down the drain and I tried not to think about whose blood it was. It could have been mine, Gabriel's, Dad's...

Using the body wash and washcloth, I scrubbed off the blood and dirt until my skin was raw. The shampoo wasn't something I had ever used, but when I was done, my hair felt clean. I had to be extra careful around my wound. It was tender and the soap burned. I could feel where Kat had cut my hair. No one would ever know unless I wanted to sport a ponytail.

I put on the clothes. They were a little tight. Kat was very slim. She was tall like me, thankfully, but I had more curves. Mom always told me that I got that from her side of the family. I was ashamed to admit it took me a long time to try and not hide them. I thought I needed to be stick thin like the other girls on the cheer squad. I was glad to be finished with that part of my life. Embracing the body I was born with, loving myself, felt like accepting a part of my family that I had never been able to meet.

Mom said her parents had died a few years before I was born, and Dad was raised by his grandmother after his parents died in a car accident. According to them, she had passed when he was only 18.

I had no siblings, no cousins, no aunts and uncles. It had always been just us.

After pulling my hair into a side braid, I laid down on the bed. It was comfortable and warm and sooner than I thought, I had fallen into an uneasy sleep.

There were colors and flashes of images. I kept seeing Trevor and Keira, but none of it made sense. The black dagger would be in my hand and then it would disappear. My dad was there, telling me to run, but I wasn't sure where to go or what I was running from.

The next thing I knew, I was standing in front of a group of figures. I wasn't sure if they were human or the Imprecors. Then I saw Gabriel, that blue light pulsing around him. He reached for me and I took his hand. The power inside us both exploded like fireworks, putting on a blue and purple light show. When I looked up at him, I could see he was trying to speak, but I couldn't hear what he was saying.

Suddenly, I found myself heading down a stone spiral staircase and into a room made of mirrors. I could see myself from every angle. It was me, but in each one I looked different. Different hair styles, different clothes, different times in my life. The only thing that remained the same was the black dagger in my hand.

There was a trail of blood running down my neck. I reached up and could feel the wound on the back of my head. It was throbbing and tender. It made me angry. I wanted it to go away. The reminder of how and why I was hurt sent rage rushing through me.

I couldn't fix the damage on the inside. That pain was too deep. It would take too much time to heal. It took too much concentration. I didn't want to deal with pain on the outside, too. I just wanted it to go away.

"Ava."

I looked up and saw Trevor standing behind me. I whirled around and came face-to-face with my mother. She reached out, her once familiar, loving hands wrapped around my throat.

I jolted awake, fighting with my sheets. When I realized I wasn't in any real danger, I relaxed. My heart was hammering. I nearly jumped out of my skin when there was knock on my door. There was no light outside my window, so I assumed I had slept all day.

"Yeah?" I called.

"It's Kat," I heard Kat say. "Can I come in?"

"Sure." I sat up, my heart still beating like a jackhammer.

Kat opened the door, her rich brown eyes taking me in. I tried straightening my shirt and pushing back strands of hair that had fallen out of my braid while I slept.

"I brought you this." She handed me a jacket.

It was leather, real leather, and had a few pockets on the inside. It was nice and expensive. I looked up at her.

"It's cold," she told me. "You'll need it. I need to look at your wound if that's okay."

Nodding, I sat on the edge of the bed and took my hair down. I leaned my head over and she gently moved my hair out of the way.

"What the hell?" she gasped.

"What?" I wondered, scared of what she saw. "Is it infected? Did I bust a stitch?"

"Um," she said and I sat up, looking at her. "Your wound...is gone."

"What?" I touched the back of head.

I felt around, searching for the spot she had stitched and the missing hair, but I couldn't find anything. Standing up, I ran to the mirror, trying to see the back of my head and knowing how stupid I looked. My dream came rushing back to me. I had wanted it to go away.

"What does that mean?" I asked her after a moment, feeling slightly sick.

"I…I don't know," she confessed. Her dark eyes searched my face. "I need to talk to Abbott."

"Dr. Abbott?" I asked.

"We just call him Abbott," she told me.

"Is he actually a doctor?" I wondered.

"He is," Kat said and her face seemed to soften. "You have every right to not trust him, or any of us, but his intentions have always been sincere. He's a good man. A little brash, but he's good."

I didn't feel like arguing with her over what constituted a good man. I was too busy wondering if I was now Wolverine. How could a wound that needed stitches just disappear? How could the hair she cut off just grow back? I felt like a freak.

I had willed this in my sleep.

"Come with me," she offered. "They're just now having dinner. I'm sure you're hungry."

I thought about it, but I didn't think I could eat anything. I didn't even feel like I wanted to. Still, I slipped on the jacket, which fit me well, and followed her down the stairs. As we descended, I pulled my hair back into a braid, mostly just to keep it out of my way.

My hair had become a shield of sorts for me. I had grown it out and the thickness and weight was like a security blanket, shielding me from the outside world.

When we entered the large dining room, the smell of cooked meat and other foods rushed forward. My stomach growled, silently, and I realized that maybe I was hungry. The other members of the group were already seated at the table, their plates full.

To my surprise, they all stood, like we were ladies and they were gentlemen. Kat walked forward and took her place beside her brother. I saw there was an empty plate between Gabriel and Pops. Since they didn't seem as if they were going to sit until I did, I walked over and took a seat. The rest of the party followed.

"You look…rested," Gabriel said to me, searching my face.

"I slept a lot, I guess," I told him. "What time is it?"

"You slept nearly all day," he confessed to me.

"I did?" I nearly stood up, but he placed his hand on mine. "Please eat. We can eat and talk."

I looked around at the food, and my stomach growled again. Someone, I was assuming Pops, had made roast with carrots, mashed potatoes, green beans, and fresh rolls.

I began putting food on my plate, aware that Kat was staring at me. When the first bit of food hit my tongue, I realized I was starving. After nearly clearing my plate in record time, Dr. Abbott spoke.

"Kat tells me you're feeling better, Ava," he said pointedly.

"Did she?" I looked at her and she shifted in her seat.

"Yes, apparently, you're doing unnaturally well," he said it like an accusation.

"Do you have a question?" I wondered.

"Has this happened before?" he asked me.

"What's going on?" Gabriel looked at me.

"I'm Wolverine," I said.

Bron signed and everyone in the room, except me, knew what he was saying.

"He wants to know what you're talking about," Kat said.

I turned and lifted my hair, showing them my head. Gabriel had no idea what it had looked like before, but he was aware that I had been injured. They all looked shocked.

"Even your hair grew back?" Reese wondered.

"I suppose so." I shrugged.

"You're taking this rather well." Dr. Abbott eyed me curiously.

"Well, in the past day or so, I've found out the supernatural exists, my parents are imposters, and more than likely dead, and I have magical powers." I took another bite and talked through a sizeable piece of roast. "I could either have a mental breakdown or, what was it you said, pull myself together."

The group looked at me as I ate, as if I were about to fall apart. I wanted to. I could feel the seam that held my mind together fraying. If I gave in though, how would I save Trevor? How would I get any answers?

"What I want to know," I took my last bite, "is how are we going to save Trevor?"

"Trevor?" Dr. Abbott asked.

"Yes, Trevor," I put my fork down, "The boy that Keira and the

Imprecors have and are probably torturing right now as we sit here and eat this delicious meal."

Dr. Abbott folded his hands in front of him; his crisp blue eyes closed and then opened again.

"I understand your worry, Ava, I really do." He tried to sound concerned, but I didn't buy it. "Unfortunately, we have no idea where Trevor is or where to start looking for him. It isn't as if we are the police and can put out a missing person's report on him. Trust me, if we knew anything, we would have done something. Our mission has always been to protect the innocent."

"I can talk to Keira," I offered. "I can just go outside. You know they're circling whatever barrier you put up, testing it for weaknesses."

"They're not out there," he said, putting his napkin down.

"How do you know that?" I was irritated and I know it sounded in my voice.

"You cut Keira and another one with that blade," Dr. Abbott said, as if that explained everything. When I didn't respond, he continued, "That blade was forged hundreds of years ago by your ancestor, Tepkunset. We've been looking for it for a very long time. How they found it, we don't know, but we are glad to have it back. It is the only thing that can end the life, if you want to call it that, of an Imprecor. Even a tiny nick can make one of them very ill. Now, Keira isn't truly an Imprecor, not yet, but she has sided herself with them, so part of her soul is tainted. I suspect she is very sick along with the other beast. They will be tending to their own."

"So we just sit here? And what? Wait for them to come back?" I asked.

"No, of course not." He smiled, looking at Pops suddenly. "Ryland will begin your training. We have to put on a good show for our guests."

Ava

I spent the rest of the night arguing with Abbott, about many things. At the top of that list was the idea he had about my place in the Mavors. The Order was something I still didn't have a complete understanding of at the moment. From what I'd gathered, both Pops and Abbott were high-ranking members, but I wasn't sure who outranked who. Still, they seemed in agreement about one thing; I had to learn how to use my abilities.

I also learned that now that they had found the one they were looking for, other members of the Mavors, from all over the world, were headed our way. They wanted to meet me. It sounded like they just wanted to see what I could do.

From what I could gather, there had been several potential descendants of Tepkunset that could have inherited her abilities. I was the only one who proved useful. The Mavors had been looking for her heir since the Imprecors had shown up again nearly 70 years ago. It had taken them at least 30 of those years to even find one of Tepkunset's descendants.

They had sent members of the Mavors out to investigate these potential candidates; Gabriel, his parents, and Pops had been assigned to me. When this piece of information was made known, Gabriel shifted in his seat and wouldn't meet my eyes. Pops spoke up and said that their intentions were only to gain intelligence. They were only supposed to interact if they were sure. I guess Gabriel had been sure.

I knew I could get angry with them, I was, but I also knew they were right about learning how to control my power. Calling it that made me feel very strange.

"So, how do we do this?" I asked Pops. "Do I carry you on my back while I lift rocks with my mind?"

"You're funny," Reese laughed. "I like her."

"She has a certain charm." Kat winked at me.

Bron glared at me while he picked at his nails. He was not a fan. I wasn't exactly sure what I had done, but he didn't like me. I guess my personality wasn't for everyone.

"To be honest, Ava," Pops said. "We don't really know what we're doing. We've never had to train someone with your abilities, and I'm sure you're far stronger than we could ever dream of. Still, we can show you what we have learned over the years, and I do trust you can master your skills."

"Sounds like a good plan." I clapped my hands together, standing up from the armchair I had been sitting in. "Or, the only plan, but it's a start. So, lead the way."

"Gabriel will train you in physical combat," he said. "I will be your mentor in the lore and other studies. The others are here to assist as well. We are here to see that your training is successful."

This all sounded so strange to me. Lore studies and physical combat. Was I about to go to ancient, secret society, warrior school?

"Okay, well, let's get started," I said, before the weight of what was happening really settled in.

Pops nodded and asked that Gabriel and I follow him. The others stayed behind while Pops led us downstairs and into the basement. He pulled on an overhead light and walked the length of the massive bottom floor. It was nondescript. It looked like what you'd think a basement was supposed to look like.

Pops stopped at a shelf at the other side of the room. He rummaged around in a box and I heard something click. The shelf slid along on a hinge. I gasped. A secret chamber? What movie was I in?

When the shelf finally stopped moving, I could just make out the outline of stairs that descended into darkness. Pops flipped a switch and the metallic steps glistened under the light. Gabriel gestured me forward as we followed Pops down. A large square room came into view and as we got closer, lights flickered on.

It was as large as a football field. It seemed to go on forever, but it was only because of the floor length mirrors that covered the walls, creating the illusion. It reminded me of the mirrored room from my dream. I shivered at the thought.

All sorts of equipment, some I recognized and some I didn't, and weapons lined the walls. There were several sparring rings, but the one in the middle looked well-used.

It wasn't hard to comprehend that this was where the Mavors trained, away from prying eyes who wouldn't understand. And now I was one of them? Is that how it worked? If I accepted being this warrior they had been waiting on, did that mean I was already a member of this ancient Order?

"Are you alright?" Gabriel asked.

"What?" I looked up at him.

"I know it's a lot," he said. "You just seem a little overwhelmed."

"I'm fine," I responded, walking forward and taking in the room. "What do I need to do?"

"There are many things, but we always start with strengthening your mental hold on your abilities," Pops said. "That means, a lot of meditation."

"Meditation? That sounds so...new age," I commented. "You know, crystals and such."

"It's not so new," he smiled, waving me forward, "These practices have been around for thousands of years."

We came to a door at the far end of the room. Inside, it was dimly lit and smelled of fresh grass and flowers. There was a soft, thick carpet that lined the floor and different sized pillows scattered here and there. A large circular seat surrounded a fire pit in the middle of the room.

"So, I just...go in?" I asked.

"You don't have to," Gabriel said. "I don't use this room. Pops does. Some of the other Mavors do for prayer and meditation."

"Gabriel has his own way." Pops smiled at his grandson, but his look of affection was laced with concern.

"I'm not very spiritual," I admitted.

"It doesn't matter," Pops said gently. "You are Tepkunset's heir, Ava. You really don't have a choice in what you believe in anymore. As far as spirituality is concerned, my recommendation is to just try. I know you want to rescue Trevor, get answers, and understand the magic that courses through you."

"Yes," I responded, even though I wasn't sure if he had asked me a question.

"Just give it a shot," he encouraged.

I think if it would have been anyone else, I would have refused. Instead, I walked into the odd little room. To my surprise, Gabriel followed me. I turned to look at him.

"Sorry," he stopped, "Someone always sits in. Meditating can be sort of intense."

"Okay." This was all really strange.

What did they expect me to do, float away into another cosmic plane? Was that possible? I felt nervous suddenly.

Gabriel gestured for me to sit down. Once I did, he began building a fire in the pit. I watched as the smoke, which smelled of hickory and flowers, swirl into an overhead vent. At least I wouldn't suffocate. It felt as though I might die from the heat, though. I peeled off my leather jacket as soon as the flames started.

"Am I supposed to need a shower after this?" I asked him.

"The heat helps you focus," Gabriel said as Pops shut the door.

"If you say so." I felt sweat run down my back. "I don't know what I'm doing."

"Just close your eyes," he said as he finally took a seat across from me. "Try to clear you mind."

"Maybe if I knew what this was for? What's the point?" I asked.

"If your abilities are like ours, then they are connected to your emotions," he said. "Mediating helps you gain control over both."

"What are your abilities?" I asked him, sure that my dreams of the dark blue light I had seen pulse around him meant something.

"It's nothing like yours," he said. "Mavors are called from all over the world because they are born stronger, faster, with the strength to withstand fights against the Imprecors. We can't do what I saw you do at the park. Our abilities are physical. Some can use magic, like Kat, but it takes years of practice and it's not anything like what you're capable of."

"None of you have ever been able to do more?" I asked him, the dream still pricking at my mind.

"None that I know of and if they had, I'm sure we would know," he said. "Now, close your eyes, please."

I sighed, but I did as I was told. Taking a deep breath, I tried to clear my mind of all the things that were swirling around it. It was nearly impossible. Thoughts of my parents and Trevor kept surfacing.

Shaking my head and rolling my shoulders, I tried a little harder. I had to figure out this ability if I wanted to help Trevor. Soon, I felt myself relax. It came on suddenly, the weightlessness. I had felt this before, when I had passed out in the girls' locker room.

I had been in this place, in this darkness. Before, I had been thrust in. It was terrifying, but this was calming, soothing. The emptiness was comforting in a way, foreign yet familiar, almost as if I were sleeping but awake.

Still, I knew that couldn't be the case, because now I saw shadows of black and grey swirling into a form before my eyes. A house seemed to materialize out of the darkness. I could see only the structure, its surroundings still shrouded in the gloom of the darkness of my mind.

Keira's house. Or rather, her host parent's house. I had only been here once to pick Keira up. At the time, nothing seemed odd about how quiet and dark it was. Looking back, I remembered how still the house had seemed and how quickly she had jumped out of the car. She was hiding something and I was too blind to notice.

It was dark out and the only light I had was from the moon. The house was in complete darkness. There were no inside lights on and nothing from the front porch. It was a large plantation style home that needed a bit of work. The white paint was peeling and some of the shutters were crooked where the screws needed to be replaced.

If I were being honest, the house, the entire situation, freaked me out. Why was I here? That I didn't have an answer for. I just knew that some compulsion was guiding me forward. Even if I wanted to stop, I couldn't. I had to keep going.

I made my way up the wide steps and pulled on the door. It came right open and I walked in. The first thing I noticed was the smell. It was rotten, like a trashcan that needed to be emptied. Trying not to gag, I made my way past the foyer and into the living room.

There was trash thrown all over the place and the furniture was overturned. Pictures hung askew on the wall, and mud and filth covered the floor. The sight made my heart hammer.

"Trevor!" I called and rushed into the next room, the dining room. He had to be here.

It was open to the kitchen, so as soon I as walked in, I could tell no one was in there. It was in the same condition as the living room, or maybe even worse. Cabinets were thrown open, food containers were broken, and their contents were splattered on the floor and countertops.

"Trevor!" I called again.

I heard a noise coming from upstairs. I bolted, thinking that maybe if he were in trouble, then I could do something. What were these amazing powers for if I couldn't help people?

I raced up the stairs, taking two at a time. When I reached the landing, I stood there for a moment, trying to determine where I had heard the noise. Just when I thought I might have imagined it, I heard a muffled cry coming from the right end of the hall.

Without hesitating, I ran in the direction of the noise. I rushed past a few open doors, but there was nothing in there but disarray. I burst through the door and for a moment, I couldn't comprehend what I was seeing. All I knew was that it terrified me.

Bolting straight up from the seat, with sweat pouring down my back, I tried pulling the scene back to me. I looked around the room as if that would remind me of what I had just seen.

"Are you alright?" Gabriel had stood up with me.

"I need you to take me to Keira's, her host parents' house," I said without missing a beat. "That's where Trevor is. Oh, God, what has she done to those people, Gabriel? Why wasn't I worried about them before? I didn't even think about them!"

"What did you see?" he asked, grabbing my shoulders.

"It was awful," I told him. "It was like the dreams I have been having, but this was new. The others were in the past. I saw something. It was something horrible, but I can't remember what it was. But, I know it's them, the Imprecors. Does that make sense?"

"Yeah," he said. He picked up my jacket. "Where does she live?"

"I've only been there once," I confessed. "But I know I can find it."

It sounded crazy. Gabriel hesitated. He trusted in my ability fully, I could sense it, but he was afraid. I suppose I was too in that moment, but I had to do something. If I didn't then that meant I wouldn't get to Trevor in time. In time for what? I had no idea, but I was determined to find out.

"They'll never let us leave," Gabriel said.

"They'll have to," I took my jacket from him, "This is our job. We save people, right?"

"You don't know Abbott and what you mean to him," he said.

"I don't care," I pushed passed him, "I'm going and if you're a Guardian, a Mavors, you'll come with me."

Gabriel stood up straighter, as if my words hit him like a gut punch. He followed after me as we pushed through the door. As if Abbott had a sixth sense, he and the others were in the training room waiting. I said nothing as we walked past them.

"Where are you going?" he asked.

"To do my job," I said.

"Ava," he called.

I flipped him off and ran up the stairs, Gabriel at my back. I could hear him cursing behind me. I didn't give him time to say much more.

Gabriel took the lead and we entered a garage. He grabbed a key and soon we were inside a large SUV. It was sleek and new, nothing like his car. I looked over and noticed his vintage roadster still in a crumbled heap in the corner.

Before Abbott and the others could stop us, we had peeled out of the garage and down the driveway. I could see them all standing on the porch in the rearview mirror. I half expected the magical barrier to prevent us from going through, but the threshold let us pass.

I could feel it though. It was like static electricity all over my body. Gabriel must have felt it too because he shivered and rubbed his face, trying to shake off the feeling.

"Turn here," I pointed after we were on the road for about 15 minutes. "And then there."

We drove a little further and my confidence wavered. What if what I saw was just an illusion and I was panicking for nothing? No, that couldn't be it. It had felt so real. I might not be able to recall what was in that room, but the sense of danger I'd felt was anything but fake.

"Here, this road," I blurted, causing Gabriel to brake suddenly.

He turned down a dirt road that we soon realized was a driveway. Eventually, a large white house came into view, the house from my vision.

"This is it," I said.

Before Gabriel had the SUV in park and the ignition turned off, I was out the door.

"Ava, wait." He grabbed me just as I was about to walk up the stairs. "If there are Imprecors in there, you can't just go barging in."

"I have the dagger," I said.

"But no training," he countered. "We need a plan."

"Our plan is to do whatever is necessary to get Trevor out of there," I told him. "I have the dagger and these amazing abilities. I managed with my...mother. I'll manage now. You're the one that's going in defenseless. I should be worried about you."

"I have this." He pulled out a revolver.

"Will that thing work on them?" I felt nervous.

"It has been blessed." He cocked the revolver's hammer. "They won't kill them, but they'll slow them down. Let me go in first. You've had no training..."

"Gabriel..."

"I don't even want you using that if you don't have to. Okay? Please?"

"Okay, alright. Let's just go."

He walked up the stairs ahead of me, gun drawn but held low. It was as if he was expecting trouble, but he didn't want to risk hurting anyone who didn't deserve it. He knocked on the door, but there was no answer. He knocked again, still nothing.

Gabriel looked back at me and then I nodded, giving him the go-ahead. He turned the knob and gently pushed the door open. We stepped in and Gabriel quickly swept the entrance. The first thing to hit me was that smell. I covered my mouth and nose for a moment. Gabriel didn't react. Either he didn't smell it or he was trained not to notice.

The living room looked exactly as it did in my vision. Gabriel stepped over a broken vase and made his way into the dining area. I was close behind him. Fear coursed through me, but I tried my best to keep it in check so it didn't overpower me.

The thought of what we might find upstairs scared me. I wanted to say that to Gabriel, but I couldn't do it. Once he swept the downstairs, then I'd let him lead me up to that room. What we'd find, I didn't know, but I knew it would be horrible.

As we headed up the stairs, my hands shook and I felt nauseous. I gulped, trying to keep the bile down. Gabriel looked back at me as if he could sense my unease. I just shrugged, and he continued upstairs. We reached the landing and began exploring every room.

Each one was in a different state of disarray. Mattresses were torn, closet doors off hinges, and clothes shredded across the floor. The smell intensified the further down the hall we went. Finally, when we were nearly to the last door, I reached out and stopped him.

"What is it?" he whispered.

"I don't know what we're going to find behind that door, but..." I paused. "It's going to be bad."

"The vision?"

I nodded. He took a deep breath, trying to regain his composure, and moved forward. I didn't move for a moment, but I couldn't let him go in there by himself. This was my fight and Gabriel needed me, as untrained as I was.

Putting one foot in front of the other, I caught up with him.

Gabriel gave me one last look before he nudged the door open with his gun. The room was cast in darkness and when he tried the light switch, nothing happened. He coughed as the smell hit him full force.

Gabriel pulled out a flashlight and shone it about the room. We saw a window at the far end that had been plastered with mud and newspaper. Gabriel made his way over and began pulling off the strips. As the dim sunlight filtered in, bits of the room came into a focus.

I scanned around as Gabriel pulled off more of the paper. Just as he removed the last strip, an image that would never leave my mind was revealed. I gasped, unable to muster up a scream, and jumped backwards.

Gabriel spun around, aiming his gun in the direction he believed the threat was coming from. But when his eyes landed on what had startled me, he lowered his weapon.

"Dear God," he said, his voice full of anguish.

Three withered bodies were laid across a king sized bed. They were in an advanced stage of decomposition, but you could still tell some features. There was no doubt that there was one female and two males. The older male and female clung to what looked like their child. The boy couldn't have been any older than 12 or so.

"It's a coven," Gabriel said. "They've nested here."

"Trevor?" I asked him, tears in my eyes.

"He's fine," a familiar voice said behind us. "Have you come to bargain?"

Keira stood at the doorway, leaning her shoulder against the frame as if we weren't standing in a room with three dead bodies on the bed.

"Keira." I moved forward, but Gabriel grabbed my arm. "Keira, why? These people—"

"Mean nothing to me." She moved into the room, and I noticed that Gabriel followed her every move with the barrel of his gun. "They were a necessary sacrifice for us, for Mother."

"We're friends, Keira," I told her.

"No, darling, I pretended to be your friend," she laughed.

"Trevor, where is he?" I asked her, suddenly very afraid. "I swear if you hurt him—"

"You'll what?" She smiled at me. "You're not even properly trained yet. Technically, this is just me against Gabe and trust me, I'm far stronger."

She doubted me, and I could feel my pride take a hit. I remembered what I did against them in the park. Could I call that power forward again?

"One more step and I'll put a bullet in you," Gabriel threatened. "And you know this isn't just a regular gun, witch."

"That gun won't do much to us," she sneered.

"Oh, it'll hurt you," he said. "You haven't been fully converted, have you? You're close. That's why the dagger's poison still stings. Where is the other one Ava got? Did she make it?"

I was listening to his words, not sure of what he was saying. Keira was with the Imprecors, but wasn't exactly one of them. Not yet. She had power though, that much was for sure.

"When did they recruit you?" he asked. "This year? Last year? Twenty years ago? How old are you? How long have you been their slave?"

"You know, your father was just as brave. You see where that got him," she told him, and I could feel Gabriel tense as he stepped forward, the gun steady in his strong hands.

"I am not my father," he told her. "You're going to back off and let us out of here or I'll pump you so full of silver, it'll be coming out of your eyes."

"You need to learn a lesson, boy." Keira's eyes narrowed. "And you don't have anywhere to go. Looks like you might just be in a bit of a pickle, sweetheart."

"Step into the light," Gabriel said to her.

She instinctively backed up.

"Step into the light," he jeered and then pointed to the bodies on the bed. "They look pretty used up to me. I bet that cut Ava gave you looks pretty nasty and with no more souls to heal you, you might not want to risk a sunburn, huh? Are you that far gone, Keira? Come on, witch, step into the light."

Keira didn't make a move. Her chest was heaving up and down. I narrowed my eyes and looked closer at her. There were dark circles around her eyes, worse than before. The skin on her face was taut and pale, almost shallow. The wound looked horrific. The skin was dying, rotting, where I had cut her. Her frame looked frail, but I knew not to be deceived. While the power of the souls of the family lying on the bed, which had rejuvenated her youth, was now fading, her strength was anything but gone.

Gabriel moved me back toward the window. Just then, figures appeared at the door behind Keira. They were cloaked and hidden in the darkness, so I couldn't make out any distinguishing features. It didn't matter though. I knew who they were.

"Gabriel," I said, fear clear in my voice.

He pulled me closer to him and opened the curtains as wide as he could. The figures hissed and sulked back a bit. The light hurt them. Gabriel opened the window and began to push me out onto the sloped roof. My shoes hit the slick shingles, but thankfully found purchase. He followed me, his gun still pointed at the figures in the room.

"Do you see a way down?" he asked me, not taking his eyes off of them.

"Not really." I began to walk the length of the roof and finally saw where we might be able to shimmy down a post of the porch.

I ran back to him, trying to keep a hand on the side of the house so I wouldn't lose my balance.

"Come on." I touched his arm, but he didn't budge.

I could see Keira and the others still standing there. I didn't doubt for a second that if the sun weren't in the sky, they would have already killed Gabriel. They needed me. Keira cut her eyes at me as if she knew exactly what I was thinking.

"Did you kill him? Did you kill my parents? Was it you that ended their lives or was it all of you?" he asked her.

"Gabriel, don't," I tried to reason with him.

Keira merely smiled at him and said, "If I did? What will you do to me?"

"You know what I'll do." He ground his teeth.

"Do you promise to make it hurt?" she teased, winking at him. "I like it rough."

"Let's go," I tugged this time, "Gabriel! Look at me."

His grey eyes blazed in my direction. For a moment. it was as if he didn't realize who he was looking at or where he was. Then his eyes settled on my face.

"Ava..." Tears gathered at the corner of his eyes.

"I know," I said, thinking about my own parents. "Not right now. She has Trevor. We have to be smart."

He nodded and looked back at Keira one last time. "I'll be seeing you."

"Promises," she sighed. "Don't worry about dear Trevor. I'll keep him safe until we meet again."

I turned Gabriel around, and then we climbed down to the porch. I hurried him to the car and shoved him inside before he changed his mind and charged back into the house.

Ava

We had driven back in silence. The only thing this little expedition had accomplished was absolutely nothing. We were no closer to finding Trevor and were nearly cornered by Keira and the other Imprecors. Abbott spent about an hour yelling at us about that fact when we returned.

We had learned that Trevor's family was missing, too. Gabriel had gone to his house to check on them, and his parents were nowhere to be seen. Keira was sure to cover her tracks, though. She'd emailed the school from his dad's email address to let them know that the family had to fly to Ohio for an emergency. Apparently, their great-great aunt was dying, and they needed to be by her side.

Bron had learned that the Imprecors had burned down my house. I sat there in shock for what seemed like the longest time. It was another way to cover their tracks. Franscisco and Melinda Black perished in the fire, along with their teenage daughter, the news was reporting. It was a natural gas leak. One spark and boom.

I had excused myself after that. I couldn't take Abbott's continued verbal assault that just seemed to be him regurgitating insults on my intelligence. For the rest of the evening, I sat in my room, trying to reconnect with whatever force had allowed me to see into that house.

Thankfully, no one interrupted me, not that they would be. As much as I tried, I couldn't find that tether I had felt earlier.

When the house was quiet and I was sure everyone had fallen asleep, I slipped on the black jacket and then slinked into the hallway. Back in my more adventurous years, I'd snuck out all the time, my parents oblivious. I tried not to think about the fact that they were gone, my home was gone, and these were now the only clothes I had to my name.

I entered the training room and the overhead lights automatically flipped on. I felt very exposed, but I was the only one there. Trying not to feel like I didn't belong, I made my way to the meditation room. I pulled open the door and nearly screamed when I saw Gabriel sitting there.

He jumped up, and the first thing I noticed was his bare chest and the large tattoo that covered it.

"I am so...I'll go." I lowered my eyes and shut the door.

As I was walking through the training room, I heard the door open behind me.

"Ava?" Gabriel called. "Are you alright? Did you need something?"

I turned to him as he slipped his shirt back on. He was covered in sweat. His dark hair was nearly dripping with it. Why did gross sweat make him look even more beautiful? I shook my head and crossed my arms over my chest.

"I just wanted to see if using the room would help me figure out where they took Trevor." I shrugged. "I've been trying all night, and it's not working."

"You're free to try," he said.

"Why are you in there?" I asked him suddenly. "Pops said you didn't use it."

"I don't," he said. "Not normally, but..."

"Trevor," I finished.

"Yeah," he said. "I can't do what you did in that room, but I can train my mind to be ready for whatever battle lies ahead."

"Well, I can't do what you did in that house," I said to him. "I need to train, and soon. I shouldn't have run away tonight."

"You just lost your whole life, Ava," he said. "No one blames you for needing a minute."

"Abbott does and I'm pretty sure Bron does as well," I sighed.

"Yeah, well, Abbott is an ass." He shrugged.

I couldn't help but laugh. He gave me a slight smile.

"Bron isn't so bad." He shrugged again. "It just takes him a little longer to warm up to people."

"It might take him a few thousand years to thaw out when it comes to me," I admitted.

"I just think he needs to get to know you," he offered.

I wasn't sure if that would really help.

"Can we start training?" I asked him. "Can you show me how to use this dagger? And that gun? Show me how to use all of this? I just want to know how to help Trevor."

"Of course, I will," he moved forward, "But first, you need to eat. We both do. Have breakfast with me, since it's now dawn, and then we'll start."

I nodded. We headed back upstairs where Pops was already cooking. He smiled at me and to my surprise, pulled me into a tight hug. I hugged him back, but let go before my emotions took over.

The rest of the houseguests came and ate their fill as well. I tried helping Pops clean up, but he shooed me away and Gabriel led me back downstairs. The others joined us as well. Kat and Reese took over the sparring ring and Bron went for the weights. I couldn't help but think that if his muscles got any bigger, they would just explode out of his skin. Lorcan smiled as he walked by and headed for the rack of swords.

"What's first?" I asked Gabriel.

"Have you ever been in a fight?" he asked me.

"Um, when I was in first grade," I shrugged, "I guess that's not a good start, huh?"

"Your abilities are more than fighting with your body," he told me. "But, you should still know in case you need it. I'm going to show you a few basic defensive moves. Once you get comfortable with it, we can move on. It's going to feel really slow at first. It's not that I don't think you can't handle more, but once you master these moves, everything else will come easily."

"Okay," I told him. "And then the dagger training?"

"I can help you there." Lorcan came up with a long sword in his hands. "Gabriel is our best fighter, but I am more skilled with the blade, right, Gabriel?"

"You are," Gabriel said after a moment, his jaw tight.

"Just let me know when you're ready, Ava," Lorcan said and then went back to his corner of the room.

I watched him swinging the blade around as if he were in a dance. He seemed to know what he was doing. Gabriel cleared his throat and I brought my focus back around to him.

We spent hours on these defensive moves he claimed were supposed to be so easy. To me, they seemed like I was twisting my body in ways it wasn't supposed to go.

"We should break," he told me.

"I'm fine," I said, my body sweaty and achy.

"Ava," he said. "It's 6:00pm. We need to eat. I appreciate your enthusiasm, but you won't be able to do much if you don't take care your basic needs like food and rest."

"You don't have to be so preachy," I huffed as I stormed past him, grabbing my jacket off the bench.

It wasn't fair to be so short with him. He was right. I was tired, hungry, and I knew I smelled awful. But I was angry. Even if I did go up there and take a shower, I didn't have any clean clothes to change into.

Barreling into my room, I threw the dagger and jacket on the desk and sat in the chair. I was breathing heavy, mostly out of anger. I couldn't just sit here smelling. Even if I had to Febreze my clothes and sit in a towel, I had to shower.

Stripping down, I got in the shower and washed the day's work off of me. I wrapped the towel around me and laid on the bed. Gabriel said I had to eat and I knew he was right, I just didn't want to put those disgusting clothes back on.

There was a knock on my door, and I quickly sat up.

"Yeah?" I called.

"Hey," it was Gabriel, "Can I come in?"

"Um," I went to the door and cracked it, "I just got out of the shower."

"Oh, sorry," he kept his eyes on mine, "Uh, Pops washed the clothes you came here in. So you could have a spare. There are some stains he couldn't get out. If you need to wash yours, I can show you were the laundry room is."

He handed me the clothes and I carefully took them from him with one hand, keeping the towel secure with the other.

"Thank you," I told him. "I do need to wash my clothes. If you give me second, can you show me where everything is?"

"Yeah." He nodded.

I closed the door and quickly got dressed. Pops had even washed and folded my underwear. It felt weird having him do these things for me. It felt even weirder that Gabriel had brought them to me. I mean, it was just underwear, but still.

When I finished, I gathered my stuff and followed Gabriel to the laundry room. After I put my clothes on to wash, he gave me a tour around the house. I knew it was basically a small mansion, but it was far bigger than I realized. There were hidden rooms and most of them were underground, just like the training room.

He showed me a long corridor that was lined with different rooms that almost made me think of classrooms. They were full of desks and the walls were lined with books. One of them had long tables and were lined with glass vials on one end and what looked like cauldrons on the other.

"Is this a school? For magic?" I asked him. "In Guntersville, Alabama?"

"Of a sort." He smiled. "We have locations like this all over the world. We utilize them when needed and get rid of them when they are compromised."

"I guess we'll be getting rid of this one soon," I said.

"Yes, I suppose so," he agreed, and I noticed the sadness in his eyes.

I guess I wasn't the only one to lose their childhood home.

"Gabriel," I stopped walking, "Why did you ask Keira about your parents? What happened?"

He stopped also and then turned to look at me. Waves of hurt seemed to roll off of him and I was sorry that I had asked. That was too personal. It had just sort of slipped out. I shouldn't pry, but he'd seemed to want answers from her.

"It happened when I was really young," he said. "It was right when we moved here. There were rumors of an Imprecors nest in Norway. I don't know why they were called by the Order, but they went. They never came back."

"I am so sorry, Gabriel," I said, reaching out and then pulling my hand back, remembering how he had reacted when I'd tried to comfort him before.

He leaned toward me, as if he actually wanted my touch this time. I just put my hands in my pockets, and he took in deep breath.

"Are you ready for dinner?" he asked.

I nodded, and we headed back upstairs. Pops had made a wonderful meal of lasagna and garlic cheese toast. There was also a lovely cobb salad with a few different dressings to choose from. I was sufficiently full, but when he tried to refuse my help with cleaning up, I didn't budge.

It wouldn't kill me to load the dishwasher, and if I were being honest, he looked exhausted. I'd noticed his hands shaking at dinner. He'd tried hiding it, and I pretended not to see. Gabriel had seemed to notice as well, so we both pitched in to help. Kat and Reese even swept the dining room and wiped things down, and to my surprise, Bron stuck around and put away all the clean dishes.

Before Bron left, he stopped me and called Gabriel over. He began signing to me and Gabriel translated for him.

"He said that you need endurance training," Gabriel said. "You got winded too quickly today. Fighting Imprecors is physical, even if you have an advantage with your powers. You need strength in all forms. He said...you really want me to say...okay, okay...he said, you're out of shape, no he's not calling you fat, you just need to be able to keep up and you need to start running, lifting weights, and drinking more water."

"Wow, gym rat," I looked at him, "Tell me how you really feel."

Bron smiled and walked away. Gabriel laughed, shrugging. I grabbed my clothes from the dryer and headed for the stairs.

"Ava?" I heard Abbott say.

I turned and saw him standing in the entryway to the study. Gabriel raised his eyebrows at me and went back to the kitchen to check on Pops. I wanted to throw my dagger at him for abandoning me.

Every time I looked at Abbott, anger flared inside me.

"Yes?" I answered, not budging from the stairs.

"Can I have a word?" He gestured toward the office.

I sighed, not wanting to ever be alone in a room with him again.

"It will only take a moment," he said.

I nodded and entered the room with my bundle of clothes. He sat at the desk, but when he noticed I wasn't about to do the same, he started talking.

"High-ranking members of the Mavors will arrive in a few days," he said, straightening his clearly expensive shirt.

"Okay." I shrugged as if that should matter to me.

"We will have a ceremony," he said. "We would like to fully induct you into the Mavors. We can fill you in on the ceremony procedures."

"Okay," I repeated.

"I had Bron venture into town and get you a few essentials." He picked up a large duffle bag from under the desk. "Seeing as you have lost your belongings."

I took the bag from him, surprised by his thoughtfulness.

"Thank you," I said.

"The clothes are rather plain," he pointed out. "Just the basics and toiletry items. If there is anything else you need, please let me know."

"Right," I nodded, "Thanks again."

"I have one more thing for you." He stood up and walked over to a garment bag. "The banquet is formal. If you wouldn't mind wearing this, I would appreciate it."

I unzipped the bag and looked at the evening gown. It was fancy and expensive. My eyes widened. This was more than a banquet.

"I'm not some show pony, Abbott." I glared at him.

"I'm not asking you to be," he said. "But there are certain ways things need to be handled. We are a very old Order, Ava, and we have waited a very long time to find you. All I am asking is that you humor us for one evening."

"While Trevor is being tortured?" I reminded him. "You want me to parade around in a pretty dress? I should train and we should look for him."

"You are training," he tried reassuring me. "And we are looking. Bron and Reese have already been back out to that house. The Imprecors have moved on. Kat is working on a tracking spell. We'll find them. Until then, our Order needs a bit of hope in the fact that we may be close to finally ending this battle with the Imprecors. You can give that to them. And keep in mind, these people are skilled warriors. More warriors mean our chances, along with your help, have significantly increased."

I took the dress from him and he smiled in relief. I didn't like this, but it seemed that the Mavors had strange and flamboyant customs. He was being decent, and I honestly didn't want to fight with anyone at the moment. We needed to work together. That didn't mean I trusted him for one second. He may say this was for the Order, but I felt that Abbott had intentions of his own.

The next few days were hard. I had yet to connect to that ability again. Gabriel was trying to teach me to channel my power into my movements. He didn't have any himself, so what he was trying to convey was merely theory. I had studied with Pops, trained with my dagger with Lorcan, and Kat was teaching me spell work. Bron put me through a lot of physical training, and Reese even showed me some archery work.

It was all interesting, and amazing, but it overwhelmed me. I couldn't grasp any of it. Anytime I thought I had the upper hand, Gabriel would knock me on my butt, Lorcan would have a blade at my throat, and I had melted at least five of Kat's glass vials. If Abbott was hoping to show me off, he was going to be sorely disappointed.

The day of the banquet, I woke up with the worst migraine I'd had in a long time. I honestly hadn't noticed they had stopped until just then. I ran for the bathroom and purged my stomach. I laid on the tile floor for a while. The coolness felt good on my face. After a moment, I heard a knock on my door.

I felt a sudden pang in my stomach. Great. Not only was my head killing me, my ovaries had decided to betray me as well. I tried to think about what day it was and realized it was about that time. I searched in the bag that Abbott had given me to see if there were any feminine products so I could be prepared.

Nothing. Great. Men!

"Ava? Are you up?" It was Gabriel. I was supposed to meet him for breakfast and then go train some before the first guests arrived.

I tried to say something, but just then I had to vomit again. He must have heard me because he came barreling into my room. I felt him grab my hair out of the toilet bowl. This wasn't the first time he had seen me barf all over the place. So, I shouldn't have been that mortified, but I was.

"I'm fine," I said when I was done.

"You don't look fine," he told me.

I made my way over to the sink and washed my mouth out. He was standing behind me as I brushed my teeth a few times.

"Is there anything I can do?" he asked.

"Not unless you can magically make my migraine medicine un-burn in a house fire." I leaned against the sink.

I wrapped my arms around my body, trying to settle my stomach. He reached out his hand and after a second, I took it. He led me back into my room and helped me into bed. I hated feeling so weak, but the room was absolutely spinning.

"Some great warrior I am," I told him with a laugh, putting my hands over my face. "If the Imprecors came now, they'd kick my butt."

"We're well protected," he said, but it was little comfort. "I'll be right back."

Like the wind, he was gone from my room. After a few hours, and me trying to fall back to sleep, I heard noises outside my door. Hushed tones and what sounded like arguing.

Kat came in without knocking. Abbott quickly followed her and then Gabriel. Good thing I wasn't in a compromising position. As I laid there with my both my head and stomach killing me, I looked up at them with murder in my eyes.

"Kat has whipped up something for your head," Abbott said. "Please drink it quickly so we can be sure you're ready for tonight."

"Your thoughtfulness is so touching." I rolled my eyes as I sat up and took the cup from Kat.

"It should be pretty fast acting," Kat said. "I've used it for others with headaches and migraines."

"Nothing has ever really helped me," I said as I drank the concoction.

"That's because your pain is magical," she said. "All Mavors have issues with their body accepting the power at first. This usually helps. I hope it will help you. I made it a bit stronger because your power is different, to say the least."

I nodded and handed her the cup. I flinched and grabbed my side as a cramp came on. It was embarrassing, but I couldn't help it if I hurt.

"Is that a normal reaction?" Abbott asked.

"No," Kat said. "Are you alright?"

"Yeah, it's not that," I told them.

"Well, what is it?" Abbott asked. "We can't have this tonight of all nights. Kat, fix this."

"The only thing that can fix this, Abbott, is some chocolate and Midol," I snapped. "Since your little care package lacked basic essentials for the female body, I either need to go to the store or have someone else go buy me a box of tampons. Considering this night is so important to you, do you want to volunteer?"

"Oh," his face went red, "Well, then, uh..."

"I have something for you, Ava." Kat was smiling.

Gabriel rubbed his hand over his face, trying to wipe away a smile. The group left, and soon Kat returned with what I needed.

"So, are you wearing a fancy dress, too?" I asked her.

"Yeah," she said, sitting down on my bed. "Think of it as a graduation. You won't be the only fledgling presented if that makes you feel better. Whenever one of us finishes their training, they are inducted into the Mavors. It usually happens on your fifteenth birthday. You're just starting late."

"Great," I sighed. "I love being behind."

"You are far from behind," she laughed.

"Are you serious?" I looked at her. "I have done nothing but screw up all week."

"Is that how you see it?" She propped herself up on her elbow, her dark eyes searching mine. "Ava, you are leaps and bounds beyond what some Mavors are twice your age."

"I've destroyed a lot of your equipment," I pointed out. "Do you not remember me setting things on fire?"

"Oh, I remember," she laughed again. "The point is, you set it on fire. Do you know how long it takes us to conjure magic? We have to study for years to even get the slightest spark, and not all of us can. You've only been studying magic for about a week and you can call an entire flame. That's amazing."

"Well, I'm still lying in the bed with period cramps," I said.

"You're only human." Kat patted my head and then stood up. "Are you feeling any better?"

"I am actually," I told her. "I think I'm going to go to the training room for a bit."

"I would tell you to take it easy, but I don't think you'll listen." She opened the door. "I, on the other hand, am going to take a long bath and do my makeup."

"Oh, dolling up for anyone in particular?" I asked in a teasing way.

"Myself," she winked and then said, "But my ex is going to be here, so I have to make her wish she never broke up with me."

I laughed as she walked away. Kat was growing on me and that made me nervous. My track record with friends was spotty.

Making my way downstairs, I grabbed a granola bar from the kitchen. When I got into the training room, I expected to see Gabriel there, more like hoping, but Lorcan was practicing with his long sword.

"Are you feeling better?" he asked when he saw me.

"Kat to the rescue," I told him. "I wanted to get in some more training today before the guests arrive. I thought Gabriel would be here."

"We can work on more dagger work," he offered.

"Sure," I agreed.

We spent the rest of the time with Lorcan showing me more ways to use the dagger. He was clearly very skilled. I wondered if he thought my skills were as advanced as Kat did. I wasn't about to ask him. I felt years behind everyone. Lorcan could do things with this dagger that I could only dream of. I half considered just giving it to him, or Gabriel, and waiting until I felt more comfortable with it.

Holding the dagger in my hand, I couldn't deny that it felt right. As soon as I picked it up, the small blade just seemed to belong with me. Still, it scared me. I saw what it had done to Keira. It held a power I didn't understand and one I was afraid to wield.

Spending time with Pops shed some light on who Tepkunset was and what she could do, which were amazing things. The more she connected with her power, the more she could control it. Her abilities allowed her to connect to the very spirit of the earth. It was all very elemental, but not in the sense of controlling the elements. They were there to fuel her power over will, over something close to creation. She didn't create life, but could mold fate. She could bless and she could curse.

I had also learned that the power came with a heavy price. She was, after all, very human. She experienced anger, sorrow, love, and everything that came with being flesh and blood. That's why meditation was so important, to control and not let her emotions get the better of her. Losing control could cost people their lives. She became both loved and feared.

Before the Mavors had lost contact with her, they'd learned that she had married and had children. None of them, that they knew of, had abilities. Soon, with the invasion of English settlers, Tepkunset and her people had been lost to time.

"Damn!" I cursed as I cut my hand on the blade.

I made my way to edge of the mat, so I wouldn't drip blood on it. It wasn't too deep, but it hurt. Lorcan acted fast and grabbed a First Aid kit. He cleaned my wound and began wrapping gauze around it.

"I'm sure you won't need this by tomorrow," he smiled at me, "since you're Wolverine."

"It's the only thing I knew to compare it to," I laughed. "Cut me some slack."

"It's fine." He finished with the tape and pressed down on it gently. "Nothing wrong with liking comic book heroes. Nerdy girls are hot."

I resisted the urge to roll my eyes. I did raise an eyebrow which just made him smile. Lorcan was shamelessly flirting with me. Not that I wasn't flattered. He was a good-looking guy, but he was several years older and he had introduced himself to me under false pretenses.

So did Gabriel, a voice in my head said.

"Ava," Gabriel's voice sounded from the door.

I jumped, as if I had been caught doing something wrong. I felt like I had betrayed him somehow. It was a ridiculous reaction. I had tried reaching out to him, and he'd pushed me away. Wasn't he the one who said we were fated? It made me want to shout at him. It made me want to punch him. More than that, I just wanted to feel his lips on mine again. Lorcan still sat there, smirking at Gabriel.

"Abbott wanted me to see how you were," he said, looking down at my bandaged hand. "The guests have just landed and will be here shortly. Perhaps we should get ready?"

"Yeah." I nodded and headed for the stairs.

Lorcan stood up but didn't move. As I took the first step, I looked back and saw that they were still both standing there.

"You guys coming?" I asked.

"In a minute," Gabriel said without turning to look at me. "Lorcan and I have some things to discuss."

Gabriel

Lorcan and I stared at each other for a moment. He smirked at me, and I felt my temper ignite. There were a lot of things I wanted to say and even more things I wanted to do to his perfectly symmetrical face. I refrained because I wasn't about to have a pissing contest with him over Ava. I knew how I felt about her. My affections for her were true.

"You wanted to talk?" he asked.

"I do," I told him.

"About Ava?" His grin deepened.

"No," I told him, and he seemed a bit surprised. "About Trevor."

"Your friend," he said.

"Yes," I replied. "Abbott told me your abilities in meditation far exceed most of the Mavors, even those with more experience."

"I've honed my abilities, yes," he confessed, and it didn't sound like a brag.

"I wanted to ask a favor of you." I hated asking him for anything. "Will you try to reach him? Will you try to reach Trevor or reach out and find him?"

"I've tried that. Pops asked me," he told me.

"Yeah, but you haven't tried it with me," I said. "Trevor is like a brother to me. With me there, won't the connection be stronger?"

"It's possible," he admitted and then continued when I said nothing. "You want me to try now?"

"If you don't mind," I told him.

He shrugged and led the way to the meditation room. When we entered, he lit the fire and rummaged around in a few of the cabinets. I had never had the inclination to look inside them, so I wasn't exactly sure what was in there.

Lorcan came back to the fire, which was already filling the room with intensifying heat. He tossed in a few dried herbs and flowers. When he began taking off his clothes, I raised my eyebrow.

"Don't get excited." He winked. "It helps me concentrate."

I narrowed my eyes at him as he stripped down to his boxers and took his place in front of the fire. He looked too close for what was safely acceptable, but the heat from the flames didn't seem to bother him. Shifting in my seat, I watched as the smoke of the fire turned a dark shade of yellow.

I assumed it was the ingredients he had added. The room smelled heavily laced with the scent of wildflowers, and I felt my body grow heavy and relaxed. It was an unnerving feeling, but at the same time, almost welcoming.

"What did you do?" I asked, and I noticed my words were slurred.

"Be quiet," he said.

I wanted to say something else, but the words were lost somewhere in my mind. My eyes closed against my will, and I felt my body slump in my seat.

Darkness swept over me like a wave. It was more than the blackness that came with sleep. It was pure and all-consuming. For a moment, I felt and heard nothing. I thought Lorcan had acted out his aggression and put me out of my misery, but I was hyperaware and knew I was conscious. Or, rather, not awake, but maybe lucid dreaming.

"You're not dreaming," he said.

"What the hell?" I turned around.

That's what it felt like. And when I did so, his face came into view. Then, slowly, the rest of his body seemed to materialize out of the inky blackness. Thankfully, he was fully clothed. I looked down and I could see myself as well.

"What is this?" I asked him.

"It's just what I can do," he said. "We all have our strengths, right?"

I looked at him. He was being nonchalant about it, but this was amazing. None of the Mavors could do this, no matter how good they were at meditation. And, if I were being honest with myself, I wasn't this good at anything.

"You're cutting yourself short," he said. "You could kick all our asses."

"Are you in my head?" I asked him.

"Yep." He smiled.

"Get out," I almost snarled.

"If I do, the connection is severed," he explained. "I'll try not to pry too much. But, thanks for thinking I'm something special."

"I never said that." I felt my nostrils flare.

"Calm down." He put his hands up. "I like you, even though you want to pummel me. You don't see how the other Mavors look at you. No one has your abilities, Gabriel. You were blessed with strength that none of us have."

"Can you find Trevor?" I asked, ignoring him.

"I'll have to search through that head of yours," he said and then raised his hands defensively. "I'll only look for memories of Trevor, just to make an emotional connection. I'll warn you though, it's going to feel really strange."

"Fine," I sighed. "How stran..."

A chill started at the top of my head and ran down my body as if someone had just dumped a bucket of ice cold water over me.

Flashes of memories played through my mind. I could see Trevor's face, memories of our life together, the first time we met, times we spent gaming, dinner at his house, all leading up to the last time I saw him. He was at the mercy of Keira, his face pale and gaunt. My heart clenched with guilt and worry.

The memories slowly faded, like the writing on a chalkboard being erased. In their place, I could see a small room with a figure huddled in the corner. I instantly knew it was Trevor, even though he was shrouded in darkness.

"Trevor!" I called.

His head lifted. But just when I thought he was going to look at me, a door opened and Keira walked through. Anger washed over me, and I moved forward.

Without warning, the scene shifted. It was like being knocked off my feet. My arms reached out for something and found Lorcan. He pulled me back up.

Looking around, I saw we weren't in the small room anymore. It was my room, but it was years ago. I knew this because I still had my dinosaur sheets. My heart sank. A noise caught my attention, and I turned toward the door just as my mother walked in.

"Mom," I whispered.

A thousand emotions flooded my body as tears pricked my eyes. My dad, who was carrying me in his arms, followed her. I was asleep, holding onto a stuffed animal. He placed me on the bed and kissed my forehead. Mom leaned down and kissed me as well, brushing my dark hair back gently.

"I hate leaving him," she said.

"I do, too," he agreed. "We'll be back soon."

"It gets harder every time we have to go." She sounded like she was fighting back tears.

"I know." He took her hand as she stood up.

"I wouldn't trade a life with you for anything, Lewis," she sighed. "This is our mission, but..."

"What kind of life is this for him?" he finished for her.

She nodded as a tear fell down her face. My dad wiped it away and kissed her gently, hugging her to his body.

"We can stop," he said suddenly.

"What?" She looked up at him.

"After this mission," he told her. "It can be our last one. We can leave. We'll take Gabe and we'll leave."

"We can't leave the Mavors." She shook her head. "We made a promise. We took an oath."

"We did," he agreed. "But Gabriel hasn't. We don't have to put this burden on him. We can give him a normal life. As normal a life as someone like us can have. He'll question why he's stronger and faster, and we'll tell him in time, but we can raise him to just be a normal kid."

"Do you really want to do this?" she asked. "And Pops?"

"Pops will understand," he said.

"And Myra? The others?" She wrapped her arms around her body.

"I don't care what they think," he said. "They'll accept it or they won't. People leave the order all the time. They're shunned, yes, but it's their choice. We can make that choice for our family, for our son."

"Okay," she nodded, "Okay. For our family."

"For our family." He hugged her again.

I stood there watching this play out like a movie as the scene faded. My parents were going to leave the Mavors. I wondered if they ever told Pops. Surely he would have told me if they had. Had they had a chance to tell anyone? Their last mission. It had been the one to take their lives. They were never able to have that normal life they had wanted.

"Gabriel?" Lorcan said and touched my shoulder.

We were thrust forward again. It felt like we had been catapulted through time and space. This time we both hit hard and painfully. Lorcan coughed, trying to catch his breath as he pushed himself up on his elbows. Groaning, I rolled over on my back.

"No," Lorcan whispered. "Wake up, Gabriel. We have to get out of here."

"What?" I raised up.

The scene had shifted to an elaborate den. I recognized it as one of the living quarters of our main Mavors compound, located in Denmark.

I had been here only once, but it was imprinted in my mind because it was right after my parents died. I clearly remembered pulling up to the imposing structure, sitting next to Pops in that cold black car.

It was like a castle with its high turrets and long halls. We had spent the summer there after burying my parents in the Mavors graveyard. That's when my training had begun. That's where I had first met Lorcan and the others.

I saw him then, a younger Lorcan, head full of soft brown curls. He was sitting in front of the fireplace, a red flame dancing in the center. Myra, his mother, was standing over him. Tears were streaming from his closed eyes.

Abbott came storming through the door. His icy blue eyes were full of rage. He looked from Lorcan to Myra.

"Lorcan, put your clothes on," he said.

I looked back and noticed Lorcan was sitting in front of the fire in nothing more than his underwear. Lorcan didn't look up at Abbott, and his eyes remained closed.

"He can't hear you," Myra told him.

"What did you do?" Abbott walked up to her.

"I haven't done a thing, Callum." Myra turned to him. "Our son is talented, but he must practice and hone his ability. We agreed..."

"I know what we agreed to," he spat at her. "But he is a child. You can't expect..."

"I am High Priestess." She stood to her fullest height. "I have a responsibility. And he is more than just a child. He's a Mavors. It is his duty. It is also your duty. We just lost the Matthews. My sweet friend Sasha is gone. Our ranks dwindle every day. Our children, as hard as it is for me to say, are our future. If we ever want to find Tepkunset's heir and prevent Thyana's rise, we must do this."

"I know that, Myra," Abbott said. "But we can't use him like this. He isn't a pawn. He is our son."

"Exactly," she said. "He is the son of the High Priestess and a very powerful Council Member. If we find Tepkunset's heir, he will make a suitable companion."

Abbott looked at her like he didn't recognize her. Myra didn't blink for a moment, as if she had just seen Lorcan's future all played out in her mind.

"Wake him," Abbott said.

"What?" she asked.

"Wake him," he said. "He's had enough practice for today. He can be your prodigy tomorrow. For now, I'm taking him to spend time with his friends."

Myra straightened her shoulders and then walked over to Lorcan. She leaned down and whispered in his ear. It was just a simple call of his name, and he opened his eyes.

I turned and looked at Lorcan. He stared at the scene before him. I could tell he had never known that exchange between his parents had taken place. When the scene faded to black, he stood there for a moment longer and then we were jolted forward again.

My eyes shot open. Both of us were back in the meditation room. Lorcan was already on his feet, putting his close back on.

"Lorcan," I started.

"No one has been able to do that before," he said with his back to me. "I'm usually the one in control in there. I guess you're stronger than you think, Matthews, because you somehow hijacked my brain."

"Lorcan, I didn't mean..." I said.

"Don't," he said.

"I just..." I began.

"I don't need your sympathy, Matthews." He rounded on me as he slipped on his shirt. His eyes looked wild. "I know exactly why I was born and bred. It's why we were all born, right? To continue the Mavors. Well, all except you, right? Your parents were ready to give it all up. Good for you."

He stormed out of the room. I sat there for a moment. Finally, I got up and followed him into the training room.

"I just wanted to say, I'm sorry," I told him, and he stopped without turning around. "I didn't mean to see that. I won't say anything. And, please, don't tell anyone what you saw."

"What? That you have loving parents?" He sort of laughed.

"No, that they were going to leave the Mavors," I said.

"It happens a lot." He shrugged and finally turned to look at me.

"I know," I said. "But, I don't want anyone knowing that I know."

"Why?" He was confused.

"Because...I just want that to be something they shared," I said.

"Sure, Matthews." He shook his head in frustration.

We stood there for a minute. There was a lot that had just happened. Secrets we didn't know we wanted to know had just been exposed, and we couldn't even keep them to ourselves. Even if we didn't want to, Lorcan and I had to learn to form some of sort of trust between us.

"Is that why you're interested in her?" I asked him.

"What do you mean?" His eyes shot up at me.

"Ava," I said. "Is that why you're so...do you see her like a job? Don't even try to pretend you aren't working some angle. I've noticed your interest, and I'm sure she has, too. I'm just curious what your endgame is."

"My parents might have my life planned out for me," he said. "And, yeah, they might want me to pursue Ava because of who she is, but trust me when I say this, I don't need their help to see that Ava is special. So no, she's not a job. I care for her."

My heartbeat quickened in my chest. I tried not to let my jealously take over, but I couldn't stop the thoughts from running through my head.

"Are you going to threaten me? Tell me to stay away from her?" he asked, a smile spreading across his lips.

"No," I said.

"Really?" He seemed surprised. "You're not going to mark your territory?"

"I don't have to," I told him. "I have never doubted Ava's feelings for me."

"So confident," he laughed.

"It's not confidence in myself," I told him. "It's in her. It's in the destiny I know we share."

"I guess we'll see." He smiled.

"I guess," I agreed.

Lorcan stared at me a moment longer. Without another word, he turned and left me standing in the middle of the training room.

I sighed and made my way upstairs to get ready for the banquet. As I showered, playing over what had transpired in the meditation room,

I couldn't help but focus on Trevor. I knew that was him in that small room. We were no closer to finding him.

Lorcan's abilities were amazing but unpredictable. I wasn't sure if it was him or me that had made his visions so unstable, but one thing that gave me solace was seeing that Trevor was still alive.

"Just hang in there, Trev," I said.

Keira

Keira could feel the poisonous magic of the blade coursing through her body. It had made her extremely weak, her bones ached, and her skin felt like dried parchment. She couldn't remember feeling this vulnerable in a very long time. One of the others, who Ava had sliced on the arm, was far worse than she was.

They would both make it. The blade had pierced none of their vital organs, so they wouldn't die. However, just a slight cut was enough to make them violently ill.

Velia came into the room of the new building they had settled in. She moved like shadows, silent and quick. Keira watched her for a moment as she moved around the room, putting the roots she had foraged from the nearby woods into a mortar. She began crushing the roots and adding in water to make it softer. After a moment, she poured it into a cauldron that was over a small flame.

Velia was old, older than all of them. She was the one who had found Keira when she was just five-years-old. Mother had sent her to Keira. She had been born with potential, but she was not the heir. Still, power coursed through her veins. She was a descendant, traces of Tepkunset's magic lived in her blood, so they brought her into the coven.

That had been 50 years ago and when she was still only seventeen in form. Mother had promised her a long life, and she had provided. That life had come at a cost. To sustain her form and feed her magic, she'd had to take the lives of other descendants and those unlucky enough to be in her path. Drunk on power, she did so gladly at first.

Now, after all these years, she wondered how long she would have to survive on scraps. Mother had promised them peace from the cruelness of humankind. Keira had suffered at the hands of her father before Velia. And, her mother had been too drunk to care. Humans were flawed, a disease on the earth.

Velia had told her of a time when her people had lived in peace. It was lush, vibrant, and they were one with nature. That was until men had come, destroying their village, killing their people, and driving them deeper into the woods. The Norse men. They had quickly forgotten all that their Mother had given them.

When they traveled to the New World, with Mother's help, they gave their thanks long enough to land. Then they no longer needed her. They clung to the green fertile fields and overstocked lakes. Her children saw beauty in the faces of Tepkunset and her people, forgetting about Mother. Thyana was a jealous goddess.

Like any loving goddess, she would remove the temptation. She would take the people, kill the land, freeze the waters. Thyana would destroy it all, piece by piece, until there was nothing left. Until all her people had was her, that would be when she would stop.

In Keira's opinion, Thyana had underestimated the Beothuk people. Tepkunset was powerful and she had the loyalty of her tribe. Not only that, the Norsemen had sided with her against their own goddess. And now, Thyana was trapped.

As pain surged through her face and body, Keira couldn't help but feel a hint of resentment for Mother. While she agreed that mankind was lost and had been for a long time, there was a part of her that believed, perhaps, Thyana wasn't the goddess for the job.

The Imprecors believed Thyana would bring a reckoning to the humans, and they would restore the earth to its former glory. Keira knew she was human, but she was also born as something more. Her loyalties to her human side had died out a long time ago, if they had even existed.

She knew what Velia was the moment they met. She had taken over her mother's body. Velia was supposed to raise her, guide her to Mother, and if she proved useful, convert her. The Imprecors began this practice as a slap in the face to the Mavors. If they could plant spies, so could they. Even though Kiera wasn't the one they were looking for, she had made a perfect addition to the coven.

Going through countless hours of practicing magic, years of it, her powers had soon become stronger than Velia's, and the old witch knew it. After all, she was a descendant of Tepkunset. Perhaps she wasn't the heir, but she was powerful.

Velia had also been the one to take over Melinda, Ava's mother. How Ava hadn't been able to detect her, with her being as powerful as they claimed, Keira didn't know. She supposed maybe her weak minded "father" had something to do with it.

"Drink." Velia brought her a cup.

Keira took the cup and drank the contents. She could feel as the magic spread through her body and settled in the cut in her cheek. Relief. The pain eased and she breathed in deeply.

"Better?" Velia asked her.

"Much better." Keira nodded. "Now, let's go get our girl."

AVA

PUTTING ON MY MAKEUP MADE ME FEEL LIKE I WAS BACK IN MY pageant days. Those were so embarrassing to recall, but my mother had insisted. She had told me they would help me build confidence and get into a good college. Thinking about times like that made me feel so lost. Even after she claimed to have taken over my mother's form she had continued to say the same things. She always encouraged me. Why had she pretended to care about my future knowing where it was headed?

I finished styling my hair and put the curling iron I'd borrowed from Kat down on the sink and turned it off. My long dark locks were curled and put into a side swept updo. I had done something similar to this for a dance once, so it wasn't hard to recreate. I looked at my reflection in the mirror and pretended for a second I was just headed to Prom instead of some weird magical induction ceremony.

For just a moment, I closed my eyes and imagined my parents were downstairs waiting for me to get ready. They were alive and hadn't been taken over by evil beings whose sole purpose was using my powers to destroy humanity. I was just a normal girl with a normal life, and an ordinary guy was going to pick me up and give me a boring corsage to match my cheap department store dress that cost way too much money.

A knock on my door brought me out of my daydream. I quickly put on my lipstick and opened the door. Kat was standing there with a wisp of a dress on. It was dark green and looked amazing on her ebony skin. Silver jewelry hung from her wrists and neck.

"Your makeup looks amazing, but why aren't you dressed?" she asked me.

"I couldn't bring myself to put it on yet," I told her as she walked into my room.

"Oh, it can't be that bad." She took the dress out of the garment bag. "Oh, Abbott went all out on this one, didn't he, and with matching shoes?"

"I suppose." I shrugged.

"Come, the guests are already arriving." She handed me the dress and pushed me to the bathroom. "Get dressed and let's go dazzle the elders."

I sighed but did as she said. The dress fit me really well. I expected it to be too big or too small. It was strange that Abbott knew my exact sizes. I tried not to let that creep me out, but I kept that thought in my mind. He was not to be trusted.

"Damn, girl," Kat said looking me up and down as I came back out.

The dress was actually really pretty. It was frosty blue with a plunging V-neckline and a sheer inset to maintain my modesty. Crafted with a sheer V-open back and a tonal lining overlaid with embroidered frosted elements, it cascaded into a flutter full length hem.

"Thanks," I laughed. "I don't have any jewelry though."

"No one is going to be looking at your jewelry," Kat said, grabbing my arm. "But, come with me and we can fix you up."

We went back to her room and she gave me a few pieces that matched my outfit. She had moved in nicely to the Matthews' home. I suspected she had been here before and that's why she was so comfortable. Or maybe Kat was just relaxed anywhere. Her room was covered in clothes, shoes, books, and apothecary wares.

We met up with Bron and Reese at the foot of the stairs. I looked around for the guests that were here, but saw no one.

"Where are they?" I asked.

"In the banquet hall," Gabriel said, coming down the stairs. "It's on the other side of the grounds, along with our guest rooms. We try to keep guests out of the main house if we're expecting this many at once."

"You're drooling," Kat leaned over and whispered in my ear.

I straightened my shoulders and closed my mouth, ignoring her comment. Gabriel was wearing an all-black suit, all the way down to his shiny black shoes, with a sapphire blue handkerchief in the pocket. Just that pop of color seemed to set him in a different light.

Gabriel had always been attractive to me. In a suit or in a plain grey t-shirt, he was better looking than any guy I had ever seen. Still, there was something different about seeing him come down the stairs like that.

Lorcan and Abbott joined us a moment later, followed closely by Pops. He looked better today, well-rested.

Soon we were out the back door and walking along a paved pathway. An extensive structure came into view a minute later. It was a modern cabin, anything but humble, with large glass windows that reached from the floor to nearly the roof. It had three pointed sections, and each one was adorned with a chimney. The trees and other plant life seemed to envelope its structure, hiding it from prying eyes.

We entered the cabin, which opened into a large foyer. Two men stood there like guards. At least, I assumed they were based on their stance and how they eyed us with suspicion. It was almost like this place didn't belong to Gabriel and Pops, as if they were guests in their own home. Perhaps they were.

"Ryland!" said a strong female voice suddenly, emerging from behind the two men.

She was an older woman with perfectly pinned up red hair, skin like ivory, and eyes a deep golden brown. The beautiful green dress she wore accentuated all of her best features, and she seemed to know it.

"My lady," he greeted her with a kiss on the cheek. "You look lovely."

"It has been too long, my friend," she returned his kiss, "Abbott, how are you?"

"I am well, my lady." He bowed slightly.

My lady? What a greeting.

"And this must be Ava." She smiled at me.

"Hello," I said, unsure if I should bow too, but thankfully she extended her hand to me and I shook it.

"I'm Myra Walsh." She smiled again.

"Myra is our High Priestess," Pops explained.

"Oh," I said, feeling suddenly nervous.

I had read about the inner workings of the Mavors in one of my study sessions with Pops. There was a hierarchy to it, a structure that helped it function. You had the High Priestess or Priest, then the Regent, and finally the Council Members. After that you were just a lowly member. The leader of the Mavors stayed in power until their death, and they were usually voted in at a rather young age.

"It's nice to meet you, ma'am...miss...I'm sorry, High Priestess." I felt my face grow hot.

"This is all new to you, Ava, it's fine." She smiled and patted my hand. "I am so sorry about what has happened to you. We didn't know that your parents were...we didn't know what the Imprecors had done to them. If we had, we would have moved sooner."

I nodded my head at her words. Myra seemed kind, but at the moment it was hard for me to trust any of the Mavors, no matter their position or rank.

"Shall we go in?" Myra asked. "There are many people who would like to meet you. Who is your escort?"

"I'm sorry?" I asked.

"It is a tradition that all new inductees have an escort, one that is already a member of the Mavors, for the ceremony," she said looking around. "Someone to stay by your side throughout the night to answer any questions you may have."

"I can."

"Me."

Gabriel and Lorcan spoke at the same time. I turned to look at both of them. Gabriel's face was red, but his head was held high. Lorcan had the biggest smirk. I rolled my eyes at him.

"Can Kat do it?" I asked her.

"That is very nontraditional." Myra looked from me to Kat. "But I don't see why not."

"Thank you," I told her.

Kat came sweeping up to me and looped her arm through mine. We followed after Myra as she led us through the double doors. The two guards looked at me with interest. Or, it seemed as though they did.

"Good choice," Kat whispered to me. "Although, Gabriel and Lorcan look completely dejected."

"Well, you said you wanted to make your ex jealous, right?" I laughed.

"Oh, and with you on my arm, I definitely will." Kat smiled. "You look hot and she will just have to deal with it."

"And thank you," I told her.

"For what?" she asked, looking over at me.

"For agreeing to do this," I shrugged my shoulders, "For being nice."

Kat nudged my hip with hers and we laughed.

Myra led us down a wide staircase into a large banquet hall full of people. I could see them staring at us. I was expecting Myra to make this grand speech and introduce me, but she merely led us to a table and showed us our seats.

Kat spent the next hour or so introducing me to people, some were the Council Members and others were just her friends. She explained to me how each district had a Council Member representative. I recalled this information from my studies, but I didn't know who they were.

Each continent, except Antarctica, had their own Chancellor, who spoke for them and that Chancellor had seven Council Members. Europe had two Chancellors because they had the most Mavor members, bringing the total number of Chancellors to seven and the Council Members to forty-nine. I was pretty sure I had met every single one of them by the time Kat was finished showing me around or showing me off.

All of them had questions about me: how was my training going, what could I do, what was my plan to defeat the Imprecors. I honestly had no clue what to tell them, but Kat always had the right words. She would simply tell them that the High Priestess had never let them down. That seemed to satisfy everyone.

The way they looked at Myra was how one looked at a savior. Kat explained that even though it was Pops and Gabriel who had found me, it was under Myra's direction and guidance. She had found the heir. Still, Pops and Gabriel were getting their own share of admiration from the crowd.

"That's her," Kat leaned over and said to me. "My ex, the one talking to Gabriel."

I had been staring at her and Gabriel for the past few minutes. The girl was about our age, but her eyes seemed much older. She had long black locks, eyes as blue as the ocean, and a body that had seen a lot of cardio. She was toned and could probably take any man in here, but there was still a femininity to her face, a softness to her lips. She was freaking Wonder Woman.

Gabriel was awfully chatty with her, and I felt my stomach do a little turn. I had no right to feel any way about him, considering I had done nothing but push him away the past week. I had even purposely avoided him tonight.

Still, when his eyes caught mine across the room, I felt my face grow hot. I about choked on my drink when he stood up and he and the girl started making their way to our table. I looked at Kat in a panic. She kept her eyes on the approaching duo.

"Hello," Gabriel said when they approached. "Ava, I wanted to introduce you to Isla Knight. Isla, this is Ava Black."

"It's nice to meet you," I told her.

"Likewise." She shook my hand and then looked at Kat. "Kat."

"Medusa," Kat took a sip of her drink. "Have you been turning men to stone with your stare tonight?"

"Only the terrible ones who thought I would ever dance with them," Isla said without missing a beat.

I liked her.

"Isla Knight not dancing?" Kat feigned surprise. "Have you forgotten how?"

"It's possible," she said. "Would you like to refresh my memory?"

Kat looked up at her and Isla stared back intensely. Gabriel and I didn't exist. I was pretty sure Isla had used me as an excuse to come talk to Kat. We both watched them with great interest.

"I'm Ava's escort," Kat said after a moment. "I don't want to be rude."

"Actually," Gabriel piped up. "I was hoping Ava would do me the honor of the next dance. So, you're free to do what you please, Kat."

Kat and I looked at each other. Apparently Gabriel was Isla's wingman and I couldn't get in the way of that.

"Um, sure," I said to Gabriel, and he took my hand.

Kat still sat there, not moving. After a moment, Isla sat down with her. Gabriel led me to the dance floor just as a new song began playing. It was classical, and I wasn't sure how to dance to it, but he didn't seem to mind. He placed his hand lightly on my waist and we began moving around the floor.

"How long have they been a thing?" I asked him after a moment. "Kat and Isla."

"For as long as I can remember." Gabriel looked over at them with a smile.

"They seem perfect for each other," I said.

"They are," he agreed. "If they could just stop fighting."

"It was nice of you to help Isla out," I told him.

"What do you mean?" he asked, looking down at me.

"By asking me to dance, you gave them some time alone." I didn't understand why I had to explain this.

"Right," he said, his grey eyes searching my face.

I felt a sudden rush of heat flood my body. Looking away, I scanned over the crowd, my anxiety suddenly getting to me. Pops had explained that the ceremony was pretty informal. They called your name, you stood before the Council, they asked you a few questions, and you committed to a sect within the Mavors.

Still, it was like I could feel that these people expected something of me, something more than just defeating the Imprecors. I didn't know how I was going to do any of it. At that thought, a sound, like bells, came over the room. Everyone stopped dancing.

"The ceremony is about to begin."

I looked for Kat and I saw her red-faced, sitting at the table alone.

"Are you alright?" I asked her.

"I'm fine," she said, but there were tears in her eyes.

"Kat..." I touched her hand.

"I'll be ok, love." She tried smiling.

"Kat, you don't have to do this for me if you don't feel like it," I said. "I'm sure I can find someone else to escort me. It's a ridiculous thing to need anyway. I can just go by myself."

"I don't want you to have to do that," she said as a tear fell from her eye.

"I'll escort her, Kat," Gabriel said.

"I'm sorry, I shouldn't have left you," I told her, my heart breaking for her.

"It's not your fault." She wiped away a tear just as another fell. "It was a long time coming. I just wish it didn't happen right now. I'm sorry."

"You have nothing to apologize for," I said.

"Gabriel, do you mind?" she asked. "I just need to go."

"I don't mind," he said.

Kat hugged me and left the room. I stood up and looked at Gabriel. He held his hand out to me, and I took it. We were always being thrust together.

Gabriel led me to the center of the room just as the last bell chimed. We stood with a small group in front of a large stage. Myra, her Regent, and the Chancellors sat in large high-back chairs, looking down at us.

They all looked so young. The girl beside me had to have just turned fifteen if that was the age requirement. Her cheeks were a rosy pink and her escort looked as though he was her proud father. I never really thought about being a part of the Mavors, having a kid and hoping they would be chosen to follow in your footsteps. What a dangerous expectation for your children.

I had to remind myself that these people were warriors. Their ancestors had brought this darkness to this land, and it was their oath to rid it of it. They were born with increased strength, speed, reflexes, and more. There was underlying magic there as well, but none of them had been able to defeat the Imprecors. That was what I was for.

The young girl looked at me in shock and then tugged on her dad's sleeve. Her father looked over, smiled, and patted his daughter's hand.

"Are you going to save us?" she asked me.

"Excuse me?" I felt my stomach drop.

"You're the heir, right?" she asked. "Are you going to save us?"

I didn't have the words. She said what everyone had been saying all night, but she didn't dance around the subject. Without speaking to her, I turned and faced the front. Just then, Myra stepped forward. She had changed into a long black robe as had the other members. I saw Pops and Abbott at her side.

"Welcome, brothers and sisters," Myra called, her voice clear and ringing throughout the hall. "We once again gather on the new moon to welcome new members into our fold. Each year, we give thanks to Mother Mara, the moon goddess, for blessing our family with her love, protection, and power. Each year, we pray she guides us to finding the true heir, and I am blessed to say that we have at last found her. We have so much to be thankful for, so please take a moment and send your gratitude outward and above."

I watched as everyone around me lifted their arms in praise. Everyone except Gabriel. He had his eyes closed and his head slightly bent, but he was otherwise unmoved. When the small prayer was over,

Myra began calling the new members forward, and she started with me.

"Ava Black." Her sweet Irish accent made my name sound even more beautiful.

Gabriel took my hand, and we moved to the center of the room. I could feel the young girl's eyes on my back. I couldn't help but feel guilty for completely dodging her question. But what was I supposed to say? I didn't even have control over what I could do. How could I make such promises?

"Welcome, Sister Black," Myra said, and everyone in the room echoed her greeting. "Today is a momentous day. Knowing that you are here with us has brought a sense of joy and a renewed determination. Your instructors have relayed to the Council about your progress, and we are all impressed with what you have to offer the Mavors."

I didn't even know that my "instructors" had told the Council anything about my training. It made sense. I was sure they reported what I was doing in training to Abbott, and he sent that on to Myra and the higher-ups.

"We only have a few questions for you." Myra smiled.

Gabriel, Kat, and the others had prepared me for what was to be asked of me. There were three questions of initiation.

1) What does the Mavors mean to you?

2) What are your plans as a Mavor?

a) Join the Council

b) Become an instructor

c) Become a scholar

d) Become a guardian

e) Study magic

And my favorite,

3) Do you swear to dedicate your life to defeating the Imprecors?

The strange thing was, I didn't fall under any of these categories. I was new, a rarity, I was the Heir of Tepkunset. I was on my own. Still, I had to choose something.

"Ava, since this is unprecedented, we would like to create a new sect of the Mavors," Myra said to me, and I nodded. "It has been approved by our Council Members. You are now the first and only Alcehmi. This sect will allow you to explore and hone your abilities. It also places you over all sorcerers. There are none like you, Ava. Do you accept?"

I wanted to tell her no. I wasn't in control of my powers yet. Kat said I could call flames, but that was the extent of my magic. I had healed myself, but that was subconsciously. All that I had done had been accidental. I started to protest, but Gabriel squeezed my hand.

"I do," I nodded, the words falling out of my mouth.

"Ava," Myra started. "Since Gabriel is escorting you, do you choose him as your Guardian?"

"Excuse me?" I was shocked and looked over at Gabriel. His face was unreadable, but I saw the surprise in his eyes for just a moment. Clearly he was not expecting this question either.

"You are the Heir of Tepkunset," Myra said to me. "There are many things expected of you. One of those things is to carry on her traits to a new generation. By doing that, you must choose a partner. Do you choose Gabriel? Or, do you have someone else in mind? We prefer they be a member of the Mavors, of course."

I looked at her for a moment and then at Abbott. He was staring at me intensely. He knew. He knew Myra was going to railroad me with these questions, and he had chosen not to warn me. Why? He was so keen on making me as presentable as possible. Why would he let me be blindsided? He had to have a reason.

Gabriel squeezed my hand again, as if to say, "Be careful."

"If you cannot choose, we can choose for you," Myra continued when I still hadn't responded. "There are several eligible and qualified guardians to be your companion."

I could feel panic rise in my stomach. This place was supposed to be a sanctuary. I had lost too much. I had just declared, publicly, to dedicate my life to the Mavors. Now, they wanted to use me like a prized pooch?

"I am not prepared to make that commitment publicly." I leaned on Gabriel for show and he moved closer to me.

Maybe if they thought I had chosen him, they would drop it. He had warned me with the squeeze of my hand, so I was hoping he was okay with this.

"So, you agree to carry on your line?" Myra asked me.

"As I said, I am not prepared to make that commitment publicly," I repeated, hoping she would drop it.

"I see," she said, and there was a long silence. "Will you show us your powers?"

This might be even worse than asking me in front of everyone if I was willing to make a magic baby with Gabriel.

Gabriel and I had spent countless hours working on my abilities. We'd tried to recreate what had happened at the park, but nothing worked. I would get a spark, but then it would fade quickly. Calling the powers to me was next to impossible.

"I am honored to be part of the Mavors, Priestess," I said to her after a moment. "You all have welcomed me with open arms, and there will never be anything I can do to repay that debt. However, I will humbly decline to put on a show for you or anyone else."

Myra's dark eyes seemed to flash with angry light. I had read her completely wrong. She was not some endearing woman who had my best interests at heart. Myra was in a seat of power and didn't want anyone threatening it. I was a threat.

I bowed to the members of the Council and walked away. Gabriel was by my side and held my hand as we sat down at the table. For the rest of the ceremony, I sat there with thousands of thoughts running through my head. At the forefront was focusing on controlling my abilities and getting the hell out of there.

Ava

It had been several days since the ceremony took place. Some guests had returned home, but most of them had stayed behind. We were, after all, at war. I threw myself into my studies with Pops, my practices with Kat, and my training with Gabriel. Myra had tried to view what I was working on, but Pops had stepped in and said that I would be glad to show them my progress at the end of the week.

The only thing was, I didn't feel like I had made any progress, even though they told me I had improved.

Gabriel and I had yet to talk about what had happened at the ceremony. I had put him on the spot, insinuating to everyone that I was planning on having his child. We had spent a lot of alone time together training, but neither one of us had mentioned what any of it meant.

The night before I was supposed to show Myra and the Mavors Council my nonexistent abilities, I stayed up late and worked in the training room. I was exhausting myself mentally. I knew that, but I couldn't stop. The power was in there somewhere and I had to find it.

"Can't sleep?" I heard a voice at the door.

I turned to see Gabriel standing there, leaning against the frame. His hair was messy, as if all he had done was run his hands through it before coming down. I could see the faint beginnings of dark circles under his grey eyes.

"No." I shrugged and continued to hit the punching bag in front of me.

I had given up on calling my powers and resorted to taking it out on the training equipment.

The sight of him caused anger to swell inside my chest. It was unfair, but since the ceremony, anything and everything he said or did just got under my skin. I wasn't trying to be ungrateful for any of his help, because out of all the people here, I knew he was genuine.

That didn't stop these feelings of contempt from surfacing whenever he was around. I tried to make sense of it, and the only thing that didn't sound insane was it wasn't him at all. I was just angry at everyone and mostly myself.

"Want some help?" he asked me, walking forward.

"With what?" I hit the punching bag harder. "Calling powers that don't want to listen?"

"You're angry," he said, stepping beside me.

"I'm frustrated," I told him.

"Have you meditated?" he asked.

"Yes, Gabriel!" I snapped. "I've done all the things you have been telling me to do. All of it! Repeatedly, and it's not working. I meditated. I prayed to God, to the sky god, to the Great Spirit, the moon goddess, to whoever you all claim is listening, and they aren't answering. Did you, any of you, ever stop to think maybe you were wrong about me?"

"Not for a second," he said, his eyes searching mine.

"Why not?" I asked. "I have. Maybe I'm strong and can do some really amazing things, but maybe I'm not her. Maybe I'm not the Heir of Tepkunset."

"You don't believe that." He shook his head.

I said nothing as I continued to hit the punching bag. Gabriel stood there for a moment and then walked toward the door. For some reason, this infuriated me.

"Where are you going?" I turned and looked at him.

"You clearly want to be left alone." He shrugged.

"Some Guardian you are," I remarked and started punching the bag again.

"Spit it out," he said, his voice laced with anger.

"What?" I turned to him again.

"Say what you're thinking," he gestured to me and then crossed his arms, "You're clearly pissed at me and it's only polite to tell me why."

"I am not mad," I told him.

"Spare me, Ava," he said, glaring. "We've spent almost every waking moment together and you've only spoken to me when necessary. If I've done something, please, let me know what it is."

"It's nothing." I turned back around.

"You don't get to do that." He marched over and stood in front of me.

"Move it, Gabriel," I told him, my nostrils flaring.

"Not until you tell me what I've done!" he demanded.

"Nothing!" I yelled. "You've done nothing! But, that's also part of the problem. We haven't even talked about what happened at the ceremony. And, yeah, I might have been quiet, but so have you. And I'm pissed off! I don't know what any of this means!"

I shoved him away from me, and he stumbled back. He was shocked. So was I. I didn't expect to be able to move him. He was just so solid. During training, I could never touch him. I felt bad for losing my cool, but I was just so angry.

"This place is supposed to be safe!" I took another step forward. "I'm supposed to trust people here? Make a life here? How? How can I when I don't know what people want from me? I've lost my entire life, Gabriel, and I don't know who to trust."

"You can trust me, Ava." He took a step toward me.

He wanted to reach out. I could see the indecision on his face. I wanted him to. I could feel the power inside me ignite. It was like I had lit a match and tossed it in gasoline.

"I...don't...feel..." I started.

Suddenly, purple light seemed to explode out of me. Gabriel went flying backwards, hitting one of the mirrors, hard. A phantom wind swirled around us as another surge of energy came rippling out of me. I was losing control and I'd hurt Gabriel.

I could see him slowly getting to his feet. Blood was running down the side of his face.

"Gabriel," I whispered.

The wind slowly died down. Gabriel leaned back against the shattered glass. I ran to his side. I reached out, but pulled my hand away, afraid to touch him. I was even more afraid he'd recoil from me.

"Stay here," I said and ran for the First Aid kit. This thing was getting a lot of use.

When I came back, he was still sitting there. The blood was now running down his cheek and neck. I used the cotton balls and cleansing solution to clean him as best I could. The wound itself was superficial, but that didn't make me feel any better. He winced when I dabbed at it.

"I'm sorry," I said, feeling tears burn my eyes.

I could feel him staring at me, so I willed the tears to stay where they were. He was the one that was hurt.

"You didn't mean to," he said.

"Don't protect me." I shook my head.

Gabriel grabbed my hand, and I looked down at him. His grey eyes were trying to say something, but I'm not sure what it was.

"That is my job," he said, and then his eyes moved down to my lips.

"Gabriel," I started.

Before I could say anything else, he'd leaned forward, his lips finding mine with ease. I should have pushed him away. This wasn't the time to share a kiss, but his lips felt so nice, so warm, so right.

I kissed him in return, touching his warm cheek with my hand. He leaned into me, his powerful hands cupping my jaw, pulling me closer. Everything about this, about him, felt right. It also felt wrong; I felt like I wasn't supposed to feel this happy while feeling so lost and broken.

Gabriel grabbed my waist, pulling me onto his lap, and I tangled my hands in his soft hair. He ran his hands up and down my back, sending shivers all over my body. His lips worked their way from my mouth to my neck, and then he crashed into my lips again.

I could feel his body vibrate with excitement as my hands made their way under his shirt, feeling the muscles of his stomach and chest. Grabbing the hem of his shirt, I pulled it easily over his head. We were only parted for the briefest of seconds, and then he found my lips again.

He leaned me back on the floor, kissing me deeply, his body hovering over mine. The tattoo I had only glimpsed once before was now on full display. I traced my fingers along the raised lines, causing him to shiver. It filled the expanse of his broad chest and went down the center until it came to his navel. The image of a large raven with dark eyes seemed to pop under the color of his olive skin.

"Sorry to interrupt," Lorcan said from the door.

Gabriel and I both sat up. I was mortified, but Gabriel stood to his full height. Lorcan looked around the room, taking in the broken glass and Gabriel's bandaged forehead.

"They're ready for you, Ava," he said, now looking at me. "I'll tell them you need a moment."

He left saying nothing else. Gabriel slipped his shirt back on and stood looking at the door. He turned his head to me and reached his hand out. I took it and he helped me to my feet. I realized that was the first time I didn't hesitate an offer of help from him, as small as it was.

Gabriel stood in front of me, pushing my hair from my face. My heart beat harder now than it had just a moment ago. He took my chin in his hand and gently lifted my face to his. Our lips met and sparks flooded my body. It was such a gentle and sweet kiss.

"I'm sorry," he told me.

"For kissing me?" I asked him.

"No, definitely not for that," he grinned, "I'm sorry I haven't talked to you. I really didn't know how. I don't know what this means either, Ava. The only thing I know is you were meant to stop the Imprecors, and I am meant to help you. And..."

"And what?" I wondered.

"I'm in love with you," he said with ease.

My heart flipped in my chest. This wasn't what I had expected him to say. Here I stood in his arms, not long ago a moment from who knows what, and now he was confessing his love for me.

"I'm not expecting anything from you," he said. "I know you hardly know me. And it sounds overly creepy, I know, considering you were my assignment and I learned all I could about you without your knowledge. I know you feel like I betrayed you, that I lied to you. And, I guess I did, but if it makes any difference, I didn't want to. I didn't mean to fall for you. I didn't want to, but you didn't make it easy. I hope one day you can learn to trust me, and I will do anything to gain that trust. I am so sorry."

There really wasn't much I could say to that. He was right. He and his grandfather and the Mavors had all betrayed my trust. The Mavors wanted something that I could not provide. But, Pops had shown me nothing but kindness, and Gabriel, he wasn't asking me for anything except forgiveness.

I stood up on my tiptoes and kissed him. He smiled against my lips, leaning down so I could reach him better. Being here, with him, with his arms around me sounded much better than going to put on a show for the Mavors Council.

"I have to go," I said, leaning against him.

"You'll do fine," he told me. "I believe in you. You just have to believe in yourself."

"I hate putting on a show for them," I clenched my fists. "I hate that they think they can control my life. I'm only doing this because I know they can help us save Trevor. After that, I'm gone. Do you understand?"

"I am your guardian, Ava," Gabriel said and kneeled in front of me.

"What are you doing?" I stepped back.

"When Myra asked who you chose as your guardian, it wasn't just something she made up," he told me. "All Mavors can choose guardians. It's a way to be protected, but also to form alliances. I am yours, if you will have me."

"Does that mean...like are you asking me to be with you?" I wondered.

"Some relationships do work like that," he explained, his cheeks red. "But not all of them. All the Council Members have a guardian dedicated to them."

"Is this a magical bond?" I asked him.

"It is," he nodded, "I will always be able to sense you, to find you. If you are in danger, I will know. My life will be yours."

"Gabriel," I shook my head, "This is a lot to ask of you."

"I am willing," he bowed his head, "I know that you don't need me, but I want to be with you. You are powerful, and I have no doubt that you will defeat any and all enemies in your path. However, with power comes danger. Please let me help you face it. Again, I am not asking you for anything other than the ability to stand by your side."

"If I say yes, will you stand up? I feel like you're proposing to me," I laughed nervously. "You're not that good of a kisser."

He looked up at me with a smirk.

"Okay, yes, you can...be my guardian." I grabbed his shoulders to pull him up.

When I did, dark purple energy swept through me and into him. I jerked my hand back as the blue light I had seen in my dreams raced through his body and settled in his eyes. He staggered for a moment and then righted himself.

"Are you alright?" I asked him. "Was that supposed to happen?"

"I...I'm not sure." He tried to stand and then sat back down. "Whoa, I'm dizzy, but I feel...amazing!"

"This is freaking me out. Are you freaked out? Why are you smiling?" I looked down at him.

"I just feel good," he laughed.

"You sound drunk," I pointed out.

"I feel like I am," he giggled. He actually giggled.

Kat came through the door and looked at us. She raised her perfectly arched eyebrows with interest.

"Um, the old people are becoming impatient," she said, looking at Gabriel. "Should I be concerned?"

"Will you please stay with him?" I asked her. "I'll explain everything when I get back, I promise."

"Okay, then," she walked over to Gabriel, "But if you throw up on me, Matthews, you're dead."

I gave one last look at Gabriel and ran from the room. My head was reeling. I wasn't sure what had happened, but there was that blue light. None of the Mavors could do that and I had only seen it in a dream. Had I done that? What bond had we just formed?

I could still hear his voice in my head, "I'm in love with you."

I wasn't ready for that. I loved my parents. It was familial love and losing them had nearly killed me. My heart might not survive loving Gabriel.

After running across the Matthews property, I finally made it to the large cabin that the Council Members were staying in. When I entered the building, two guards directed me to a different area than I had been to on the night of the ceremony.

They opened a set of doors and ushered me inside. I was going to say thank you, because it was my nature to be polite, but they were gone before I could speak.

The Council Members sat at a table in the middle of a large training room. Thankfully, they had decided on normal attire and not their intimidating black cloaks. I walked up to the table, and the setting reminded me oddly of cheerleader tryouts. Hopefully, they weren't expecting me to do a cheer and a back handspring.

"Good morning, Ava." Myra smiled. "I've been looking over reports of your progress this week, very impressive. I hope you don't mind that we switched your training with Kat to a more seasoned instructor."

"Of course not." I shrugged.

"Gabriel has also said that you are gaining more control over your ability." She looked at her papers.

A part of me wondered how much Gabriel had lied. I could still feel that power from earlier surge inside me. Maybe he knew something that I didn't.

"Would you mind showing us?" Myra asked.

Her request sent unchecked rage through my body. This woman really wanted to be in control of me and everything around her. She had created a sect for me, but I really think it was just to keep a closer eye on what I was doing and to keep me isolated. She knew there would be no one else to join the sect because no one else had my abilities. Then, she tried to force me to publicly commit to having an heir of my own with someone I hardly knew. Now, here I was using my abilities for her benefit.

"Priestess, I hope that the reports in front of you also convey that I am not in full control of my abilities," I told her.

"I understand your friend, Trevor Bishop, has been taken by the Imprecors," she stated.

"Yes," I confirmed, eying her warily.

"We are doing all we can to find him, I can assure you," she sat back in her chair, "But, I know that you and Gabriel made a failed attempt at a rescue. Until we know you are in control of your powers, you will not be allowed out in the field."

She was pushing me. If she wanted a show, she was going to get one. I planted my feet on the floor, stretching my arms out at my side, calling to the power that had come to me earlier. A slight wind ruffled my hair and I watched as it rustled through the papers on the table. The occupants sat up straighter, looking at me with intense interest.

I called for the power. I wanted that light to fill my body with warmth and to zap the hell out of that table. Thinking of Trevor, of what he might be going through, I focused my mind and energy on pushing the power toward them.

A wall of energy of purple light and silver lightning formed around me. The Council Members stood up from their chairs. Abbott was impressed, terrified, but impressed. Pops' eyes were wide with amazement.

I sent the wall toward them in a rushing wave. It pulled the wood from the floor, sending splinters and nails flying in all directions. The glasses on the table shattered, spraying them with sand like dust and water. Just as the purple wall was about to reach the table, I stopped it and let it explode forward, sending all of them stumbling, focusing my effects on everyone but Pops. I didn't want to hurt him. At the end of it all, he was the only one left standing.

"How dare you!" Myra stood up.

"I told you my powers were uncontrollable," I feigned innocence.

"Is that so?" Her nostrils flared. "Well, then I suppose you aren't ready for field work just yet."

"If you don't think I am, then I'm not," I told her.

Myra was trying everything to get a reaction out of me.

"Have you chosen a guardian?" she asked.

"I am not ready..."

"To make that public," she finished for me as she sat her chair up and straightened her silky blue shirt.

She eyed me with curiosity. I wondered if she knew I had chosen. What had happened between Gabriel and I was still so new. It was no one's business.

"There are certain ways things are handled here, Ava," Myra said to me. "I suggest you become familiar with them."

"Yes, Priestess," I told her. "May I go?"

"Dismissed." She waved her hand, and I left with a smile on my face.

I found Gabriel and Kat in Gabriel's room. It was the first time I had been in there. He was pacing the room while Kat sat at his desk.

"There you are!" he nearly yelled when I walked into the room.

I jumped at the greeting. He came rushing over and crushed me in a tight hug.

"My ribs!" I croaked.

"Oh, sorry," he laughed.

"What the hell?" I asked. "Is he still acting like this?"

"He's actually calmed down some." Kat stood up. "I practically had to threaten his life to get him to stay. Do either one of you want to explain to me what is going on? Did he take drugs? Gabriel, did you sneak into my stash? I told you that stuff is experimental; I don't know what it does."

"No, it's nothing like that." I shook my head.

I told Kat what had taken place in the training room, leaving out all the touchy stuff. She was silent for a long time and then a big smile spread across her face.

"This is going to make Myra lose her mind," she laughed. "Do you know what you've done, Ava?"

"Uh...no?" I confessed.

"This isn't just a bond," she said. "Come on, let me show you."

We looked at Kat as she left the room. She snapped her fingers like an impatient mother tired of repeating herself, and we jumped into action, following her into the hall. Soon we were in her room and she was rummaging through all of her books.

"Now, this isn't part of the main course of study," she said as she picked up a green leather book. "Makes sense, I bet they never wanted anyone to try."

"Try what?" Reese walked in and plopped down on Kat's bed, eating from a bag of chips. He offered some to us, but I shook my head. Gabriel, on the other hand, took the entire bag and started devouring the chips.

"To form a Guardian Bond," she said as she flipped pages.

Reese looked at me and then looked at Gabriel, who had finished the bag and was wiping his hands on his shirt.

"You're kidding me." He sat up.

"I think it happened," Kat said and stopped on a page. "Aha! This is why Myra wanted to know so bad if you had picked a guardian."

She handed me the book. I started reading the passage.

"Holy crap," I breathed.

"What?" Gabriel asked.

"I...we..." I handed him the book so he could read it.

He looked down at the book and for a second, he stopped moving. I could see him swallow deeply and then look at the rest of us.

"I think I made you into something else," I told him. "But how is what I did any different than what you guys do?"

"You made him like you basically," Kat explained. "According to legend, Tepkunset did the same thing with Erik and a few other of the Norsemen. I'm pretty sure this is why we take guardians to begin with. The Mavors are hoping to unlock some magic with us. The bond is strong, and it is sealed in magic, but none of us are strong enough to make any real change. However, you are, Ava."

"Do you think Myra wants me to do this more than once?" I asked her.

"Probably," she nodded. "The old hag."

"Kat!" Reese warned her. "She is our Priestess."

"I call it like I see it." She shrugged.

I read the passage again. When Tepkunset was fighting the Imprecors, she used her magic to protect those who fought with her. They followed her, became her protectors, her guardians, while she trapped Thyana. She empowered the warriors with unearthly abilities.

Those warriors would go on to form the Mavors. While their magic was passed down and remained strong, it wasn't like what it was before. According to the book, a warrior that was bound to Tepkunset would share in nearly all of her abilities. Their lives would be longer and harder to take. Any warrior could dedicate their life to Tepkunset, but she had to bless them, accept them.

I looked at Gabriel. I had accepted him in so many ways, but in the process, what had I done to him?

"She probably wanted you to choose Lorcan," Kat was saying.

"Why him?" I looked up from the book.

"He's her son," she said. "And Abbott's."

"Say what?" I questioned.

"Yeah, they aren't together though," Reese explained. "It was an arrangement to produce a child, that's it. Lorcan was basically raised by his nanny. That doesn't mean he isn't just like them, power hungry. I bet he knows exactly what Myra wants from you."

"Holy crap, can you imagine if you guys did have a baby?" Kat said suddenly.

"What?" Gabriel and I exclaimed together.

"I'm just saying." Kat laughed at our faces. "You being the heir and Gabriel now being empowered by your magic...I'm just saying, your baby would probably be pretty powerful, too."

"So, I'm just a magic baby maker for her," I said. "She can't control me, but if she gets my child, well, then she can raise it however she wants."

"That's messed up," Reese said.

"You can say that again." Kat nodded.

"This is all speculation, right?" I asked. "You don't think this is really what she wants? The Mavors were created to rid the world of the Imprecors, not this, right?"

"I know it was created for something good," Kat said, shrugging. "I don't know if it stayed that way. And, if I were you two, I'd keep this bond of yours on a need-to-know basis. At least until you find out what she wants."

"Right," I said and looked at Gabriel.

"If we want this to stay a secret, I need to get out of here," he said. "I feel like I'm about to explode."

"Right," I said again and stood up. "And you two are okay with keeping this between us? I know you're close with Abbott."

"Abbott was our mentor," Kat said. "I respect his position in the order, but this is beyond that. This is people's lives we're talking about here. So, yeah, you can trust us."

"Yep." Reese saluted me like a soldier.

I nodded my thanks and grabbed Gabriel by the arm to lead him out of the house before he tore it down with all of his pent up energy.

Ava

We took a walk around the property. Well, Gabriel was taking quick, long strides, and I had to jog to keep up. The energy coursing through him was unparalleled. I could practically see the blue light under his dark skin.

"Gabriel," I grabbed his arm, making him look at me, "You have to try to calm down."

"I'm trying," his voice had a hint of fear in it, but his face showed joy.

A few of the other Mavors were on the walking trail. I moved out of their way as they passed. They nodded their heads to us, eyeing us curiously. Or, maybe I just thought they were. I was nervous. I didn't want anyone knowing what was happening to Gabriel.

"Is there anywhere we can go that's away from people?" I asked him.

"Yes." He grabbed my hand, and we took off.

We ran for what seemed like forever. By the time we reached a densely wooded part of the property, I was out of breath. Leaning on my knees, I saw Gabriel had led us to a treehouse.

"Come on," he said to me.

"You want me to climb now?" I wheezed. "And why do you look like you could run a marathon?"

"I've never felt so alive," he smiled, "Come on!"

He took my hand and led me to the tree. We climbed the wooden ladder until we reached the base of the structure. Gabriel pushed open the trap door. After he made his way inside, he grabbed my hand and helped me through.

It was dusty, but everything was in its place. I walked around looking at all of the different things that Gabriel must have collected over the years. There was a box of Pokémon cards, a treasure chest full of plastic army men, and various other toys for a much younger child. He hadn't been here in a long time.

A map was pinned to one of the walls. It was of the city of Guntersville, the lake taking up most of the large canvas. There was a red pin and as I moved closer, I noticed it was on my street, on my house. I turned to look at him.

"We found you pretty early on," he said. "I'm sorry."

"You don't have to do that." I shrugged. "It...doesn't bother me as much as it did. I understand."

Gabriel nodded, turning to look at the map. All that energy was still rippling through him. I could almost see it. But his mind seemed to be a million miles away. Or, maybe it was years.

"How long has it been since you've been here?" I asked him.

"Is it that obvious?" he wondered, not looking at me.

He had moved to one of the shelves, looking over the seemingly random objects.

"You just seem lost in thought," I told him, moving closer to him. "Do you want to talk about it?"

"No," he said, but then he looked at me. "Yes."

"I'm here for whatever you need, Gabriel," I told him.

"The day I learned they died, I was here," he told me.

"I am so sorry," I said.

He gave me a sad smile. Picking up a box off the shelf, he went and sat on the floor of the treehouse, next to the boarded-up window. Tiny slivers of sunlight filtered through the slats, dancing upon his dark hair.

He opened the box and pulled out a few photographs. They were wrapped in plastic, but had been yellowed with age.

"That's them." He handed me a picture.

Gabriel looked so much like his father it was shocking. They had the same grey eyes, a slightly arched nose, and strong jawline. He had his mother's smile though, full lips, warm and inviting.

"They're both so beautiful," I said to him. "You can see each of them in you."

"You think I'm beautiful?" He smiled at me.

"You know I do." I looked over at him.

Gabriel reached over and touched my face. A surge of static electricity passed through us. It was almost painful, but at the same time, invigorating. I jumped slightly, feeling the spot his fingers had been, and then looked up at him.

He leaned over and gently pressed his lips to mine. That same feeling enveloped my body. I looped my arms around his neck, pulling him to me. Gabriel's body hovered over me, the contents of the box scattered and forgotten on the floor. His lips were warm on mine, warm and delicious.

For a moment, I forgot about all the implications of being Ava Black and him being Gabriel Matthews, two young adults with the fate of the world on their shoulders. I was just Ava, a girl who had found a boy who adored her and who she cared for in return.

His hands moved down my body, resting on my hip. Gabriel stopped, looking down at me, desire in his eyes.

"I don't ever want to stop kissing you." He smiled, blushing.

"I don't want you to either," I laughed. "But, I think you should right now. We are completely alone and if you keep kissing me, I don't think I'll have the willpower to make you stop."

"Right," he said, moving slightly away from me.

"It's not that I don't want to," I looked away from him, "I know Rob made me sound like a complete whore."

"Ava," his brow furrowed, "You don't have to explain anything to me. I don't care about Rob. I don't care if you slept with him or anyone else. That doesn't make you anything other than human. The only thing I care about is you, just you. Never think I care about things like that."

I grabbed his shirt and pulled him down, crashing into his lips. My hands moved into his hair, pulling him as close to me as I could.

"I thought we needed to stop," he said between my onslaught of kisses.

"We do," I laughed.

"I mean, I'm not complaining, but..." He smiled down at me.

"Gabriel..." I looked up, feeling like at any moment, I could and would give him all I had. "I..."

Suddenly there was a boom that shook the entire ground and the small treehouse we were in. Gabriel toppled over and when he tried to right himself, another boom quaked through the ground again.

"What the hell?" I yelled.

Another explosion, and this time I heard something crack. I tried standing up, but as I did, I felt another wave shake us and we were blown straight out of the tree. I could feel myself sailing through the air, debris hitting me in the face.

The only thing on my mind was Gabriel. I didn't want him to get hurt. I reached out for him, feeling nothing but air. I could feel my power come alive inside me; it searched for him and I felt it wrap around his body.

We both hit the ground, hard but unharmed. Pieces of the tree and the wooden structure landed around us. They fell like rain, but none of it touched us. My power had created a shield around us, cushioning our landing and protecting us from the fallout.

Gabriel and I got to our feet just as a group of people moved over the hill, shrouded in the coming darkness.

"Mom?" I whispered.

I wanted to kick myself. She wasn't my mother. Keira was walking beside her. Her beautiful face was gaunt, but she looked much better than the last time we had met. Instinctively, I pulled the dagger from the sheath at my side.

"Stop!" I yelled, and the group before me halted.

"I see you're coming into your power," my mother called to me. "Good."

"Are you sure about that?" I said to her. "It seems like you are all pretty much screwed because if you take another step forward, I'll shred you."

"Ava, I think you and I should be properly introduced," she told me. "This mask I'm wearing is rather tiresome."

"No, thanks," I told her, squaring my shoulders.

"It's in your best interest," my fake mother said to me. "Because after we broke through your protection spell, we made a little stop by your compound and dropped off a few friends. I believe one of them is keeping your grandfather company, Gabe."

"You better not—" he started.

"You have no leverage here, boy," she snapped at him. "Now, Ava, where were we, ah, yes, my proper name. First, let me shed this skin."

The figure before me, who looked like the woman I had called Mother for my entire life, stepped forward and transformed before my eyes. It wasn't beautiful. It was terrible, grotesque. Bones moved and popped. Her skin seemed to melt before my eyes. I could feel bile rise in the back of my throat. I wanted to move away from her, but fear rooted me to the spot.

When she'd finished, the thing standing before me was hardly human. She was tall, taller than even Gabriel, with grey skin and long skinny fingers. She looked exactly like the monsters from my nightmares, the ones who had taken the life force from those girls. I knew now that those girls had been actual people, actual victims. The thought filled me with unhinged rage.

"Now, that's better," she smiled at me, her mouth a crooked line, "I am Velia, High Priestess to Thyana, our Mother, our Goddess."

"Full offense, but you're fugly as hell, bitch," I said to her.

"Oh, my delicate feelings," she sneered. "There are things far more important than your looks, Ava. Or, have you learned nothing?"

"Oh, I have." I shrugged. "But you can't even use the 'at least I'm not ugly on the inside' comeback."

"Enough!" Keira stepped forward.

"Know your place," Velia said to her.

"I know my duty." Keira moved another step up. "And it is to bring her to Mother. While you're out here exchanging insults, she waits."

They looked at each other for a moment, a silent war between them. I could see the power struggle. Keira was still too human to take her on and she knew it. She backed up and let Velia step forward. As she did so, a figure was shoved before us.

"Trevor." Gabriel moved, but I held him back.

The protective orb I had placed around us was still intact. No one else could see it, but I could feel it. I didn't want them to know it was there. Not yet.

"Let him go," I told her.

"We will," Velia said to me. "If you come with us."

"Not happening," Gabriel said, his eyes brimming with that blue light. "We've been here before. She's not going anywhere with you, not in exchange for anyone."

"What about in exchange for you?" Keira asked. "I know she cares for you."

"Come and get him," I challenged.

My words seemed to enrage her. Keira balled up her fists and a bolt of dark green energy struck out at us. It ricocheted off the orb and nearly hit Velia in the face. I smirked at her, and her face contorted into an ugly sneer.

"Look who's been holding out on us, Gabriel," I said. "When did you learn all of that?"

"I've always had power," she said. "Why do you think they wanted me?"

"And you chose to side with them?" I asked her. "You don't have to. Come to me, Keira. Be with us. Be with me. I care for you."

I could see the glazed look in her eyes as my magic took her over. Keira walked toward us, each step a struggle. She was fighting it. I could see it, but I could feel it more. She was strong. It was possible she was stronger than me. I believed it when she suddenly stopped, breaking free of my compulsion.

"You don't know me, Ava." Keira smiled at me. "But I know you. This tough girl persona is just an act. Your whole life has been a show. Don't get me wrong. You play your part well. The fallen star. The girl once at the top now on the outside looking in. Someone who has learned her lesson and is trying to right her wrongs. Please. We both know you were your true self whenever you were walking on the necks of the peasants. You felt powerful, but not as powerful as you do now, right? You could just snap your fingers and have anyone do your bidding. It feels good, doesn't it? I know because I feel it too. You're begging me to join you, but really, Ava, you should join me. It's so freeing here. We aren't confined to any rules. Mother feeds us all the power we need. She could nourish you, too. Your power would be endless with her."

"You're so lost, Keira," I told her, sadness in my voice. "That's not freedom. I would be her slave. Just like you are."

"I hope Mother sees you for what you are," Keira finally said. "You are not worthy of her attention. The power you have is wasted. It should have been given to me! I think I might just take it. If I can take the others' energy, I can take yours."

"You will not touch her!" Myra came over the hill, Abbott and a few others behind her. I could see Kat, Reese, and Lorcan. Each of them had their long swords. They were bleeding from various places, but seemed otherwise unharmed. I saw Gabriel scan the crowd for Pops, but he wasn't among them.

Relief washed over me, despite being scared for Pops. Reinforcements had arrived. I was hopeful that we could do something, maybe finally end this war and save Trevor.

Some of the Imprecors turned their attention to the approaching Mavors. They hissed, raising their elongated arms in a defensive motion. I could sense their desire for violence. These creatures were not afraid of us. They fought a righteous war, and we were in their way. They would rip us all to shreds to get what they came for. Me. They would kill to take me to their Mother.

"Now," Velia nearly whispered.

The Imprecors moved with inhuman speed. They spread across the open field like ants when someone steps on their hill. The Mavors moved quickly as well, but the Imprecors were on them, slashing with their long nails.

Gabriel and I charged forward just as more of them came out of the tree line. How many of these witches were there? I lined one up and was running straight for it when I was tackled by another one from the side. We both went skidding to the ground. Dropping my knife, the thing was on top me, its gaping mouth and sharp teeth snapping at my face.

Using one arm, I held it back and searched for my blade with the other. The thing shrieked so loudly it felt like my ears might bleed. I could see darkness around it and knew it was the Imprecors' magic. I wasn't sure why everyone and everything had a different hue, or essence, when they used their magic, but I could see it now.

It brought up its hand, and I could see the magic energy gathering in its palm. I wasn't sure what spell it intended to use on me, but I didn't want to find out. Using a move that Gabriel had taught me, I shoved my foot upwards and flipped the thing over my head.

Seeing my blade to my left, I grabbed it and turned over just as the Imprecor was coming back for me. I rammed the blade into its guts, twisted and pulled up. The thing screamed and then exploded into hot embers. I jumped back, feeling the heat of its death on my skin.

Another of the Imprecors charged at me, and I used my power to lift it off its feet, throwing it into a group of its coven buddies. They crumbled under its weight, becoming a tangled mess.

A large group of the beasts came out of the tree line. As I turned to them, I saw they were headed straight for Kat and Isla. They were preparing to face at least thirty Imprecors. I headed toward them, but suddenly Gabriel was there. Even from this distance, I could see the dark blue light building within his arms. He lined up one of the beasts in his sights and pulled the trigger of his gun. I watched as the magic within him seep into the weapon and explode outward, turning the gun in this hand into a canon like weapon.

The Imprecors, and even Kat and Isla, were knocked off their feet. He hadn't meant to use the power within him. He looked around, our eyes meeting. There was fear and wonder dancing behind his eyes. I nodded, and he helped Kat and Isla up as more Imprecors took the place of the ones he had momentarily taken out of play.

I began moving toward them and then I felt a sharp, white hot pain erupting from my shoulder. I turned, seeing that Keira had come up from behind me while I was distracted. A blade was sticking out of my shoulder. I tried turning away from her, but she took another dagger and shoved it into my lower back, right under my rib cage. I could feel my breath leave me in a painful gasp.

"You have never met anyone like me, Ava," she whispered in my ear. "I'm like your mirror, but the biggest difference between us is I know how to use my power."

She twisted the blade in my side. I hissed, feeling my power and anger rise. Using both, I grabbed a handful of her hair and flipped her over my shoulder. She landed on her back in front of me. It was a bad idea, but I yanked her blades from my body. Blood instantly soaked through my shirt.

"You might bleed out before this is all over," Keira said, standing to her feet.

I threw her blades down, squaring my shoulders. Pooling my power into a ball of purple light in my hands, I stared her down.

"You're right. I might," I told her, feeling the world around me tilt. "But you're wrong about one thing."

"What's that?" she sneered.

"I know how to use my power." I threw the light at her, the ball of energy hitting her directly in the chest.

Keira went flying back, crashing into the Imprecors. I could see Velia amongst them. She came charging forward, her black light of energy swelling around her. There was something or someone else with her. I could see it just out of the corner of my eye. I ran toward her, trying to meet her energy with my own.

Just as we were about to meet, a red streak of light hit us both, sharp pain sending us crashing to the ground. Images flashed through my mind. Barren land, new growth, blood, birth, death. It came like waves. I couldn't understand what was playing before my mind. And the sounds were overwhelming. The wetness of something slithering, the crunching of leaves, the cracking of bones, waves on rocks, scuttling of insect legs.

"You have caused so much trouble, little girl," a voice said above the noise in my head. "I think we've seen enough."

Finally, I was able to open my eyes. Looking up, I saw a being above me, hovering over the scene on the ground below.

"Thyana," I breathed.

I knew her. She was the Mother of all things deep, dark, and earthy. I could smell the dampness of wet grass in my nostrils. I could feel the dew that clung to a blade of grass on my skin. I knew in my bones that if I were lost in the forest, she would be there, watching me.

She created life, but it wasn't anything that sought the light. It was things that burrowed, dug into the earth, seeking the shelter of the darkness and cold.

Mother was pure magic, ancient and old. She called to the magic within me. My body wanted to go to her. We were kindred spirits. I saw the other Imprecors slowly make their way to her, bowing in reverence. Even the Mavors were having a hard time looking at her.

While we were made from the same magic that ran through this soil, we were far from the same. Our energy came from the same source, but hers had been twisted with the hunger for power, the hatred from humanity. We were not the same.

"Why do you fight me, child?" she asked, feeling me recoil.

"You are not my mother," I told her. "You took her from me a long time ago."

"So bold." She smiled.

Her features finally came into view. This was what it was like to look upon a goddess, all irrational beauty and unnerving fear. She was from the earth and her features reflected that; skin like soil, hair red as flames, eyes as green as the fields. She wore a cloak of the deepest amber with a crown of animal bones upon her head.

While she looked human, her features were sharper, more angular. Her cheek bones were set higher and her ears came to a point. Her teeth were pearly white, but they, too, ended sharply, nearly cutting into her lips when she talked.

"I'm not bold," I shrugged my shoulders, "I just know what's right."

"What's right?" she laughed; it was almost girlish. "What's right for the bird is chaos for the worm. Right and wrong are subjective, especially to lesser beings."

"And we're the lesser beings?" I asked her.

"They, Ava, they are the lesser beings." She gestured to the Mavors and I glared at her. "Why align yourself with them when you were meant for greater things?"

I glanced at Gabriel. It was a mistake. In that moment, I had let my guard down. She was able to ease into my thoughts, my feelings; I could hear inside my soul.

"Ah," she said to me. "Love. So very human of you. Just like Tepkunset. She loved my son."

"Your son?" I looked at her.

"He was one of many," she waved her hand, "Where do you think the line of Mavors came from? How do you think they are so instilled with magic? I gave them the very magic they use against me. Ungrateful. He sacrificed himself for her and she allowed him to. You don't know the true story, do you? I can see it on your face. The Mavors don't even know their own history. Tepkunset gave up her power to seal me away. Her lover was dead. She was in pain. She made a rash decision. She gave up who she was for a man."

"She sacrificed what was most precious to her to save her people," I countered.

"She was weak," Thyana spat. "But, smart. She made a blood sacrifice, spilling her own blood, giving up a piece of her soul to lock me in the cage."

"And how are you free now?" I asked her.

"Because of you," she lowered herself further to the ground, "All of this was meant to be. The Mavors found you where and when they needed to. This land was where I was sealed. All I needed was a drop of your blood spilled in battle on the soil Tepkunset entombed me. Now, I am free. Goddess, Mother, Thyana, Reborn. And before you get any ideas, that same spell won't work again. I've worked magic against it. But, I thank you for shedding blood for me, Ava."

I looked at Keira. She smiled up at me. I wanted to choke the life out of her. Her blade had shed my blood. She had brought Thyana forward.

"Guard your thoughts, Ava," Thyana said to me. "She is your sister."

"She is nothing to me," I said through gritted teeth. "Neither are you."

"And they are nothing to me." She gestured to the people around me.

She waved her hand, and red energy encircled the Mavors warriors, wrapping around their bodies. They crumbled to the ground, clutching at their throats and their chests. Their mouths were open in silent screams as the earth moved beneath them, roots moving upwards, snaking around their bodies, pulling them in.

I couldn't allow that to happen. These people were my friends. Even though I didn't particularly care for some of them, and I definitely didn't trust the other half, they were innocent people. I couldn't let them give their lives for me.

Gabriel was going to hate me. I could just imagine the anger, the betrayal. I couldn't see any other way. If I could save them and find a way back to him, I would. I had to. I wanted to live. I didn't just want to survive this. I wanted all of us to live. And I wanted to live with him by my side, away from all of this. No more Imprecors or Mavors.

We would carve out our lives, our own little treehouse in the woods somewhere. A place we could fill with small treasures and beautiful memories. And, if we had children one day, they would be protected from this life. They wouldn't have their parents taken from them. They wouldn't be raised by imposters.

"Stop!" I yelled. "Please, don't do this. I'll do whatever you want. Just let them go."

"You care that much?" Thyana looked at me, satisfied.

"I do." I could feel tears sting my eyes. "Let them go. Give us back Trevor. I'll come with you. I'll...I'll serve you."

"Swear it." Her smile fell and her true power began to show. "Swear your life to me."

I turned to Gabriel. I could see the look in his eyes, the pleading. He was begging me to find another way. Looking around at them, the red tendrils of power encased their bodies, and I didn't know what else to do. I couldn't fight her. I wasn't strong enough. She would kill them all.

"I swear," I said finally.

Thyana released them. They fell to the ground in a heap. Gabriel jumped to his feet and began running toward me. I stood there, waiting for him, to feel him in my arms one last time. I reached out, his hands just inches from mine, and suddenly darkness closed around me.

Gabriel

I stood at the window in my room, looking out at the grounds of the Mavors compound. It had been exactly two weeks since we had faced the Imprecors and Thyana. I leaned my head against the frosty glass, still feeling exhausted from that fight; a fight that had taken everything from me.

I could still see Ava as she stood in that field, reaching for me. The look on her face haunted my thoughts. She was terrified. She didn't want to go. What she had done was to save them, to save me.

I would never forget watching Thyana take her...eat her. That's what it had looked like. The goddess had enveloped Ava, absorbing her into her own body. And then they were gone, all of them. I had stood there for a very long time, waiting for her to come back.

For the longest time, I had been so angry with her. And then I was angry at myself for feeling any resentment against her at all. Pops said it was natural. I knew what Ava had done was selfless. But I couldn't help but feel like she had abandoned me. She had left me behind.

But if I knew anything, I knew her. Ava wouldn't have done this without a plan. That's what I kept telling myself. She knew something, a way out. I had to help her from my side of things. And I had to do it before Thyana destroyed everything. I had to believe she was still alive.

There were already reports of increased numbers of disappearances. The Imprecors were feeding and doing so without fear of repercussions. They had their Mother to protect them now. Thyana had sworn to reclaim the world, rebuild it in her own image. She was powerful, but she was incapable of doing that with Ava in play, so Thyana had removed her. But had she?

I knew that Ava had sworn her allegiance to Thyana, but there was no way she would help her destroy the world.

I had been tracking the disappearances and the bodies that showed up not long afterwards. I hated that this was the way I was tracing her movements. When there was another report, my heart sank, and I was filled with disgust that my heart also brimmed with hope that I was another step closer.

I'd tried getting Trevor to help me, but he couldn't tell me much about his time with Keira or the other Imprecors. They'd kept him and his family locked away, and Keira had toyed with his mind so much that he wasn't even really sure what he had seen. The only thing he knew was that they were kept in a cellar or a cave. He said it was damp and wet.

Trevor had been through it. His entire family had, but Trevor definitely got the worst of it. Keira had used him like a puppet. What was even worse, she had used him like her own personal snack pack. Anytime she felt low on energy, she would take some from him. Trevor said the last time he recalled being in control of his own body was the day Ava had found him and Keira behind the school.

He said that was the first time Keira had syphoned energy from him. It was the first time she had snaked her way inside his thoughts. The way he explained it to me, it was like being a prisoner inside his own mind. There were so many times he was screaming, but nothing came out. He said if he even tried to say something, it would be like fire exploded inside his body. The only way to quench the flames was to push the words back down.

The Mavors helped Trevor and his family get back home. Before they left, I took Trevor to the side.

"I'm really sorry," I told him. "If I had known...I just wish I could have done something. And...I'm not trying to sound insensitive, Trevor, but if you remember anything, please call me."

"I will," he said; his small body shivered. "But, if I am being honest, I don't want to remember."

I nodded and watched him leave. Trevor had been my friend for so long, and I couldn't help but feel responsible. I had brought Trevor into this mess just by knowing him.

I doubted our relationship would ever be the same. The Mavors had offered to move them to another town or state, to give them a fresh start, but Trevor's parents refused. They said Guntersville was their home and, despite what they had been through, they would stay and heal as a family.

Trevor's father, a man I had always respected, made me swear I would find Keira and put an end to her.

"I don't understand any of this," Mr. Bishop had told me. "All I know is my son is hurting and there is nothing I can do about it, but you can. And as a man who has made his fair share of mistakes, I know that look in your eyes, Gabriel; you can't blame yourself. I know in my heart you would never put Trevor in danger purposely. That doesn't change the fact that they hurt him. So, do an old man a favor and kill the evil bitch that did it. And you go help Ava. She's a good girl."

"Yes, sir." I shook his hand, swearing to do just that.

Kat, Reese, and Lorcan found me in the library a few days later. I had been poring over lore, studying the patterns of the attacks, trying to find anything that would lead me to Thyana and then to Ava. I was coming up with absolutely nothing, and it was driving me mad.

"Hey, there, bud," Kat said, sitting down at the desk I was occupying. "These two are too afraid to say anything, so I'm just going to lay it all out there. You smell, you look like hell, and you need to eat. I know you're trying to find Ava, but you will not do her any favors if you fall over dead from malnutrition or kill yourself from your own stench."

My head shot up in her direction. I said nothing as I looked at her and then to Reese and Lorcan. They hovered in the doorway, as if stepping into the room would put them in my line of fire.

They had all seen what I had done on that field and Kat had experienced it firsthand. Ava had changed me, released my abilities. There was no way of keeping that a secret now. People were either afraid of me or curious.

"Kat," I said.

"Gabe," she said, mimicking my tone. "You are no good to her or anyone else in your current state. Look, I can't imagine what it must feel like, losing the person you love like that. But, if you want to help her, you have to take care of yourself. Go eat something, sleep, and for the love of God, go take a shower."

Taking a deep breath and wanting to unleash all of my pent up rage on her, I looked down at myself. It was as if I hadn't seen myself clearly in so long. Kat stood up and walked over to me.

"You are not alone," she reached out and took my hands, "We care for her, too. We will help you...let us."

"I...I don't even know what I'm looking for." I could feel myself crumble. "I keep looking and none of it is leading anywhere...and... what? What is it?"

"There is something you should know," Kat sighed.

"It's my mother," Lorcan came forward, "She's lost it completely."

Reese followed in after him. And to my surprise, Isla entered after him, walking up to Kat.

"She's declared Ava an enemy of the Mavors," Kat told him.

"What?" I growled.

"She just announced it in the Council meeting," Kat explained. "She claims Ava willingly left with Thyana and is now considered our most wanted."

"That's a lie." I was in disbelief. "Ava was practically...eaten alive. We don't even know...if..."

"You know," Kat said. "Myra knows, too. She's alive."

"There's more," Lorcan told me, and I could feel that newfound power surge within me. "Please don't fry the messenger. I'm here for Ava."

"How do I know you aren't working for your mother? Spying to see what I've found?" I asked Lorcan, taking a step closer.

"You know how I feel about Ava, Gabriel," Lorcan said it like a challenge. "I would never do anything to put her in danger."

"What else did Myra say?" I asked after a moment.

"Anyone who is found helping Ava will be considered a traitor and executed," Kat said.

"This doesn't make sense," I shook my head, "Ava's existence was prophesied to help the Mavors. Our whole society was focused around finding her. Why would Myra paint her to be a villain?"

"Ava is powerful," Kat shrugged, "Myra is in a seat of power. She doesn't want to let that go. If she can't use Ava, or her love child, she'll get rid of her."

"I'm leaving," I said suddenly.

"What?" Kat looked at me as I walked out of the library and toward my room.

"I will not stop helping Ava, and Myra knows that," I told her, their group moving toward my bedroom as I began packing a bag. "She'll come for me. I'm leaving. I'll find Ava and help her, but I can't do it from here."

"I'm coming with you," Lorcan said.

"Me, too," Reese announced.

"Reese?" Kat looked at her brother. "I want to help Ava too, but do you think this is the best way to do it? We have resources here."

"I'm going, too," Isla said, and Kat's eyes widened. "I know I just met her, but she didn't go with Thyana willingly. I was there. She sacrificed herself for us. Myra is lying. I cannot sit by and let Myra destroy this order. I cannot sit by while an innocent Mavors is held hostage by the Imprecors."

"Fine," Kat huffed. "I'm going too because you idiots are going to need my help, but you know what this means, right?"

"Yes," I said, slinging my bag over my shoulder. "We'll all be hunted down."

We began walking out of my bedroom door when Bron walked in. He crossed his arms, looking down at all of us.

"Where are you going?" Bron signed.

"Who said we were going anywhere?" I asked, signing back.

"I'm not stupid, Gabriel. I saw Kat run from the meeting. I knew she was coming here. And I knew you would leave. So, where are you going?" Bron asked again.

"I have to help her, Bron," I shrugged, "Are you going to stop me? Take me to Abbott?"

Everyone was watching us. Bron said nothing for a moment.

"I'm assuming you're all going?" Bron wondered.

They nodded, and Bron rolled his eyes.

"Fine. Someone needs to be the spy. They'll never suspect me. I'm too loyal to Abbott. I'll be your eyes and ears. Well, so to speak." Bron smiled. "Help her, Gabriel. We have to stop Thyana. I know she's a literal goddess, but we can't forget Keira. She's dangerous."

"Thank you, Bron," I signed, and I hugged him. "The rest of you grab what you need and meet me in the garage. We leave in five minutes. If you aren't there, you aren't coming."

Epilogue

AVA

I felt her take me, bring me to her chest, like a mother comforting a frightened child. Her heart beat against my ear, fast and powerful. Then there was pain as she held me tighter, squeezing me against her breast.

She opened wide, her chest taking me inside. Warm, wet fingers pulled me, settled me against the heart that beat like the pounding hooves of untamed beasts.

Then there was darkness. I couldn't hear anything. I couldn't feel anything. I couldn't see anything. I couldn't even move. Time seemed to mean nothing here, wherever here was.

I woke up in a cold, damp chamber. Opening my eyes, I saw I was lying on a cot with no coverings. The ceiling and walls were stone, covered in vines and other things that grew in the wet darkness.

I sat up and placed my feet on the ground. The floor was only dirt. Mushrooms of varying sizes and shapes grew along the edge of one wall. It had a smell, not foul, but unsettling.

Turning, I saw a door. There seemed to be light coming through it so I cautiously took a step forward, trying not to make a sound as I peeked through the wooden slates. I didn't hear or see anyone, so after a moment, I turned the knob and stepped out into a long hallway.

It seemed I was in some type of building. The floors and walls were stone. It made me feel like I was in a castle, something you would read about in a storybook. Large torches lined the hall and I could see more doors behind and ahead of me. What I didn't see was an exit.

I took a step forward and heard a voice. It seemed to surround me, or maybe it was within me.

"I see you, Ava," Thyana said to me, her voice like a whisper in the wind. "Come to me."

Without meaning to, I took a step forward and then another one. She was controlling me. Resisting her, I dug my heels into the ground and held onto the doorframe.

"Come to me, child," she told me again, her voice louder. "You swore your allegiance to me. You must obey."

My feet betraying me, I made my way through the maze of halls. Finally, I reached a set of double doors. Sweat dripped off my chin from the exertion of trying to resist Thyana's power. The doors opened, and I walked inside.

The chamber was dimly lit with torches. It was vast, and the Imprecors lined the walls. I looked up, barely able to see the ceiling. There was an altar and Thyana was seated above it. This was almost like a cathedral. It was her temple.

"At last," Thyana said, and I saw Keira at the goddess's side. "The little goddess has graced us with her presence."

"I am no goddess," I said as Thyana forced me to my knees.

"The Mavors have hidden so much from you, Ava," she told me. "Do you know who Tepkunset truly was to her people? She was no mere mortal. She was like me. We came from different regions, from different parts of the world, but we were made from the same power that brought forth life on this planet. She was my sister. Why do you think you can will things into existence and the other Mavors cannot? You have been blessed by the Goddess Tepkunset. Just as she has blessed Keira."

I looked at my former friend. She was fierce and beautiful as she stood next to her master. Her bright blue eyes glowed with the power that coursed through her body.

"It breaks my heart," Thyana caught my attention, "We could have been amazing together, ruled together. But she was corrupted by man, by Erik. They were meant to worship us, to nourish us. And what did she do? She fell in love with one. Disgusting. You could do what she was meant to, Ava, rule with me."

I saw Keira tense. She didn't like this.

"With a little guidance, you could be strong enough." Thyana tilted her head, looking at me. "You've only had a taste of power in your insignificant life. I could show you true power. I could give life everlasting. You've already sworn your allegiance to me. All you have to do now is give me your soul."

"I kind of like my soul," I shrugged, "So, I'm going to pass."

"You should watch your tone," Keira threatened.

"Do not worry yourself, Keira," Thyana waved her hand, "She will learn."

A door to the side opened and two Imprecors brought forth a struggling form. They threw her down at my feet.

"Frankie?" I looked at her in shock.

"Ava?" Frankie had tears running down her cheeks, a bruise forming on her face.

I couldn't explain the feeling in my chest. I wanted to rip Frankie limb from limb. I had felt hatred toward Frankie for a long time, but this was different. Frankie disgusted me. I wanted to destroy her. To devour her. My eyes shot up to Thyana.

"What have you done to me?" I felt true fear for the first time since standing before the goddess.

"I've only awakened the desire within you, Ava," Thyana explained. "Humans are nothing more than cattle. Their life force comes from the core of the earth. It is sweet and satisfying. It is here for us to partake in. They were never meant to rule. Especially not humans like this vain, selfish girl. You know what she is, Ava. The world would be better without her. Think of all the pain she has caused. You know I am right."

"Ava," Frankie pleaded with me, grabbing my legs. "Please, help me."

"Take what is yours, Ava," Thyana said to me "Take it. Take her soul. Feel it course through you and your power will be undeniable. Join me."

I felt my mouth water. My body shook with desire. I reached down and grabbed Frankie by the throat, lifting her easily off her feet. Frankie's eyes flashed wide with terror. I wanted to do this. Why? Had giving myself over to Thyana really changed me that much? Had I become an Imprecor? Was I a goddess?

"You deserve this," I said, tears forming in my eyes, as Frankie struggled to breathe. "If anyone deserves this, it's you."

I felt my power build inside me and call to the life force inside of the girl in my hands. Her soul was small, but powerful. The taste was already there, on my tongue, making my body tingle with energy. I brought the girl closer to me, feeling the power inside of my body take over. I saw blinding white light and heard a crashing sound as a large hole in the wall exploded, showering us with rubble. The Imprecors scattered, hissing at the bright sunlight.

Dropping Frankie, I stared up as the light grew, reaching the darkest corners of the room. I could see a figure standing before me, so bright and beautiful I had to shield my eyes.

It was a woman, with raven hair and earthy skin. Her nose was strong and her chin was narrow. I knew that face. She came forward, touching my cheek, a sad smile on her lips. She wore a long skirt and a wraparound mantle with an intricate woven design. There were colors that seemed to swirl around her face and body as if she herself were a prism, casting a rainbow reflection all around her.

She looked like me. I looked like her. Either way, I could see my face in hers. I could see my mother's face, my grandmother's face. It was as if I could suddenly see all of them who had come before me in her dark eyes.

Suddenly, I felt white hot pain as she shifted, phasing through me.

"You were meant to save the children of the earth, Ava, not destroy them," she said to me. "There is a darkness in you that will be hard to resist, but you must. Go. Go now!"

The light dissipated, and I fell to the ground. I saw Thyana behind the throne; Keira was shielding her with her body. The light had burned her, her skin was red and angry, but she was still mobile. She glared at me.

I grabbed Frankie's hand. We ran toward the sunlight and burst forth through the hole in the wall, never slowing down.

To Be Continued.

Dear Reader,

Thank you for reading The Sacrifice of Ava Black. Please consider leaving a review on Amazon. I also love hearing from readers. Feel free to send me a message at one of the following links:

Facebook: https://www.facebook.com/TDTAGP
Twitter: https://twitter.com/agporterbooks
Instagram: https://www.instagram.com/agporterbooks/
TikTok: https://www.tiktok.com/@agporterbookz

If would like to keep up with my writing progress and author events, be sure to sign up for my newsletter: https://agporterbooks.wixsite.com/author/newsletter-1

Or join my Facebook group: https://www.facebook.com/groups/1421756684770187

Happy Reading!
A.G. Porter

Also by A.G. Porter

The Darkness Trilogy:

The Shadow

The Forsaken

The Redeemed

Short Stories:

The Armor of Dusan

Poetry:

Pieces of My Heart

Pieces of My Soul

Made in the USA
Columbia, SC
23 August 2021

43210686R00154